WILL TANNER, U.S. DEPUTY MARSHAL

A STRANGER IN TOWN

William W. Johnstone
with J. A. Johnstone

PINNACLE BOOKS
Kensington Publishing Corp.
www.kensingtonbooks.com

PINNACLE BOOKS are published by

Kensington Publishing Corp.
119 West 40th Street
New York, NY 10018

PUBLISHER'S NOTE
Following the death of William W. Johnstone, the Johnstone family is working with a carefully selected writer to organize and complete Mr. Johnstone's
outlines and many unfinished manuscripts to create additional novels in
all of his series like The Last Gunfighter, Mountain Man, and Eagles,
among others. This novel was inspired by Mr. Johnstone's superb story-
telling.

All Kensington titles, imprints, and distributed lines are available at special quantity discounts for bulk purchases for sales promotions, premiums,
fund-raising, educational, or institutional use. Special book excerpts or
customized printings can also be created to fit specific needs. For details,
write or phone the office of the Kensington sales manager: Kensington
Publishing Corp., 119 West 40th Street, New York, NY 10018, attn: Sales
Department; phone 1-800-221-2647.

ISBN-13: 978-0-7860-3931-9
ISBN-10: 0-7860-3931-7

First printing: November 2016

10 9 8 7 6 5 4 3 2

Printed in the United States of America

First electronic edition: November 2016

ISBN-13: 978-0-7860-3932-6
ISBN-10: 0-7860-3932-9

CHAPTER 1

Deputy Marshal Ed Pine rode into the tiny settlement gathered around the railroad at Muskogee in Indian Territory early in the afternoon. Without stopping, he rode straight through on his way to Creek policeman Sam Black Crow's cabin three quarters of a mile west of town. The diminutive Creek woman hoeing weeds in the garden next to the house paused to watch his arrival. When she recognized the deputy, she walked out of the garden to greet him. "Deputy Pine," she called out.

"Clara," Ed Pine replied. "I reckon Sam ain't here," he surmised upon seeing the empty corral by the barn. "I saw the padlock on his office, so I didn't bother to stop in town."

"Sam go to Tahlequah this morning," Clara said. "Big fight, one man die. He go to help Cherokee police."

"Well, I'm sorry I missed him," Pine said. He had counted on some help from Sam, since the Creek policeman had sent the telegram reporting the train robbery at the Muskogee station. He had assumed that Sam would expect a deputy in no more than two days' time from Fort Smith. "If he gets back anytime soon, you can tell him that I'm here to see if I can pick up the trail of those men who robbed the train."

"I tell," Clara said.

Clara offered to fix some food for him, but he declined, thanking her for the offer before turning the sorrel back toward town. He would have to find out anything he could in town, and the first place he decided to try was Luther Brady's Trading Post. Sam Black Crow had said in his wire that he suspected the robbery was done by Ben Trout and Brock Larsen, a couple of outlaws from Kansas. Brady's was the hangout familiar to all the outlaws in the territory, and would likely be the one place they might have shown up.

"Well, if it ain't Marshal Ed Pine," Luther Brady slurred when the deputy marshal appeared in his doorway. He made no effort to hide the contempt in his greeting. "If you're lookin' to buy a drink of likker, you're outta luck. You bein' a lawman, you oughta know I don't sell no spirits. It's against the law."

Accustomed to Brady's sarcasm, Ed didn't respond until after he looked over the cramped room, paying particular attention to the only customers in the store, two men seated at a small table beside the stove. "I expect the two gents sittin' at the table are drinkin' coffee outta those cups, right?"

"Dagnabbit, Pine," Brady complained, "I ain't sellin' whiskey to no Injuns. You got no call to come down here hasslin' me over a drink between friends."

Pine slowly shook his head and gave Brady a wry smile. "I swear, Brady, I could almost believe you, except for the fact you ain't got no friends. But I didn't ride all the way over here from Fort Smith to catch you sellin' illegal whiskey." He walked on over to the counter and laid his Winchester rifle on it while still keeping an eye on the two at the table. He had already decided they were of no concern to him, but long years wearing a badge had taught him not to be careless in the Nations. "Now pour me a shot of the same coffee those fellows are drinkin'," he said. "I had a dusty ride and I could use something to cut that dust."

Brady reached under the counter and pulled out a whiskey bottle and a couple of shot glasses. "I'll have one with you," he declared. "This is my own private stock. Like I said, I don't sell no whiskey."

"Course you don't," Pine said. "You're just offerin' me a drink, right? No charge, 'cause that'd be against the law."

"Right," Brady replied, obviously perturbed.

Pine watched while Brady poured the whiskey. Pine tossed it down. Then he said, "Ugh, that's awful stuff. Wish I had a barrel of it."

"What *are* you doin' in these parts?" Brady finally asked.

"Whaddaya think?" Pine replied dryly.

"Train robbery at Muskogee station," Brady said, not really needing any time to think about it.

"That's right," Pine said. "Two fellows robbed the Katy, right in the station, and we've got witnesses that said it was Ben Trout and Brock Larsen, down from Kansas."

"You don't say?" Brady replied. "Ben and Brock, huh? If that don't beat all . . . all the way from Kansas. I don't recollect seein' them boys around here."

Pine responded with a tired shake of his head. "I swear, Brady, as many lies as you've told in your life, looks like you'd be better at it by now. I got a witness that said he saw 'em walkin' in your front door the day before the train got robbed."

It was a lie, but it served its purpose, for Brady scowled painfully and replied reluctantly. "Well, that ain't exactly true," he said. "It was two days before they held up the train—I mean, it was two days before the train was robbed. I don't have no idea who done the job."

"Right," Pine responded. "Two days before, so I reckon they might notta been in town when the Katy was robbed, right?" There was little doubt in his mind that the holdup was the work of the two notorious outlaws, now that he had confirmation that they had been there. Trout and Larsen had robbed trains down in Texas and had stayed one step ahead of the Texas Rangers. It figured that they had deemed it better for their health to take their business to Oklahoma Indian Territory and closer to Kansas. It was important to know if they had worked alone or had some more men with them, so Pine lied again. "This witness said they had several men with 'em."

"Your witness musta been drunk," Brady said. "Wasn't nobody with Ben and Brock."

"Is that a fact?" Pine replied. "And they were just passin' through? Don't expect they told you where they were headin'?"

"Nope," Brady answered smugly, "and I didn't ask 'em."

Pine picked up his rifle. "Well, you've been more help than you know. Thanks for the drink." He turned and headed for the door, certain now that he would be dealing with only the two outlaws, and feeling no need for a posse to chase them. Still, he would have deputized Sam Black Crow to help him, if Sam had not ridden up to Tahlequah. The problem to be solved first was to find out which way the outlaws went after they robbed the train. He figured it could be any direction but east. That left a hell of a lot of territory to search and amounted to a waste of time unless he could pick up their trail. The Texas Rangers had not been able to catch up with Trout and Larsen, and now it was time to see if he would have better luck.

Outside Brady's Trading Post, Pine stood for a moment, looking up and down the once deserted street of the tiny settlement. After a moment, he decided to go talk to the stationmaster in hopes he had not been too frightened during the robbery to remember which way the train robbers had fled. He led his horse down the short street to the railroad tracks and the stationmaster's shack.

"Are you a deputy marshal?" Elmore Wiggins asked when the tall, rail-thin lawman came up to his window. When Pine said that he was, Wiggins asked, "It's a little bit late to show up looking for those bandits, ain't it?"

"Maybe," Pine allowed. "Depends on what you can tell me to help me out."

"All I can tell you is two men popped up from behind my shack when the train pulled to a stop. One of 'em stuck a gun in my back and marched me to the cab of the engine and kept me and the engineer at gunpoint while the other one went through the passenger car robbing the passengers. Then he hollered for the guard inside the mail car to open up, or he was gonna shoot the conductor and the engineer. Then when the guard opened the door, he shot him down—just because he didn't do it fast enough."

"Did you see which way they headed outta town?" Pine asked.

"Hell no," Wiggins said. "They made me and the engineer and the conductor get in the mail car. Then they shut us in and took off. There weren't no way I could tell which way they went."

"I saw which way they rode outta town."

Pine heard the voice behind him and turned to find a short, broad-shouldered man approaching from the forge across the street. "My name's Tom Shepherd," the husky man said. "I own the blacksmith shop. I saw them two fellers ride out from the railroad tracks and hightail it on the road to Okmulkee. It didn't occur to me that they mighta just robbed the train."

"Okmulkee, huh?" Pine responded, thinking about the odds of tracking the outlaws on a common wagon road. "And that was two days ago," he pondered aloud.

"I'm thinkin' you might be able to track 'em, anyway," Shepherd continued. "I put new shoes on both of their ridin' horses the day before. They had a packhorse, but it didn't need shoein'. Them new shoes oughta cut a right sharp track, though."

"Might at that," Pine said. "Much obliged. "I'll go have a look right now."

There were several roads out of Muskogee. Some were little more than Indian trails, with the main wagon road running north and south along the railroad tracks. Between the general store and the stables, however, a narrow road headed due west, which led to Okmulkee if a man followed it for close to forty miles. Pine had ridden it a couple of times before, and as he stood there holding the sorrel's reins, he gazed down the trail before him, trying to think of any potential spots where the outlaws might have it in mind to hole up. He couldn't recall any, so he had to conclude the men he chased had just been intent upon heading into the wilds of Indian Territory, with no particular destination in mind. Steeling himself for a long scouting trip, he wished he had brought a wagon, a cook, and a posseman to use as a home base. "But I didn't," he sighed aloud, "so I'd better get to it. They're just gettin' farther away while I'm standin' here."

When he examined the dry ground, he found

that the blacksmith had been correct in assuming there would be clear tracks to follow. There were a great many other tracks going in both directions on the road, but none that looked to be recent. So the tracks left by the two newly shod horses were clearly distinguishable from the others. At least it would give him a start. He climbed into the saddle and started out on what he anticipated to be a long search. For a moment he considered wiring his boss that he would likely be gone awhile, then decided against it.

After keeping a careful eye on the narrow wagon track for the first couple of miles, alert for any signs indicating the outlaws had departed the road, Pine picked up the pace. It appeared they were intent upon heading for Okmulkee. So he held the sorrel to a comfortable lope, stopping every mile or so to make sure he could still find the distinct hoofprints. The outlaws had continued on the road for what he estimated to be about fifteen miles before he realized that the tracks had disappeared. He dismounted to take a closer look to be sure. They had left the road somewhere behind him and he had missed it. Figuring they had evidently decided to rest their horses at that point, he turned back and led his horses while he searched for their tracks. There was a narrow stream some fifty yards behind, so he felt sure that might have been the spot where they left the road. It was the only stream he had crossed since leaving Muskogee. His hunch proved to be right, for he found a hoofprint at the edge of the stream, a sign that the outlaws had sought to disguise their trail by riding up the stream. It had been an unnecessary precaution, he thought, for there had been no one to give chase until now, and he was a hell of a long way behind.

After following the stream for several hundred yards over a rolling, treeless prairie, he came to a wooded area and the remains of a campfire in the center. That being as good a spot as any to rest his horses, he decided to stop there as well. There was no real urgency in his quest to catch up with Larsen and Trout. He was following a trail that was over two days old, so he had no notion of overtaking them until they decided to stop for a while longer than an overnight camp.

The outlaws' tracks out of the camp were easily seen. They led out toward a low range of hills a couple of miles away, so after Pine's horses were rested and watered, he set out in that direction. As he approached the hills, he noticed a gulch that appeared to cut right through the tallest section. Apparently the outlaws had noticed it, too, for their trail veered off and headed for it. When he entered into the shadows of the narrow gulch, he was reminded that he was running out of daylight and would need to find a place to camp before much longer. *This chase might last for a week or two*, he thought, his last thought before he felt the impact of the bullet that slammed into his chest. He grabbed the saddle horn in an effort to keep from falling, but the second shot, near his collarbone, knocked him from the saddle and landed him hard on the ground. A hundred thoughts whirled around his head during the few seconds he lay there unable to move. He had ridden blindly into an ambush with no sense that he was anywhere close to the men he chased. He was badly hurt, he figured, because he could not feel his body, and he was helpless to defend himself. Unable to make his hand move to pull his Colt from the holster, he knew he was done for.

"Watch him, Brock," Ben Trout warned his partner as Brock rode down from the slope and pulled his horse up beside the body lying still on the ground. "He might be playin' possum."

"He ain't playin' no possum with that shot I put dead center his chest," Brock said, keeping a steady eye on the body while his partner rode up beside him.

"How do you know that was your shot?" Ben demanded. "I'm thinkin' that was my shot, 'cause I had a bead on him and fired while you was still waitin' for him to get closer."

"The hell you say," Brock fired back. "You shot too damn quick. You hit him, but it was my shot that knocked him outta the saddle."

"Ain't no sense in arguin' about it," Ben insisted as he stepped down to look the man over. "Let's see if he's carryin' any money on him." He started riffling through Pine's pockets. "Look here!" he suddenly called out when he pulled Pine's jacket aside to reveal a badge. "He's a damn lawman—one of them marshals outta Fort Smith, I'll bet!"

"Lemme see," Brock said, and stepped down to take a look for himself. Seeing that it was, in fact, a U.S. Deputy Marshal's badge, he automatically looked back over the way Pine had ridden to make sure there was no one behind him. "How the hell did he get on our trail so quick?" They had been in no particular hurry once they had fled the town of Muskogee, thinking there was no danger of anyone in the small settlement coming after them. After all, they figured, they had robbed no one in town. Their business had been with the railroad. When Ben had spotted a lone rider from the top of the hill, approaching the gulch, they had assumed it was an outlaw looking to cut himself in on their successful robbery.

"We'll see about that," Trout had said. "We'll settle his bacon right quick, and pick up a couple of horses for our trouble."

"I reckon we shoulda kept goin' instead of layin' around here," Brock fretted.

"Maybe," Trout replied. "But right now it looks like this wasn't bad luck a-tall." He paused to chuckle. "Except for him. And it looks like he's all by his lonesome. If he ain't, he wouldn't be leadin' a packhorse. He'd have a wagon somewhere with his supplies and most likely a posseman or two. He oughta got shot, ridin' out here in Injun Territory by hisself. This is outlaw territory. A lawman signs his own death warrant when he sticks his nose west of the railroad."

"There's liable to be another'n when this one don't come home," Brock said.

"I expect there might," Ben allowed. "So I reckon it don't make no sense to hang around this little creek any longer, even though it'll most likely be a while before they send another marshal to look for this one. We'll be long gone up at Buzzard's Roost by then."

"I hope them cabins are still standin'," Brock said, thinking about the cluster of log cabins built by outlaws on the run from Kansas, Colorado, and Texas over the years. Starting with a single cabin built by Kansas stagecoach bandit Elmer Sartain in a secluded valley near the Cimarron River, the camp had grown to three such rough abodes. At different times, the little outlaw community had been the temporary home to any number of bank robbers, rustlers, murderers, and thieves. To date no lawman had ventured there, probably because it was in the middle of nowhere and hard to find. Buzzard's Roost was Ben's name for the hideout, because he could never remember the man's name who created it.

"They was in pretty good shape when we was up there two years ago," Ben said, replying to Brock's comment. "They most likely still are." Turning his attention to their present windfall, he said, "Let's take a look at our new horses." He paused briefly to pull Pine's gun belt from under his body before following Brock to retrieve the deputy's horses.

"I kinda hate to leave this spot so soon," Ben remarked when they had packed up and tied their newly gained horses on lead ropes. "It's a good spot to camp."

"I reckon," Brock replied, more interested in the fine pair of boots he was in the process of pulling off Ed Pine's feet. "A little bit loose," he decided when he tried them on, "but they oughta do just fine." He looked up at Trout and grinned. "I'd let you try 'em, but your feet are so damn big, you'd have to cut the toes off 'em." Stamping his feet on the ground, testing the fit, he looked down at the shoeless body and said, "Thanks a lot, Marshal—glad you come along." He wedged his old boots under the ropes on one of the packhorses, then turned back to Trout. "We can use the extra supplies he brought with him, too."

"Yeah," Ben said. "But we're gonna need a lot more'n what we've got to last us awhile, so we'll pick up what we need on the way to Buzzard's Roost." He climbed into the saddle then and followed Brock, who had already started across the creek.

Behind them, the man lying on the ground in the shadows of the narrow gulch heard Brock's parting remark. He exhaled painfully and blinked his eyes open, but he could not move his arms or legs without excruciating pain. Pretending to be dead had saved him from another final bullet, but now he wished he had taken that bullet. It was obvious to him that he could not help himself. He had no choice but to lie there feeling the blood pumping out of his body and waiting out a slow, painful death. It was not a pleasant way to die.

CHAPTER 2

"You wanted to see me?" Will Tanner asked when he walked into U.S. Marshal Daniel Stone's office over the jail.

"Yeah, come on in," Stone replied. "I've got a job for you, if you're up to it." He knew Will was still wearing a bandage on his shoulder from his last assignment into Oklahoma Indian Territory, but he was convinced that Will was the best man for the job.

"I reckon I'm up to it," Will said.

"You ain't heard what it is yet," Stone said.

"I'm ready to ride," Will insisted. "I've already sat around Fort Smith long enough. What's the job?"

"Ed Pine," Stone replied. "I'm afraid he's run into trouble up in the Creek Nation. While you were trackin' the last one, I got a wire from Muskogee that two men held up the MKT train there and killed a guard in the process. The Creek policeman, Sam Black Crow, was pretty sure it was Ben Trout and Brock Larsen from up in Kansas that did the job, 'cause he had reports that they'd been seen west of Muskogee. They've been working as far down as Texas, even though the marshal in Kansas Territory said that was where the two first showed up. Anyway, I sent Ed over there to see what he could find, and there's been no word from him. That was a week ago, and I ain't heard nothing from him."

Will nodded, understanding Stone's concern. Muskogee was a two-day ride at the most from Fort Smith. "So you think something must have happened to Ed," Will said, "and you want me to go see if I can find out?"

"That's right," Stone said, and waited for Will's answer.

"Well, it's a little late in the day now," Will said. "I'll start out first thing in the mornin'."

"Good," Stone said. "You can take what's left of the day to round up a cook and a posseman to go with you." He made the suggestion knowing full well that his newest deputy marshal had not made any arrangements in that regard. It was supposed to be a standing order that any deputy riding into the Nations was required to take a posseman with him, so he felt it his duty to remind his deputy. He was not surprised at Will's response.

"All the same to you," Will said, "I work better by myself."

"I figured you'd say that," Stone replied. "Ed said the same thing, and now I ain't heard a word from him. So, doggone it, Will, you be careful. I've got paper on those two, and they're a mean pair. And you know Ed Pine ain't a greenhorn lawman. He's been ridin' for me for over six years, so if they got the jump on Ed, they're liable to be trouble for anybody."

"I'll be careful," Will assured him.

After leaving Stone's office, Will rode his buckskin gelding back to Vern Tuttle's stable and pulled his saddle off. Turning Buster loose in the corral, he turned to greet Vern, who was coming from the tack room just then. "I'll be leavin' early in the mornin'," Will said. "My gun Buster a double portion of oats. I'll be takin' the bay for a packhorse. Since I don't know how many days I'll be gone, I reckon he could use some oats, too."

"Headin' out again already, huh?" Vern asked. "Where you off to?"

"Goin' over in the Nations," Will replied, "over toward Muskogee."

"You need to get in the storeroom?" Vern asked.

"Not till in the mornin'. I'll load up then." He kept a fair amount of supplies and ammunition on hand in a corner of Vern's storeroom for a few cents additional on his stable rent. He really had no place to store the supplies at Ruth Bennett's boardinghouse, anyway, and it was a much more convenient arrangement at the stable where he kept his horses.

It was wash day at Bennett House, which Ruth Bennett had taken to calling her home. She thought it gave the boardinghouse a better image of a legitimate lodging establishment, more like a hotel. She and her daughter, Sophie, were out in the backyard hanging sheets on the clothesline when Will came from the stable, so he went around back to let her know that he would be out of town for a number of days.

"Well, look here," Sophie called out cheerfully, "somebody's come to help hang up the wash."

Accustomed to her teasing, Will replied, "I reckon you'd do better to get Garth Pearson down here to help you with that. He'll most likely be needin' some trainin' on how to be a good husband." His playful remark caused him to picture the timid and polite courtroom clerk who had made a proposal of marriage to Sophie. Already possessing the opinion that Sophie was too free-spirited for the mild young man to handle, Will had no doubt that she could train Garth to do pretty much anything she wanted. He didn't allow his thoughts to linger there, however, for he was still trying to deny the disappointment he had felt when Sophie told him that she had accepted Garth's proposal. While Sophie laughed in response to his remark, he turned his attention toward her mother. "I just thought I'd tell you that I'm leavin' town in the mornin'. Ain't sure how long I'll be gone, but it'll be for a spell, I reckon."

"Oh . . . all right, Will," Ruth said pleasantly. "We hope it's not a dangerous trip you're taking." She had allowed herself to become fond of the soft-spoken young deputy marshal, now that Sophie had accepted Garth's proposal. For a time, she had worried over her daughter's seeming infatuation for the untamed cougar that resided behind the passive exterior. She had known only too painfully the uncertainty of a relationship with a lawman riding the Indian Territory, and she had feared for a time that Sophie might be making the same mistake.

"Just business as usual, I reckon," Will replied. He looked at Sophie. "Like I said, I don't know how long it'll take, but I expect I'll miss the big weddin'." He attempted to make his tone as casual as he could while thinking he didn't care to be around to witness the marriage.

"I hope you aren't planning to be gone that long," Sophie responded. "Garth wanted to have the wedding at Christmas."

This was news to Will, and not especially good news. He preferred to get it done quickly and get it over with, like removing a bullet before it festered. Christmas was three months away. "Why is that?" he responded.

"So his parents can be here," Sophie said. "They live in Little Rock, and Judge Pearson can't get away before then. So that's quite a ways off."

"That is a long time," he said, thinking out loud. Then he looked quickly at Ruth, who was watching his reaction. "Well, anyway, I'll be leavin' in the mornin'."

"Are you going before breakfast?" Ruth asked.

"Yes, ma'am, I expect so," he answered.

"Come by the kitchen before you go," she said. "I expect I'll be starting breakfast. I'll probably be able to give you some coffee and a cold biscuit—maybe a fresh biscuit, if it's not too early."

"Thank you, ma'am, that would be mighty nice of you." He turned and headed for the house.

Ruth pulled another wet sheet from the basket and shook it out in preparation to hang on the line. She paused to look at Sophie, who was still watching Will as he walked away. Feeling her mother's intense gaze, Sophie turned to her. "What?"

"Nothing," Ruth replied. "Hurry up with those sheets—we've only got so many hours of sunshine left."

Sam Black Crow stepped outside the rough cabin that served as his headquarters in Muskogee, seeking a breath of fresh air. He had built the cabin to be close to the Indian Union Agency that consolidated the police of all five nations under a central command. It was a chilly day, typical late September weather, and he felt the need to empty his lungs of the heavy ovenlike air inside the small log building with its iron stove. He stood on the front step, surveying the peaceful street of the small settlement, enjoying the feel of the cold air as it penetrated his shirtsleeves. There seemed to be no one about on the short street that ended at the train station, as he looked toward Tom Shepherd's forge and back again toward the general store on the opposite end of town. He quickly shifted his gaze back to the store when something caught his eye on the road beyond. It was a rider, leading a packhorse, but still too far away to identify.

He remained outside on the step, watching the rider approach. He could determine now that it was a white man, but not one he was familiar with. *A drifter?* He considered. *Maybe . . . and maybe an outlaw on the run, looking for the safety of Indian Territory.* The thought irritated Sam. The territory had too damn many fugitives from white man law, outlaws who knew the Indian police had no authority to arrest them. More than likely the stranger would stop in Muskogee no longer than it would take to buy any supplies he might need before disappearing in the wild country in the western part of the territory. Still, it would be Sam's responsibility to keep an eye on him until he left town, in case the rider was inclined to get his supplies without paying for them. In that case, Sam would be happy to lock him up in the shed behind his office until a deputy marshal arrived to take him into custody.

Will Tanner sat tall in the saddle, his body moving gently in rhythm with the big buckskin's motion. He saw the lone figure watching him from the short stoop of the little log building near the middle of the one street and wondered if he might be the Creek policeman. If not, at least he could tell Will how to find Sam Black Crow, so he guided Buster straight toward him. A few minutes later he rode up to the cabin and pulled Buster to a stop. "Afternoon," Will said. "I'm lookin' for Sam Black Crow. Can you tell me where I can find him?"

Sam studied the stranger intensely before answering. "Right here. I'm Sam Black Crow. What can I do for you?"

"My name's Will Tanner. I'm a deputy marshal, and I'm looking for Ed Pine. He came out here after you sent the telegram about the train robbery."

"Right," Sam said, and continued to study the deputy. There was a grim look of confidence in the solemn gaze that seemed to be measuring him. "I've heard of you," Sam said. "You're the man who settled with Max Tarbow and Eli Stark."

Unaware that he had already earned a reputation in the Nations, Will simply repeated his reason for being there. "Have you seen Ed Pine?"

"No, I'm afraid not. He came through here, but I was up at Tahlequah at the time. Cherokee policeman sent me a wire, said he needed some help, so I reckon I just missed Ed. Tom Shepherd told him which way those two train robbers had run, and Ed went after them. I'm sorry I can't tell you much more than that." He pointed toward the road between the general store and the stables. "Tom said they set out on the road to Okmulkee, and Ed went after them. That don't give you much to go on." He paused for a few moments while Will was obviously thinking it over. "You want me to go along with you to look for Ed?"

Will considered that for a brief moment before declining. "No, I reckon not. You've got your own responsibilities here in Muskogee."

Sam shrugged. "Ain't nothing I need to stay close for."

"I 'preciate it," Will said, "but I reckon I'll be movin' on right away." He didn't confess that he much preferred to work alone, with no neck to worry about but his own.

"Suit yourself," Sam said.

"Good to know I can count on you if I need you," Will said in parting, and pulled Buster's head around toward the blacksmith's shop. "I'll check with Tom Shepherd on my way outta town."

"Good luck," Sam said. "Hope you catch up with Ed. He's a good man. I've worked with him on more than one job." He stepped back up on the front step and paused there to watch Will as he headed toward the blacksmith shop. He wasn't sure what he thought about Dan Stone's newest deputy. He was surprised when he turned down his offer to accompany him. Maybe what Sam had heard about Will Tanner was true. Maybe he was a lone hunter.

There wasn't much more that Tom Shepherd could tell him, except what he had told Ed Pine about the new shoes on two of the horses. "Much obliged," Will had told him, and started out, just as Ed Pine had, on the road to Okmulgee, with nothing to go on but a few tracks now several days old. To further hamper him, it was getting along late in the afternoon, and daylight would soon be running out. He would have to think about finding a spot to camp pretty soon. With that thought in mind, he paused to let Buster and his packhorse drink when he came to a small stream. It occurred to him that it was the first water he had come to all the way from Muskogee, and it might be all there was for a good many more miles. While he was deciding whether or not to take advantage of it and make camp, he noticed a few hoofprints coming toward the stream from the opposite direction. It was enough to cause him to dismount to take a look. After closer examination, it was plain to him that someone had left the road here and ridden up the stream. Whether or not it had been the men he hoped to find, he could not say. For the tracks were now too old to determine, even if they were the sharp prints from the newly shod horses the blacksmith had told him about. But at least they might lead him to a known camping spot. *Might as well take a look*, he thought. *I've gotta camp somewhere pretty soon, and I just might get lucky*. He climbed back into the saddle and turned Buster upstream.

After following the stream for a hundred yards or so, he could see what appeared to be a grove of oak trees some distance ahead. They were conspicuous in that they were the only trees he could see over a wide expanse of prairie. As he expected, there was a small clearing in the center of the trees, and the remains of a couple of fires. Whoever left the tracks had evidently made camp there. The question in his mind was, who was he following? He could not be sure the tracks found were left by the train robbers, Ed Pine, or someone else entirely. It was the only trail he had to follow, so he decided to stick with it, thinking it a better possibility than returning to the wagon road to Okmulkee and assuming the outlaws were going there. He relieved his horses of their saddles and packs and let them drink. He didn't bother to hobble them, knowing that Buster would not wander far from him, and the bay packhorse would not stray far from Buster. There was plenty of wood for his fire, so he built it in the ashes of the fires before his.

With the first rays of morning light, he revived his dying campfire enough to boil some coffee before climbing into the saddle again. Coffee was all he needed before starting out. He would fix something to eat when he stopped to rest the horses. While he waited for the small metal pot to do its work, he studied the hoofprints around the stream— some looked to be recent. He could not say for sure how many horses had been there. And he was equally uncertain if they had all been at this camp at the same time. But he was assuming that some of the tracks belonged to Ben Trout and Brock Larsen and the others were made by Ed Pine at a later time. It seemed the only situation that offered him any chance of catching up with Pine, so he decided to follow the trail until he caught up with whoever had left it and hope his hunch was right.

He had not ridden far from the camp when the tracks he followed veered away from the stream. Looking in the new direction, he spotted a line of hills in the distance and guessed the tracks were heading toward a gulch perhaps two or more miles away. It was some trouble to follow the trail across the prairie, even though the broken stems of dry grass had not had time to recover due to the cold fall weather. The direction never varied, taking him to the entrance of a narrow gulch. From habit, he paused before the entrance and scanned the two steep sides of the gulch before urging Buster on. Walking his horses slowly, he entered the narrow confines of the two steep walls, his eyes darting back and forth from one side of the gulch to the other. It was easy to imagine it as a perfect ambush setup, with ledges on each side, close to the top of the tree-covered hills.

His gaze was brought back to the ground when Buster stumbled on a loose rock on the floor of the passage. The big gelding recovered at once, but something on the ground caught Will's attention, and he pulled Buster to a stop while he took another look. It appeared that something had been dragged from the middle of the gulch, leaving scuff marks in the dirt and gravel. It was not so much the marks that caused him to quickly dismount to take a closer look. It was the large, dark stain that formed a ragged circle in the dirt. The stain was several days old. He was pretty sure it was blood, but was it left by man or beast? Whatever left it had been dragged from the spot, so it seemed likely that it had been a deer or antelope that had been dragged away to be butchered somewhere else. Although that seemed the most logical explanation, he knew he was not going to be satisfied until he confirmed it, still thinking about the perfect ambush site he was riding through. If his hunch about the tracks he had decided to follow was right, then Ed Pine rode through this gulch on the trail of the outlaws. Since there had been no contact from Ed after he left Fort Smith to pursue the outlaws, could the reason be that he might have been ambushed here? *Damn it all*, Will thought, *I've got to find out.*

If the outlaws ambushed Ed here, why did they take the body? The only reason could be that he wasn't dead, but it didn't seem likely they would want to take him prisoner. *For what purpose?* It seemed much more likely that they would kill him and leave the body. *I'm gonna have to take the time to find out what happened here,* he told himself, disappointed to be further delayed in the chase. *I hope to hell I find the remains of a deer at the end of this trail in the gravel.*

Leading his horses, he started following the scuffed-up trail across the floor of the gulch. After only fifty feet, it took a turn and headed toward a clay recess under a cliff. Hidden from the center of the gulch, Will discovered a hollowed-out hole several feet deep. The trail ended there, but there was still no body or animal carcass. It had evidently been dumped in the hole, however, because he saw more bloodstains in the clay. Becoming impatient now with signs that didn't make sense, he decided to abandon the mystery of the dragged carcass and get back on the tracks of the horses he had been following. But he paused yet again, stopped by the discovery of a single moccasin print near the edge of the hole.

He dropped to one knee to examine the track. Judging by the size, it had been left by a young boy or perhaps a woman. After looking around for a few minutes, he discovered more tracks, coming and going. He concentrated on the footprints leaving the hole under the cliff and leading in the direction of the other end of the gulch. Near the mouth of the passage, he found more hoofprints, these from an unshod horse. The evidence seemed to be painting a different picture of what had occurred in this gulch. He considered the possibility that Ed Pine might have been ambushed by a group of rogue Indians, seeking to capture weapons and ammunition. Now there was no decision to be made. He had to find the Indians who had left these tracks, and soon, although it might already be too late.

He tried to imagine why the Indians wanted to capture a deputy. If in fact Ed had been ambushed by a rogue band of warriors, it would have made more sense for them to kill him. Maybe they figured it best to hide his body. When he followed the obvious trail out of the gulch, he found confirmation that the body was taken somewhere, for he discovered the distinct tracks of a travois, heading north along the base of the hills. Determined now to find out just what had happened in that narrow gulch, he stepped up into the saddle and followed the distinct ruts left by the travois.

For a distance he considered to be close to a mile, the tracks led him along the hills until coming to a small stream where the ruts left by the travois ended. He didn't have to guess which way the Indians had taken when they got to the stream. A faint wisp of smoke wafting up through the trees on the hill told him there was a camp back up the stream. *They damn sure better be eating deer meat*, he thought as he drew his rifle from the saddle scabbard. Leaving his horses tied in the trees, he moved cautiously up the hill toward the smoke, which he estimated to be less than a quarter of a mile away. As he continued to edge closer, he decided that it could not be a very large camp, for he couldn't hear any sounds of activity other than the occasional whinny of a horse once in a while.

Finally, he could see that he was coming to a small clearing in the trees ahead, so he became even more cautious, stopping often to look around him to make sure he wasn't walking into an ambush. A few yards farther, he came to the edge of the clearing. Moving as close as he could and taking cover behind a large oak tree, he was surprised by what he saw. Expecting to find a hunting party, he discovered instead a lone tipi near the center of the clearing. From some faint imprints in the grass, it appeared that there had been a dozen or more tipis there at one time. There was a fire burning in front of the tipi, and off to one side near the stream a couple of ponies grazed on the short grass along the bank. Will scanned the clearing from side to side, but there was no sign of anyone in the camp until a young Indian boy emerged from the tipi with a bucket. He walked to the edge of the clearing and scattered the contents, which appeared to be water, on the ground. Then he went to the stream and filled the bucket. When it was full, he placed it in the coals of the fire and sat down to watch it. After a while, the boy tested the water with his finger, waited a while longer, then picked up the bucket and carried it into the tipi. Knowing he had to see the inside of that tipi, Will took another precautionary look around the clearing before he left the cover of the tree and ran to follow the boy.

Walking Bird took the bucket of water from her grandson, Walter Strong Bow, and placed it beside the man lying on a bed of blankets near the center of the tipi. After testing the temperature of the water, she dipped a cloth in it and was in the process of wringing it out when she gave out a little cry of surprise. The boy jumped back in fear also, startled when the tipi flap was suddenly thrown aside and the opening was filled by the imposing form of a white man, his rifle ready to fire.

Equally surprised, Will was stopped for a second by the discovery of Ed Pine lying deathlike on the blankets, his bare chest and shoulder bound with cloth bandages. It was plain to see that the woman was trying to help the wounded deputy. The boy, now recovered from the initial shock, began to slowly back away toward a bow and quiver hanging on the wall of the tipi. "Hold on," Will cautioned softly. "I'm a friend." When the boy stopped, Will asked, "English?" He looked from the boy to the woman. "You speak English?" They both nodded, still not certain he meant them no harm. Will pulled his coat aside to reveal his badge. "I'm a deputy, just like him. I came to look for him." They both relaxed somewhat. During this time, there had been no sign of life from the prone figure of Ed Pine. Will moved on inside the tipi and dropped to one knee beside him. After a moment, he turned to the woman. "How bad is he?"

"Very bad," she answered, no longer afraid of Will. She placed her hand on her breast. "This wound very bad. I think maybe he die." Then she put her hand on her shoulder. "This wound bad, too, but not like chest wound." She wanted to say more, but looked to the boy for help.

"My grandmother got the bullet out of his shoulder," the boy explained. "But she can't dig the bullet out of his chest. It's too deep. She's afraid it might kill him if she tries."

Will nodded slowly to the old woman to let her know he understood her caution. He bent low over Ed then, looking for some confirmation that he was still alive. Feeling for a pulse, he was surprised when Ed's eyelids opened halfway and he spoke. "Tanner?" he gasped feebly.

"Yeah, Will Tanner," he answered. "Are you gonna make it?"

"Don't know," Ed slurred weakly. "Maybe not."

"Did you see who shot you?" Will asked. "Was it those two you were trackin'?"

"I rode right into it," Ed said, laboring with each word. "Happened so fast I didn't know what happened, but it was them. I know that."

Will nodded. "You're in pretty good hands here," he said, trying to give him courage, even though he wasn't overly confident that he could survive the chest wound. "You just rest up and let it heal. She'll help you get stronger." He hoped he was telling him the truth. Turning back to the boy, he asked, "Did you bring him here?" The boy nodded. "What's your name?"

"Walter Strong Bow," he answered.

"Tell me how you found him."

"I was hunting," Strong Bow said. "I followed some deer tracks into that notch between the hills. I didn't know the two white men were up on the hill, and when I heard them moving down, I hid in a hole under a cliff to wait for them to leave, but they didn't leave. They shot the deputy when he rode in the gulch and left him to die. They took his horse and his weapons. They even took his boots. But he was not dead, so I dragged him to the hole where I was hiding and left him there while I ran back to get my pony. My grandmother Walking Bird helped me carry him up the creek to her tipi."

"You and your grandmother are doin' a good thing," Will said. "His name is Ed Pine, and I know he's beholdin' to both of you." It struck him then that it was pure chance that Strong Bow had been there to help Ed. "What happened to the rest of this camp?" he asked. "Why are just the two of you left here?"

"We were a small village that wanted to live in the old way," Strong Bow said. "But the people decided to join the others who settled near Muskogee. My grandmother would not leave. She says she is too old to learn new ways, so she will stay here until she dies. I could not leave her, so I am staying with her to take care of her."

The situation left Will in somewhat of a quandary, knowing that his chances of trailing the train robbers were getting slimmer the longer he delayed going after them. But he didn't feel right leaving Ed without knowing if he was going to make it or not. He knew the woman was right. If she went digging into Ed's chest, looking for that bullet, she'd kill him for sure. *Hell,* he thought, *there ain't anything I can do for him. At least I can go after the men who shot him.* "Did you see which way the men were headin' when they left that gulch?" he asked.

"Yes, they headed west, maybe toward Okmulkee," Strong Bow said. "But when I was hiding in the hole, I heard them talking about going to a place called Buzzard's Roost."

"Buzzard's Roost?" Will replied. "Do you know where that is?"

"No," Strong Bow replied. "I've never heard of such a place—I don't know where it is." He remembered something else he had heard then. "One of them said they would reach the Cimarron in two days. Maybe that's where Buzzard's Roost is." He remembered something else as well. "One of them said they had to get more supplies on the way to Buzzard's Roost, but he didn't say where."

Will thought about that for a few moments, trying to recall the country between the gulch and the Cimarron. "I don't think there is anyplace to buy supplies between here and there." He tried to make a judgment on what part of the Cimarron might be a two-day ride from there. "They might be thinkin' about goin' through Okmulkee. There's a store there." It wasn't much to go on, but they might be able to make it to the Cimarron in two days, even if they stopped in Okmulkee. He just hoped he might be lucky enough to strike the two outlaws' trail away from the gulch. Kneeling beside Ed again, he said, "I'm gonna leave you here with Walkin' Bird and Strong Bow while I go after the two that dry-gulched you, but I'll be back to take you to Fort Smith when you're well enough to ride." He looked up at the old lady. "Is that all right with you?" She nodded, so he turned back to Ed. "It looks like Walkin' Bird has done about all she can do for your wounds, so I reckon the rest is up to you. But I'll be back. You can count on that, so you get busy healin' up." He turned to the boy and his grandmother. "I'm much obliged to you for takin' care of him. I don't know how long I'll be gone, but I'll leave you some supplies to help you out till I get back." His remark was met with nods of relief and a grateful smile on Walking Bird's face. He was right in guessing their supplies were running short and would soon be running out if Ed began to recover enough to eat. "I'll go fetch my horses," he said, and left the tipi.

When he returned with his horses, he took most of his basic food supplies off the bay packhorse—coffee, bacon, beef jerky, flour, salt, and dried beans—and gave them to Strong Bow to put away. He glanced around the inside of the tipi, then asked the boy, "What kinda weapons have you got?"

"Only my bow," Strong Bow replied, "but it is a strong one, like my name."

"I reckon that'll have to do, 'cause I ain't carryin' any extra weapons," Will said.

"He is a good hunter," Walking Bird interjected proudly. "He finds much game."

Will nodded to her and smiled. "I believe you. He looks like a strong hunter." Looking at Strong Bow, he asked, "How old are you?"

"I am fourteen summers," he answered.

"Well, I don't believe there's anybody better to take care of Ed than you and your grandmother, and you have my thanks. I don't know what kinda luck I'll have chasin' those two outlaws, but I'll get back here as soon as I can."

They followed him out of the tipi and stood watching him step up into the saddle. "I take care of Ed," Walking Bird said, calling her patient by his name now. "You be careful they don't shoot you."

"I will," he said.

CHAPTER 3

There were several good hours of daylight left when he returned to the gulch where Ed had been bushwhacked, so Will searched the western side of the narrow passage between the hills, hoping to find a clear trail to follow. Luck was with him, for he found some tracks that looked to be made by at least five horses, and they were heading in the direction taken by the outlaws, according to what Strong Bow had told him. These tracks stood apart from a few others, which were from unshod horses. Will figured those had probably come from Strong Bow's pony. He took a brief second to look at the sky. It was already late in the fall, and so far there had been no threat of snow. If the weather held, he figured he had a half-decent chance of following the outlaws' tracks, even though they were old, maybe until they reached the Cimarron. "Best not waste any more time," he told the buckskin and gave Buster a nudge with his heels.

Almost as soon as the tracks cleared the line of

hills, they swung more toward the south. Will figured that if they continued in that direction, they would return to the original trail on the road between Muskogee and Okmulkee. Evidently the outlaws had veered off in a little more northerly direction out of Muskogee, hoping to disguise their trail in the event there was a posse after them. Since the ambush of Ed Pine, they had obviously felt it safe to return to an original plan to go to Okmulkee. Apparently he had been right when he figured the only place they could buy supplies was the general store in Okmulkee. A few more miles confirmed it when he struck the wagon road and could find no tracks indicating they had crossed it and continued south. He was still some twenty miles east of Okmulkee, but his horses were rested, so he decided he could make it to the little town before dark.

Buster and the bay were both willing, but it was a bit farther to Okmulkee than Will had figured. So it was well into twilight when Will rode into the growing settlement on the Deep Fork River, a tributary of the Canadian. He walked his horses slowly past the darkened two-story log Council House built by the Creeks, and continued toward a scattering of buildings a short distant down the road, some of which showed signs of life. The largest of these had a sign that proclaimed it to be BURNS DRY GOODS. A small addition built on the side of the store had a sign over the door that read U.S. POST OFFICE. There was a CLOSED sign on the door. Will pulled up to the hitching rail and dismounted.

After looping the reins over the rail, he took a couple of minutes to look over the three horses already tied at the rail. They showed no signs of having been ridden hard recently, telling him their owners should be of no concern to him. He stepped up on the short stoop, opened the door, and paused to look the room over. There were three round tables along one wall of the store, with a half wall dividing them from the main store. Four men, three of them looked to be cowhands, were seated around one of the tables playing cards. A quart-sized fruit jar was on the table and each man had a glass. Unconcerned by the presence of illegal whiskey, Will looked toward the other end of the room and a two-section door that identified an inside access to the post office. Both halves of the door were closed and padlocked.

Watching him from behind a long counter, a husky man with a full head of bushy gray hair and a beard that matched, silently measured the stranger. Will was not surprised by the cautious reception on the part of the owner. It was unlawful to sell whiskey in the Nations, but that did little to slow the brisk business in stores like this one. Almost all the spirits sold were moonshine, mostly corn whiskey, which was doubly galling to the government because there was no tax paid on it. Closing the door behind him, he walked over to the counter. By this time, his presence had been noticed by the card players, and conversation at the table stopped momentarily while they paused to stare at him. The bushy-haired man behind the counter finally spoke. "Somethin' I can do for you?" His eyes, under heavy brows, quickly shifted back and forth between the stranger and the four men, painfully aware of the half-empty jar on the table.

With more important things to worry about than the owner illegally selling whiskey, Will sought to put the man at ease. "Yes sir," he said as he propped his Winchester against the counter beside him, "I'm gonna be needin' some supplies—figured maybe I could buy 'em from you."

"Why, sure," the owner replied, immediately relieved. "That's what I'm here for." Ready to do business now, he said, "My name's Jack Burns. This here's my store."

"Pleased to meet you," Will said, but refrained from introducing himself. He began calling off a list of things he needed. There were quite a few, since he had depleted his supplies to make sure Walking Bird and Strong Bow had enough to take care of Ed for a good while.

"Ain't seen you in town before," Jack said, still curious. "Passing through?" He suddenly paused when Will reached down to steady his rifle when it threatened to slide from the front of the counter.

Realizing that Jack had seen his badge when his coat had opened slightly, Will quickly tried to put him at ease. "Yep, just passin' through—got some business to attend to north of here."

Jack was immediately cautious, however. "Is your

name Will Tanner?" he asked nervously, having heard of Dan Stone's newest deputy.

"How'd you know that?" Will asked. When Jack failed to reply, Will said, "That's my name, all right, and I'll tell you something else. I ain't had a drink of any good corn likker in quite a spell. If that stuff in the fruit jar is fit to drink, I'd like to buy a shot."

"You know I ain't supposed to sell moonshine," Jack said, thinking it a waste of time to try to lie his way out of trouble.

"Look, Mr. Burns, my mind is on something more important than you sellin' whiskey to those boys at the table. So we'll just forget about that if you can give me the information I need."

"Why, that's right decent of you, Marshal," Jack replied. He reached under the counter and came up with another fruit jar and a couple of glasses. "Like I said, I don't sell none of this, and I don't give none to Injuns. I just keep a little on hand for personal use." He paused while he poured Will's drink, then added, "And to offer a drink to friends." He believed Will when he said he wasn't concerned about his whiskey business, but he still thought it best not to admit he was selling it. "Tell me what you're needin' and I'll get it up for you."

Will called off the rest of the things he needed and watched Jack as he fetched each item, all the while aware of the apparent interest from the card table in his business with the store owner. Their conversation, loud and rowdy when he first walked in, was now being exchanged in hushed tones, almost whispered, in fact. They had evidently heard

Jack call him "Marshal." Maybe his first impression of three of them as cowhands was not necessarily the correct one. As with his lack of interest in Jack Burns's whiskey business, however, he was also unconcerned with the men at the table. More than likely they were some of the many drifters, most of whom were petty thieves, who sought refuge in the Nations. The task driving him now was to bring to justice the men who robbed the MKT, killed a guard, and left Ed Pine for dead. Regarding the card players as mere distraction from serious business, he returned to focus on Jack Burns. "Now, maybe you can tell me about the two men that rode through here a couple of days ago," he said to Jack.

"What two men?" Jack replied. "There ain't been nobody special that I recall—just the usual ranch hands that work along the Deep Fork River and a few drifters, like there always is."

"I thought we had us an understandin'," Will said. "I don't give you any trouble about your whiskey, and you give me a couple of honest answers. Maybe I got it wrong, and you'd rather have me get back to what the U.S. Marshals Service is payin' me to do."

"No, no, now, wait a minute," Burns quickly replied, lowering his voice to a whisper. "I ain't doin' nothin' illegal aside from sellin' a little bit of moonshine to a few strays that come through town, but I've got a reputation to consider." He glanced nervously at the table on the other side of the half wall. "The biggest portion of my moonshine customers are drifters on the run from somewhere. If the word gets around that I ain't careful what I tell a lawman, I wouldn't have many customers before long. I'll tell you what I can. Let's just keep it quiet." Raising his voice again, he said, "No, sir, I don't sell no whiskey. Now, I'll give you a hand carryin' your possibles out to pack on your horse." He winked at Will as he picked up a sack of coffee. "Then we can settle up. I won't charge you nothin' for grindin' them coffee beans for you."

"'Preciate it," Will said. "It sure beats poundin' 'em between a couple of rocks. I'm gonna get me one of those coffee mills one of these days." He picked up a sack and followed Burns out the door to his horses.

Jack started talking immediately, as if anxious to get it all said as quickly as possible. "You're after Ben Trout and Brock Larsen, ain't you?" Will nodded. "Well, they was here, all right, three nights ago, bought a fair amount of goods, then headed straight outta town."

"Which way?" Will asked.

"I don't know," Burns said, talking even faster now. "Out the north road, I think. I don't know where they was headin'. They didn't say."

At least he now had confirmation that he was on their trail. "Where's Buzzard's Roost?" Will asked.

"Where?" Jack replied at once. When Will repeated the question, Jack said, "Beats me. Danged if I've ever heard of it."

"On the Cimarron River?" Will pressed, but Burns shook his head again. From his expression, Will decided he was truthful in his reply. "Well, never mind, we'll go back inside and settle up."

Inside again, Will waited while Jack totaled up his bill. "I'll take another shot of that whiskey," he said. "It ain't half-bad for moonshine." Jack pulled the bottle from under the counter again and refilled Will's glass. "You can put this on the bill if you want," Will said.

"No, sir," Jack responded. "It's on the house."

"Much obliged," Will said, then tossed it down.

Unfortunately, Jack had spoken a bit too loudly. Already overly curious about what the store owner had to say to the deputy marshal, the four card players' conversation had stopped, and the game halted while they strained to hear. Upon hearing Jack offer a second free drink to the lawman, one of the men was moved to protest. A tall, angular man with a white scar splitting about a week's growth of beard, got up from his chair. "If there's gonna be any free drinks offered, then I reckon we sure as hell oughta be the ones gettin' 'em, since we've already bought two jars of this damn rotgut. I don't see no reason to waste it on a damn lawman, anyway." His words were accompanied by several grunts of agreement from his two partners. The fourth hand in the game, a smallish man wearing a black hat and morning coat, pushed his chair away from the table, but remained seated. Will figured him for a professional gambler who obviously had no inclination to participate in any trouble that the tall man initiated.

Will had not really seen this coming. He had figured the three men playing cards with the gambler might possibly be wanted somewhere for cattle rustling or petty theft of some kind. But he had assumed them likely to avoid any confrontation with a lawman. It appeared now that they were going to be more trouble than he cared to deal with at this point. Equally concerned to head off any trouble, Jack was quick to reply. "Maybe you're right, Nate," he said. "I gave the deputy a free drink because he bought a fair amount of goods from me. I reckon you and the boys deserve one, too, since you've given me a lot of business."

The offer was not enough to satisfy Nate Bingham. Emboldened by the generous amount of Jack's corn whiskey he had already consumed, he had no intention of letting an opportunity to make a name for himself pass. He had heard of a deputy marshal named Will Tanner, and the word was that the sandy-haired lawman was hell on horseback. It would be a mighty big man who shot Will Tanner, and there would not likely be a better situation than the one offered him now. Tanner was riding alone, deep in outlaw country, and Nate had Sonny Thompson and Pete Scoggins to back him. "Well, now, that's more like it, Jack," Nate blustered. "But I don't cotton to drinkin' with no low-down lawman." He turned his full attention toward Will then. "You got no business in this place where decent men are drinkin'. So the sooner you get your ass back on your horse and get yourself east of the railroad, the better chance you've got of gettin' back to Fort Smith alive."

"Be careful, Nate," Sonny Thompson murmured. "I've heard some things about this jasper."

"Shut up, Sonny," Nate said, his eyes focused on

the surprised lawman. "There's three of us against
him. What's he gonna do except crawl outta here
like the damn dog he is?" He leered wickedly at Will
then, even more confident of his advantage. "What
are you gonna do, lawman? It's just you all by your
lonesome, without nobody to back you up."

"Maybe we oughta just let him go," Pete implored.
Like Sonny, he was afraid Nate had let the whiskey
cause him to bring a posse of deputy marshals hard
on their trail.

"The hell I will," Nate blurted. "I'm callin' him
out." Yelling at Will then, he repeated the question.
"What are you gonna do, lawman?" He took a wide
stance with his hand hovering barely inches above
the handle of the .44 he wore on his hip. "You're
stinkin' up the air in here."

Standing at the counter, his back partially turned
toward the belligerent drunk, Will did not move.
Truthfully, he didn't know what he was going to do,
still mentally kicking himself for not considering the
potential for trouble from the three. He glanced
briefly at Jack Burns when the alarmed store
owner cautiously backed away from the counter
in an obvious move to get out of the line of fire.
How the hell did I get myself in this situation? Will asked
himself. But instead of fear, irritation was his pri-
mary feeling, and impatience for having been
delayed in his hunt for the killers he had tracked
this far. His challenger was strictly out to gain a
reputation for himself by calling him out, but
Will was sure Nate had no fair contest in mind.
Neither did Will, for that matter, so he tried to stall

the confrontation and maybe persuade Nate's two pals to stay out of it. Maybe, if he stalled long enough, he might see an opportunity to come out of this alive. "You're callin' me out, are you?" he finally spoke. "What's it gonna be, face-to-face out in the street? Or are you figurin' on the three of you just blazin' away as soon as I turn around?"

"I reckon you'll just have to wait and find out, won't you, lawman?" Nate replied smugly.

"I didn't think you had the guts to stand on your own against me," Will said, still with his back half-turned toward Nate. "Which one of you will claim that it was you that did the killin'? Hell, you're just all mouth. Without your two friends, you ain't got the spine to stand up against me." He could see that his taunting was getting to his assailant, but he still had gained nothing but time. He needed a piece of luck of some kind to gain an advantage. By pure chance, it came in the door at that moment.

"Hey, you old crook! You still sellin' moonshine?" Billy Avery yelled out as loud as he could as he pushed through the front door. He swaggered toward the counter, a wide grin parting the gray whiskers that covered a good portion of his face, unaware of the situation he had walked in on. His outburst had startled everyone in the store, and all but one had reacted by unconsciously looking toward the source. Billy was about to blare out again, but the expression on Jack Burns's face told him something was wrong. Aware of the three men standing at the half wall glaring at him then, he started to back away toward the door. Nate Bingham turned back toward the counter when he heard the distinct sound of a cartridge being cranked into the chamber of a rifle. He found himself staring at the business end of a Winchester 73 and the cold eyes of the deputy marshal.

"Hold on there a minute!" Nate sang out fearfully, his hand still hovering over his holstered pistol. "Don't go doin' nothin' crazy!" He looked quickly toward Pete and Sonny, who were just as stunned as he. "There's still three of us," Nate blurted desperately. "You can't get us all before one of us gets you."

With cold, hard eyes that promised a deadly storm to come, and his rifle leveled at Nate's belly, Will locked his gaze upon the would-be assassin. "You'll be the first to go down. If I see any one of you reach for a weapon, you'll get the first bullet, big mouth. I'll also get one of your pals before the first gun is drawn. I don't know how quick any one of you can draw your pistol and fire it, but I'm damn sure how fast I can cock this rifle after I shoot you down. And I'm bettin' on myself to get you and one of your friends for certain. I don't know for sure about the one left, but I'm thinkin' I've got a good chance to get at least one round in him before I'm done. If you don't believe me, then one of you make your move, and we'll see."

A dead silence fell over the room for several long moments after Will's deadly proclamation left his antagonists in a state of indecision. The warning had been delivered in a confident, factual manner, calmly and without any sense of fear, effectively leaving all three outlaws uncertain. The tables had turned dramatically on Nate, and when Sonny took a couple of steps backward, Nate blurted out, "Don't go for that gun!" He was convinced that Will would do as he promised, and the muzzle of that Winchester was looking right at his gut.

Knowing they were effectively stopped, Will didn't waste any time. "Now, here's what we're gonna do. I'm gonna let you boys off easy this time just because I've got more important things I've gotta do than waste time on two-bit thieves like you." He nodded toward the still-astonished little gray-haired man who had blundered into the midst of the confrontation. "What's your name, mister?"

"Billy Avery," he stammered, and took another step backward. "I ain't out to cause you no trouble. I'll just be on my way."

"You just hold it right there, Billy," Will said. "I've got a job for you. I want you to step over there behind those three and lift their guns outta the holsters and bring 'em over here and put 'em on the counter." Billy hesitated, not sure he wanted to be involved, so Will prompted him. "Hurry up. Don't worry, the first one that moves will get shot." Billy nodded nervously, but did as he was ordered. Without taking his eyes off the three outlaws, Will said to Jack, "Pull me a few feet of rope offa that roll on the end of the counter, Mr. Burns." He watched then as Billy walked behind the three and carefully drew the first two handguns, one by one. But when he reached for Sonny Thompson's .44, Sonny, thinking Will was distracted for a moment when Jack Burns moved to get the rope, decided he had time to get off a shot. The muzzle of his .44 had not cleared the holster when the tenseness of the room was shattered by the sharp report of the Winchester. Sonny's weapon dropped to the floor while he staggered backward to land on his back, clutching his right thigh. It served as a cue for the frightened gambler to quietly take his leave.

"You shot me!" Sonny howled, as if surprised.

"I did," Will replied manner-of-factly, "and it was out of the kindness of my heart that I didn't shoot to kill." He glanced at Nate then. "I can see by the look on your face that you're wonderin' now, 'Did he cock that rifle after he shot?' Well, I've got a question for you. Do you see a spent cartridge on the floor anywhere?"

Before Nate could reply, Billy blurted, "I see it. It's yonder, up against the counter." Clearly impressed by the deputy's lightning reactions, he added, "I swear, you musta cranked that lever before that bullet hit that feller's leg."

"Pick up his pistol," Will said to Billy, and waited while the now-excited little man hurried to bring the weapons to the counter. "Now, Mr. Burns, I wanna see how good you are at tyin' knots. Bring that rope." With his rifle trained on the outlaws, Will led Jack to stand behind them. "Put your hands behind your back," he ordered Nate.

"You're mighty damn lucky you got the jump on me," Nate spat angrily, "or things woulda turned out a whole lot different." He was regaining some of his bluster, now that it appeared that the deputy was not going to kill them.

"Put your hands behind your back," Will repeated. When Nate still did not comply at once, he rapped him sharply beside his head with the barrel of his rifle. Nate was staggered, almost falling, but immediately stuck his hands behind him while Jack bound his wrists together. When it was Pete's turn, he already had his hands behind him, having seen what it cost not to respond. Using the one long length of rope, Will had Jack loop the free end around the wrists of both men, drawing them close together. Will turned to the wounded Sonny then, who was still lying on the floor. "Get up and stand next to 'em."

"I can't stand up—you shot me," Sonny protested pitifully. "I need a doctor."

"You've still got one good leg," Will said. He reached down with his free hand and grabbed Sonny by the collar. "Gimme a hand," he said to Jack, and the two of them stood Sonny up and bound him up with his partners. Now that he had the three of them tied up and no longer a threat, he had to figure out what to do with them. He had already lost too much time because of the unlucky encounter, and he didn't like the idea of wasting any further time with them. "There's a Creek Lighthorse policeman headquartered here, right?" he asked Jack.

"That's right," Jack answered, "Marvin Big Sky. He's most likely down at the Council House."

"I'm here," a voice from the front door announced,

and Will turned to see a broad-shouldered man with long black hair in two braids down his back. He carried a rifle in his hand. "I heard a shot, so I came to see." He took a long look at the three men tied together before turning to address Will. "Are you Will Tanner?"

"I am," Will answered.

"I heard you were coming," Marvin said.

"How'd you hear that?" Will asked. "There ain't no telegraph in Okmulkee, is there?"

Marvin smiled. "Indian telegraph—works faster than white man's wire. Sam Black Crow sent word."

"Well, I'm glad you showed up," Will said. "Maybe you can help me out here." He took him aside and told him the circumstances that led to the capture of the three men and the wounding of one of them. "They're just three saddle bums that got a little too drunk. The problem is they're holdin' me up from doin' what I was sent over here to do. Have you got a jail where you could hold these prisoners for a day or two, so I can get back after Brock Larsen and Ben Trout?"

"We got a lockup room in the bottom of the Council House," Marvin said. "I can hold 'em there." He shook his head slowly when Will told him that Ed Pine had been shot. "That's bad news about Ed. He's a good man."

"Yes, he is," Will said. "And I sure appreciate your help. I'm losin' too much ground on the pair that shot him, and they're two killers that I don't want to get away."

Marvin shrugged indifferently. "I'll lock 'em up.

You planning on takin' 'em back to Fort Smith with those two train robbers if you catch 'em?"

"No, I ain't gonna fool with these three," Will was quick to explain. "I just wanna get a head start in case that one I shot, or the tall, lanky one wants to get even with me for that welt on the side of his head. Most likely, they'll leave your town as fast as they can when you cut 'em loose. We'll just call it disturbin' the peace and let 'em go."

"I'll take care of it," Marvin said. "Glad to help."

"I appreciate it," Will repeated. "If that Indian telegraph is still workin', you might wanna get word to Sam Black Crow that Deputy Ed Pine is lyin' shot up about a half day's ride west of Muskogee. An old Creek woman named Walkin' Bird and her grandson are takin' care of him till I can come back for him. Maybe he knows where her camp is. There ain't nobody in the camp but her and the boy." He paused then. "One last question: Do you know where Buzzard's Roost is?"

"Never heard of it," Marvin said. "What is it?"

"Supposed to be an outlaw hideout somewhere up on the Cimarron, but damned if anybody knows where it is." He turned back toward the counter, where his three prisoners were standing sullenly waiting. "Come on, I'll help you take these three to the Council House, then I've gotta get ridin'."

"We can't walk nowhere all bunched up like this," Nate protested when they were told to start toward the door. "And Sonny with only one good leg." Sonny groaned painfully to confirm it.

"It's either walk up there in a bunch or get dragged

up there by a horse," Will informed him. "So you might as well get started."

Outside, Will climbed into the saddle and herded the bound-up trio up the street to the Creek Council House. Marvin Big Sky rode one of the outlaws' horses and led the others. It was an odd, slow-moving parade, led by a grumbling, cursing knot of outlaws trying to stumble together in an effort to all move in one direction. Billy Avery walked along with them, enjoying the show. When they reached the Council House and saw their accommodations, Nate protested again. "This ain't nothin' but a smokehouse under that stone house."

Marvin grinned. "It's got a stout door and a good lock, though, in case you're worried about somebody breakin' in on you."

"This place is for Injuns," Pete Scoggins complained. "You ain't supposed to put no white prisoners in an Injun jail."

"That's all right," Marvin replied. "You boys ain't prisoners, you're guests of the Creek Nation. We hope you enjoy your visit with us."

While Will held his rifle on the prisoners, Marvin untied them and hustled them into the twelve-foot-square, windowless room. Will almost felt sorry for them when Marvin latched the door and closed the padlock. "That's a helluva place to spend any time," he said to Marvin.

"Ain't it, though," the Creek policeman replied with a chuckle. "When I let 'em out, they ain't likely to wanna come back to Okmulgee."

"What about food?" Will asked.

"There's a Creek woman that'll cook for 'em. Don't worry, I'll feed 'em, but I reckon I'm gonna have to charge you for their food."

"I figured," Will said. "I'll leave you enough money for three meals each. How much does the Creek woman charge?"

"Twenty-five cents," Marvin answered. "Won't cost you nothin' to take care of their horses. I'll let 'em eat grass."

"Maybe I can talk Dan Stone into payin' me back if I add it to my expenses for this trip." He had already spent extra for Ed Pine's food, but Marshal Stone had always treated him fairly on expenses so far. "I reckon I'd best get started," he said to Marvin, and walked back toward his horses.

"It's almost dark," Marvin said. "You might as well stay here tonight. My place ain't but a half a mile from town."

"'Preciate the offer," Will replied. He decided Marvin was right. It was already too dark to even try to pick up any tracks the two outlaws might have left him.

CHAPTER 4

After making camp close to Marvin Big Sky's cabin on the Deep Fork River and eating a fine supper provided by Marvin's wife, Will left at first light to return to town in hopes of striking Ben and Brock's trail. Jack Burns had told him he thought the two outlaws rode out the north road three nights ago. That would make it four nights now, and as he realistically expected, he couldn't distinguish between the tracks he searched for and the many others on the road. "Well," he sighed aloud to Buster, "I reckon we've gotta switch from trackin' to hopin'." He climbed into the saddle and started out the north road to search for a place that nobody had ever heard of, never mind knowing where it was.

He continued on the road as it led past several small farms until he found himself at the last farm and the end of the road. The sun was high in the sky now, even though it had warmed the frosty prairie very little. Will estimated that he had ridden about seven miles, only to find a surprised Indian farmer driving a horse and cart toward him. The farmer pulled his horse to a stop and waited while Will rode up beside him. "I'm a U.S. Deputy Marshal," Will said. The man nodded, but did not speak, clearly puzzled to find a deputy approaching his homestead. "I don't suppose you saw two white men pass your farm in the last several days, did you?" The man solemnly shook his head. *I didn't think so,* Will thought, figuring then that he had been following a road to nowhere. He already knew the answer, but he asked the question anyway. "Does this road end here, or is there another piece of it farther on?"

"End here." The man finally spoke.

"Figured that," Will groused, frustrated, knowing that the two outlaws had no doubt left the road some miles back, and he had missed it. The tracks were just too old. "Much obliged," he said, and turned Buster back the way he had come. Going back over the road, he realized there were any number of places where the outlaws could have abandoned the wagon road out of town, and there was very little chance of his finding the right one. A picture of Ed Pine lying in that tipi, most likely dying, came to his mind, and he resolved anew to find his attackers. With no trail to follow, he decided he might as well head west to strike the Cimarron River. When he got there, he would scout the river until he found Buzzard's Roost. It wasn't much of a plan, but it was all he had.

* * *

A day and a half's ride brought him to the Cimarron, striking it at one of the many loops of the snakelike river and leaving him with still no idea where to look for Buzzard's Roost. His choices were two: follow the winding river in search of the outlaw camp, or turn around and go back to get Ed Pine. Thinking again of the two killers that bushwhacked Ed, he chose the former and decided to follow the river west, so he made a mental note of his starting point and set out along the bank.

He spent the rest of that day riding the bank of the river with absolutely no sign of a cabin, or even tracks to indicate anyone had ridden there before him. When darkness forced him to make camp, he was already of the opinion that he was on a fool's mission, but he was not inclined to admit that he would not eventually find Buzzard's Roost. He told himself that he had chosen the wrong direction to search in, so he crossed over the wide, shallow river to make camp, planning to start back in the other direction in the morning.

He awakened the next morning to a sky overcast by heavy snow clouds. By the time he reached the point where his search had started the day before, a light snow was falling. After resting the horses, he started following the river in the opposite direction from that taken the night before. As the afternoon wore on, with no sign of anything resembling a camp, he came to the conclusion that he was a damn fool. He had no idea what he was looking for, just betting on luck, and he began to wonder if there was such a place as Buzzard's Roost. He was beginning to give serious thought to the notion of returning for Ed Pine and taking him back to Fort Smith, which might have been the thing to do in the first place. At least the snow had stopped, after leaving a light blanket of perhaps an inch and a half. It was then that he came upon a camp. Rounding one of the many bends of the Cimarron, he spotted what appeared to be one man tending a campfire. Will stopped immediately, guiding Buster up into the trees that bordered the river, pretty sure the man had not seen him.

With his rifle in hand, Will dismounted and left his horses tied while he worked his way up closer to the camp on foot. A clump of laurel bushes growing near the edge of the water was as close as he could advance without coming out in the open, so he knelt there while he tried to get a better look. What he had first thought was an Indian turned out to be a white man dressed in hides. He was not close enough, however, to tell much more about him, since the man was turned partially away from him as he tended some meat over his fire. After a few more minutes, without turning around, the man suddenly spoke. "Well," he called out, "you comin' in, or are you just gonna set there in them bushes?"

Startled, Will hesitated for a moment before rising to his feet and answering. "If it's all right with you, I reckon I'll come on in."

"Come ahead then," the man replied.

Will left the cover of the laurels and walked

across a wide expanse of flat bank, his rifle carried in one hand by his side. Feeling a little perturbed at himself for having been spotted, he paused a few yards before the fire to look around the camp to make sure there was no one else there. The man turned to consider the unexpected visitor to his fire, and for a few moments the two strangers studied each other intently. Will decided the man was older than he had at first thought, for there were faint streaks of gray woven in the Indian-style braids he wore. There was a frank expression of curiosity in the lean face, and none of fear. When the man spoke again, it was a simple question. "You on foot?"

"My horses are back there in the trees," Will answered. He paused to study the man's face again, deciding there was no evil intent in his manner, merely curiosity. "I'll go back and get 'em." He nodded toward the meat roasting over the flames. "Whaddaya cookin'?"

"Rabbit," the man said. "Ain't a helluva lot, but I reckon there's enough for two of us."

"Got any coffee?" Will asked.

"Not for about two months," was the reply.

"No problem," Will said. "I've got plenty, and maybe some sowbelly to help that rabbit out a little." His remark brought a gleam to the stranger's eyes. Will walked back to the trees to bring his horses in.

When Will returned, leading the buckskin and the bay to the water's edge, the man watched him, unconsciously nodding his approval for Will's seeing to his horses' needs first. He got to his feet and extended his hand. "The name's Oscar Moon," he said.

Will shook his hand. "Will Tanner," he said as he took a closer look at the thin, lined face, sporting no hair other than a bushy mustache, which was streaked with gray like his braids. He wore an expression that seemed to convey he had nothing to hide.

"You a deputy marshal?" Moon asked.

Surprised, since his badge was inside his coat, Will asked, "What makes you think that?"

"Your horses," Moon replied. "I ain't never seen a marshal ridin' any old crow-bait horse. And them look like stout horses, 'specially that buckskin."

"Maybe I stole 'em," Will countered.

Moon took a harder look at his visitor. "You ain't got the look of a horse thief," he finally decided.

Will laughed. "Well, you're right, I ain't a horse thief, and you're right again. I am a deputy marshal."

"Kinda thought you might be," Moon said. "Whaddaya doin' up here in Osage country?"

Before answering, Will got his coffeepot and some coffee from his packhorse. Then he unwrapped the slab of bacon to slice. "I'm lookin' for a couple of train robbers who murdered a train guard and possibly a deputy. They rode up this way," he said when he returned to the fire. "Maybe you've run across 'em—Ben Trout and Brock Larsen."

"Can't say as I have," Moon said. "But I ain't been down this way for a while. I got a place up on the

Arkansas River where I do most of my trappin' and huntin'."

"Maybe you know where a place called Buzzard's Roost is," Will said.

"Buzzard's Roost?" Moon repeated, and thought for a moment before shaking his head. "Nope, never heard of it, and I know the Cimarron and Arkansas country as good as any man, I reckon. What is it, a town?"

"No, from the little bit I know about it, it's just a couple of cabins, an outlaw hideout. And I think these two outlaws I'm lookin' for were headin' there. All I know for sure is that it's on the Cimarron somewhere."

Moon thought about that for another moment. "I don't know about no Buzzard's Roost," he said. "The place you're talking about sounds more like Sartain's. Feller name of Elmer Sartain built a cabin there quite a few years back. He was a stagecoach robber as I recollect. Over the years, it got to be a regular hangout for outlaws on the run, and there's three cabins there now. Only, it ain't on the Cimarron, it's on Muskrat Creek that empties into the Cimarron. There's a woman name of Elmira Tate who lives in one of the cabins, and she does the cookin' for whoever's there at the time. Sartain ain't there no more. Winter before last, he got throwed off his horse when he was tryin' to chase a pack of wolves away from a stray cow. The wolves jumped him when he hit the snow. He chased 'em off, but one of 'em bit him pretty bad. I reckon he got the poison in it, or somethin', 'cause a couple of weeks later, he took to his bed with fever and woke up one mornin' dead." Moon nodded solemnly to emphasize the finality of it. "Ever since Sartain died, Elmira took it over and has been runnin' it like it was hers."

To Will, that surely sounded more like the place the outlaws were seeking. He had to consider the fact that Buzzard's Roost might just be what these two called the hideout, their own pet name for the group of cabins, and not how anyone else referred to it. "Sartain's, huh?" he asked. "I reckon you most likely know where that is, right?"

"Why, sure," Moon responded. "I used to take a deer or an antelope in there once in a while for Elmira to cook. They'd pay me good money to bring 'em fresh meat, but I ain't been down this way since early summer." He paused to scratch his chin whiskers. "I reckon I oughta ride over that way to see if they need some fresh meat. I might be able to run up on a herd of deer down near the shallows where there's a natural crossin'. I came up that way yesterday and there was plenty of sign." He gave Will a sharp look then. "Course, I can't go ridin' in there with a deputy marshal. That'd be the end of my business dealin's with the crowd that stays there, and might be the end of my life." He cocked a suspicious eye at Will. "You know, I ain't broke no laws, myself. I just sell a little meat from time to time to get enough money for some cartridges and such. Sartain's is about as far south as I get in Injun Territory. I've sold meat to other camps, but they're up around Wichita."

Will couldn't help smiling. "And you don't supply anything but deer meat, and antelope, and other wild game," he chided. "Not ever a stray cow from one of the cattle ranches in the Flint Hills, just north of the Kansas line, I suppose."

"Oh mercy, no," Moon replied at once. "That would be cattle rustlin', and I sure ain't no rustler."

"I'm glad to hear it. I thought I had you figured for an honest man," Will said, even though he would have bet a month's pay that the residents at Sartain's most likely enjoyed good Kansas beef on a regular basis—and a fair amount of it probably came from Moon. "I sure don't wanna risk your business dealin's with the lady there," Will said, "so I won't ask you to take me there, but I'd sure consider it a favor if you could just tell me how to find it. Whaddaya say?"

Moon gave it a second's thought before answering. "I reckon there ain't no harm in that." He paused while he continued to ponder the right and wrong of revealing the location of the outlaw hideout. "Course, you'd keep in mind that Elmira and her boy ain't outlaws, wouldn't ya? They just take care of the place and Elmira does the cookin'. That's just how she earns her livin' now that she's too old for whorin'."

"That's understood," Will assured him. "I'm not interested in anybody there but Ben Trout and Brock Larsen, and that's if they're even there." This was a fact, even though he would have probably been justified to make an arrest of anyone he found at the huddle of cabins. They were most likely wanted for something somewhere. And that included Elmira, for providing a hideout for fugitives wanted by the law. The fact of the matter, however, was that he didn't come prepared to transport a whole gang of prisoners back to Fort Smith. With no wagon and no posse, he'd have a hell of a time managing more than the two he came after. He could see by the worried look on Moon's face that he didn't care to take any part in introducing a U.S. Deputy Marshal to the residents of Sartain's. So he attempted to put him at ease about it. "As a matter of fact, I had just as soon nobody else at Sartain's finds out I'm a deputy. You think you could keep that under your hat?"

Moon responded to that suggestion right away. "I sure could. I think that's a right smart thing to do." He paused then when he thought to ask, "You mean you're fixin' to walk in there without even a how-de-do and just shoot 'em down?"

"No," Will answered. "I don't mean that a-tall. In the first place, I don't even know what these two fellows look like. I mean to arrest 'em and take 'em back to Fort Smith for trial. But I need to get into that camp and make sure I arrest the right two. There might be more than just Trout and Larsen in the camp, so that's why I don't want anybody to know I'm the law—even after I'm gone, if possible. I might need to look for somebody at Sartain's again sometime. So once I find out which ones are the two I came for, I'll see if I can't get a chance to catch 'em away from the camp."

Moon mentally chewed on that for a moment, then decided that he would be all right with it. He liked what he had seen so far of the deputy marshal and figured it wouldn't hurt to count him as a friend. And as long as Elmira and her guests had no knowledge of that friendship, his business with them shouldn't be endangered. He believed Will when he said he had no intention of hauling Elmira and everybody else at Sartain's off to prison. As far as Larsen and Trout were concerned, Moon had never heard of them, and if they had done what he said, they oughta be arrested and hanged. "I'll take you to Sartain's," he announced.

"Good," Will said. "I appreciate it. How far is it from here?"

"About five miles, maybe six," Moon replied. He looked up at a sky already losing the last rays of the setting sun. "You wantin' to go there tonight?"

"I think in the mornin' will be better," Will answered. "I wanna look the place over good before I go ridin' in there—at least find out how many are in the camp."

"That suits me," Moon said, "especially since I've already set up my camp, and my rabbit's about done, and I'm smellin' that coffee now. In the mornin'll be just fine."

Will awoke to find the campfire already blazing with new life, and the coffeepot sitting in the coals, but no sign of Moon close by. He realized that he had slept pretty soundly, something he had not planned to do, and he immediately scolded himself for his carelessness. He could have just as easily found himself sporting a slit throat this morning, if he had been wrong in judging Moon harmless. He returned his .44 pistol to his holster, having slept with it tucked under his arm, and climbed out of his blanket. He noticed a line of tracks in the snow leading toward the trees. A moment later, Moon appeared at the edge of the trees, having answered a summons from Mother Nature. "Mornin'," he called out as he strode up to the fire, still buckling up his pants. "I believe that sowbelly and coffee we et for supper kinda freed me up a little in the bowels. I ain't had a call for three or four days. Livin' on nothin' but deer and rabbits will do that to you—ain't enough grease in 'em to keep things movin' easy." He spread a small flap of deer hide on the snow on the other side of the fire and sat down, crossing his feet Indian style, and filled his cup. "I warn't sure whether you wanted to get started before breakfast or eat first. But I figured you'd need some coffee either way."

"You figured right," Will said, still feeling a little chagrined at having slept so soundly. "Coffee will do for me, though, and maybe a piece of jerky." He was anxious to find this outlaw camp. Already, he had lost too much time in his pursuit of Ben Trout and Brock Larsen.

When their horses were saddled and ready, they finished the pot of coffee and got under way. Much to Will's surprise, Moon led them back along the riverbank, retracing the route that Will had ridden the day before. They came upon a couple of places where small streams emptied into the river. Moon passed them all, continuing on until stopping short of a deep horseshoe bend in the river where a low mesa forced the water to flow southward before resuming its direction toward the east. "Muskrat Creek," Moon announced factually.

"Where?" Will asked, seeing no sign of a creek joining the river.

Moon pointed toward the back of the horseshoe where the river ran right up to the rocky face of the steep mesa. "Yonder," he said. "You can't see it from here unless you know what you're lookin' for. The creek runs underground from the other side of that hill. You have to go to the backside of the hill to see it. If you was to ride across the river right there, you could feel the water from the creek pourin' through the rocks below the waterline." Will shook his head, amazed. Without Moon's help, it seemed extremely unlikely that he would ever have stumbled upon Muskrat Creek, even knowing where to look for it.

They crossed the river near the lower end of the mesa, then rode back until coming to a formation of hollow rocks on the backside of the incline, close to its steepest part, where the slowly moving creek disappeared into the rocks. "There you go," Moon said. "Goes right under the ground." He turned in the opposite direction then to follow the now clearly seen course of the creek with his eyes, as it ran straight north to disappear into a tree-covered line of hills about two miles distant. "I'll ride with you to them hills. You can see Sartain's from there, but it's all open country between the hills and the cabins. So I'd best not go any farther with you—too easy for somebody to see us from the cabins." Will nodded and turned Buster to follow Moon's lead.

When they reached the hills, they rode up the slope above the creek and dismounted. "Come on," Moon said, and looped his reins over a low tree limb. "We'll leave the horses here." Will followed him to the highest point of the hill, by an oak that had been struck by lightning sometime in the past. "Yonder's Sartain's," Moon said.

As Moon had said, there were practically no trees for an expanse of about three quarters of a mile. Although the banks of the creek were bordered by clumps of laurel and berry bushes, Will could see that it would be impossible to surprise anyone at the cabins coming from this direction. There was very little cover until the creek entered a grove of oaks where the cabins were built. "That's the original cabin, the first one on the west bank of the creek," Moon said. "It's the biggest. Elmira moved into it when Sartain died. That 'un right across the creek from it was built by Sartain, too. The little one, next to Sartain's, was built by two fellers on the run from Colorado Territory for stealin' horses. They didn't stay in it but a year is what Elmira says. The last time I was here, there was a whore name of Darlene Futch livin' there."

Will took a long look at the collection of cabins,

wondering what the present population of the little outlaw conclave was on this day. From where he stood, there was no way to guess, since the cold fall weather kept the occupants inside by the fire. There was smoke coming from all three chimneys, however. He was further hampered by the fact that he could see no horses to even give him an estimate. When he asked where they were, Moon told him the horses were grazed on the tall grass prairie on the other side of the trees. "There ain't no barn," he said, "When the weather gets real bad, they just bunch the horses up under the side of the hill in the trees."

"Well, I reckon the only way I'm gonna find out who's in there is to take a little ride in and see," Will concluded.

"Looks that way, don't it?" Moon agreed. "Well, like I said, it won't do for me to be seen ridin' with you, just in case you run into somebody down there who knows you. So I reckon I'll head on back toward the river. Good luck. I hope you can catch them two you've been chasin'. I'm liable to run into you again before long, if you ain't kilt or somethin' "

"Right," Will replied. "I appreciate your help. I might notta ever found this place without your help. I've got a couple of sacks of extra coffee. Why don't you take one of 'em for your trouble?"

"Well, now, that's mighty neighborly of you, Will. I would surely appreciate that. I don't know when I'd get a chance to get some."

Every time I turn around, I'm giving my supplies away

to someone, Will thought. He reached inside his coat, pulled his badge off his shirt, and put it in his pocket as they walked back to the horses.

Moon stood there for a long while, his sack of coffee in hand, watching the deputy as he rode off down the hill. Will Tanner struck him as a young man with his head in the right place. He decided he liked the sandy-haired lawman, and he hoped he would be around for a while, because he did seem to have no hesitation about taking chances. And that could be dangerous with the crowd that hung out at Sartain's.

CHAPTER 5

Not at all certain he was doing the smart thing, Will nevertheless guided Buster down from the top of the mesa to intercept a path running along the side of the creek. Maybe it would have been more sensible to wait until dark and try to scout the camp before riding in. That would at least have given him an opportunity to get a count of their horses, so he could have made a fair guess on the number of men who were there. Or maybe not, he told himself. And anyway, he had to identify the two men he was after, so he decided the best way to find out who everybody was, was to simply ride in and say howdy. The decision was made for him when he saw a couple of men suddenly appear beside the larger cabin when he was still two hundred yards from the camp. The men both carried rifles and walked to the edge of the creek where the path turned toward the cabins. Will made no move to hail them, but continued his casual approach. They watched him carefully as he pulled up to a stop some twenty yards short of them.

"Howdy," one of the men, a short, heavyset fellow, greeted him. "You lost?"

Will looked from him to the other one, who was tall and skinny in contrast to his partner. "Maybe," Will answered. "Depends."

"On what?" the skinny one asked.

Will took a casual glance at the cluster of cabins behind the two men before answering. "On whether or not this is Sartain's," he said.

"Whatcha want with Sartain?" the heavyset one asked.

"I don't want anything with Sartain," Will answered, showing a hint of irritation at the questions. "From what I was told, Sartain's dead, but the word I got said a feller could find a hot meal and a place to rest his horses for a spell at Sartain's. So I reckon what I need to know is, is this Sartain's or ain't it? 'Cause if it ain't, then I'm wastin' my time jawin' with you two jaspers."

"You're in the right place, stranger," a female voice called out from the door of the cabin, as Elmira Tate stepped out on the single step. "Don't pay no attention to Slim and Coy, come on up to the house." She took a couple more steps from the door and stood watching Will, her hands on her hips, as she took an assessment of her new visitor. A rugged-looking man, and well mounted, he did not strike her as the typical drifter to show up at her door. "What brings you out this way?"

Will walked his horses up slowly to the cabin. "I

reckon I'm gettin' tired of my own cookin'," he said. "I was told a man could buy a good meal here."

Elmira smiled. "Well, you was told right. Who told you?"

"Oh, a feller I ran into in Wichita," Will replied. "Don't recall his name." Out of the corner of his eye, he noticed a man now standing in the door of the cabin directly across the creek from Elmira's. He was also holding a rifle. *That's three*, he thought, and wondered if there were more. A large woman younger than Elmira, with wide shoulders and hips to match, came outside then to stand close behind Elmira. She made no attempt to disguise her obvious appraisal of their visitor.

"We're kinda particular who shows up to eat here," the heavyset man said, openly suspicious.

Will looked him hard in the eye, glanced at the skinny man standing next to him, then shifted his gaze toward the man standing in the door of the cabin. "It doesn't look like it," he said.

His reply caused both women to laugh. "Well, I reckon you're right about that, ain't he, Darlene?"

"Amen to that," Darlene answered. She smiled warmly at Will then and asked, "You ain't got anybody close on your tail, have you?"

"Reckon not," Will answered. "I wouldn't have come straight here if I did."

"Well, I reckon you're welcome, then," Darlene said, then grinned and added, "as long as you ain't runnin' because you're wanted for killin' a whore someplace." She laughed in appreciation of her joke. "We've already cleaned up from breakfast, but there's still some coffee on, and we might have a biscuit or two left, if you're hungry." She glanced at Elmira to get her nod of approval.

While they had talked, a sturdy young man joined them, also coming from Elmira's cabin. "Eddie can help you take care of your horses," she said, nodding toward the young man, "unless you're of a mind to ride on right away."

"Coffee and a biscuit sounds too good to pass up," Will said. "And it wouldn't hurt to rest my horses for a spell. Course, I expect to pay you for the food. I was figurin' on stayin' around long enough to try one of your meals, if that's all right with you. It's been a while since I've set at a table."

"Good," Elmira said. "Come on in after you take care of your horses. Eddie will show you where to let 'em graze."

Eddie nodded to Will and started to lead the way past the third cabin toward the back of the hill. As Moon had described it, the hill was not as big as it looked when approaching it from the Cimarron. And the backside of it formed a steep flat overhang that afforded some protection for the horses in bad weather. Beyond the hill, he saw horses and half a dozen cows grazing on an open prairie. "You thinkin' 'bout movin' your stuff in the cabin with the other fellers?" Eddie asked.

"I don't know," Will said. "I ain't decided. I've got to keep ridin' on up into Kansas Territory before the weather gets much worse. Besides, it looks like you folks might be crowded already."

"Ah, we've had more'n this stayin' here," Eddie

said. "There ain't but three stayin' in that cabin across the creek, and it's had more'n that in it before. We've even took in one or two in the cabin with Ma and me from time to time. And Darlene's had a few stay with her. Matter of fact, there's two fellers stayin' with her now." He grinned broadly. "They didn't wanna bunk in with Coy and Slim and Pop."

"Is that a fact?" Will replied, interested. "I didn't see anybody besides the three fellers back there." He had a strong feeling it was the two he was after.

"They took off this mornin'," Eddie replied. "Said they was gonna ride up to Scully's tradin' post on the Arkansas. I think they're lookin' to trade a couple of horses and an extra saddle and some stuff they brought with 'em. Pop says he thinks that saddle belonged to a lawman."

Will was certain now that he was on the right trail. "What makes him think that?"

"I reckon 'cause they was talkin' mighty big about not worryin' 'bout any of them marshals outta Fort Smith. And that was a right fine-lookin' horse and saddle, decent-lookin' packhorses, too."

"And you say they took off this mornin'?" Will asked, concerned now that he might have just missed them.

"Yeah, but they said they'll be back for supper," Eddie replied.

Looks like I'll be staying for supper for sure, Will thought. "Pop thinks it's a lawman's saddle, huh? Pop, is that your daddy?"

"Hell, no," Eddie replied at once. "That's just

what they call him. He rode in with Slim Branch and Coy Trainer. They've been here for the better part of six months. Ma says if they don't come up with some more money pretty soon, she's gonna kick 'em out." Holding the bay's bridle, he asked, "You want me to take the bridle off?"

"No, I'll leave the bridles on for now," Will said, then pulled Buster's saddle off, removed the packs from the bay, but left the pack saddle on. He left them there at the foot of the hill and told Eddie he'd take them to the cabin if he decided to stay overnight. He figured he'd have to make a show of moving his things into the cabin later, but for now, he took his rifle and saddlebags with him back to Elmira's cabin. It was his intention to plant the thought in their minds that he was carrying something in the saddlebags that warranted his keeping a constant eye on them.

"You're in luck," Elmira sang out when Will and her son walked in the door to find the three men who had confronted him seated around a long table. "There's a couple biscuits left, and I even had a slice of beef we cooked from a poor ol' cow that wandered in here lost a few days ago. Set yourself down and I'll pour you some coffee. It's fresh, since everybody decided to have some with you. Coffee costs money, but we figured we'd all get acquainted, since you ain't ever been here before—it being the polite thing to do."

Will got the hint, and since he wanted to give the impression that he was flush, he reached in his pocket and pulled out a roll of bills. "I'll buy the coffee," he said, and peeled off a couple of dollars. "Is that enough?"

"Why, that's mighty generous," Elmira said, her smile almost constant now. "You might as well meet everybody in our little family. You already know me—I'm Elmira—and Darlene, and my son, Eddie. These two outstandin' gentlemen that met you with loaded rifles are Coy and Slim. This here's Pop," she said, referring to the man Will had seen standing in the doorway.

"No hard feelin's," Coy said

"None taken," Will answered. "It pays to know who's comin' to call in this territory."

"So whadda we call you?" Darlene asked.

"Walker," Will replied. It was the first name that popped into his head.

"Well, Mr. Walker, welcome to Sartain's," Darlene said grandly.

"What part of the country did you come from?" Pop Strawbridge asked.

"Colorado," Will replied.

"What line of business are you in, Walker?" Pop inquired. "Me and my partners, here, are in the cattle business. Maybe we've worked in some of the same parts of Colorado."

Will paused to study the older man. Judging by his worn-out clothes and boots, he didn't doubt that the old man had chased along behind a good many cattle in his life. But he would bet that the three of them had never stolen more than a handful of stray cows at any one time. He thought of Eddie's remark earlier, that if they didn't come up with some more money, Elmira was going to cut off their rations. The slab of beef he was now chewing was no doubt how Pop and his partners paid for their time at Sartain's. "I don't think so," Will responded to Pop's question. "I'm in the minin' business. I don't know anything about cows, except the best place for 'em is in a biscuit." He looked at Elmira and smiled.

"Minin' business, huh?" Pop asked. "There's a heap of mines up near Denver City. Was you workin' up that way?"

"Old man, you ask a lot of questions," Will said. "Whaddaya say we just all drink our coffee now?"

"That sounds like a good idea to me," Elmira said, thinking she detected a little irritation in Will's tone. "That's one of the rules around here: nobody asks a lot of questions."

"Hell, I was just makin' conversation," Pop said. "It ain't none of my business what he does. I didn't mean to get too nosy."

"No problem a-tall," Will said. "Yeah, I worked some up near Denver, all over as a matter of fact. Whatever it takes to make a livin'."

"Amen to that," Pop replied. "We're all in the same boat for sure." He formed a quick opinion of the stranger at that point. He had an idea this Walker, or whatever his name was, might be more than a small-time cattle rustler like he and his two partners. The three of them had been the only visitors at Sartain's for a good many months, that is, until the other day when those two who moved in with Darlene showed up. Ben and Brock Brown they said their names were. They said they were brothers, and they made a lot of big talk about how they weren't worried about any lawmen following them into Indian Territory. Pop had a pretty good idea that the horses and spare saddle they talked about trading might have something to do with that. They claimed they had known Sartain and had been at the camp before, several years ago, but Elmira didn't remember them. Bringing his thoughts back to the latest stranger to show up at Sartain's, he decided this fellow, Walker, might be more dangerous than the brothers. For one thing, he didn't talk much, and it was always the quiet ones a fellow ought to watch.

After they killed the pot of coffee, there was plenty of time left before supper, so Elmira ordered them to clear out of her kitchen, so she and Darlene would have room to work. "I reckon you can throw your stuff in with Pop and the boys," she said to Will. "You might decide to stay on awhile, and there's plenty of room in that cabin."

"I might at that," Will said, confident now that he had found the fugitives, not at all misled by their claim to be brothers. They had not even bothered to use false first names. It did seem curious that they thought it necessary to use fake names at all, since most all guests at Sartain's were outlaws. He supposed they did it so the other residents in the cabins wouldn't start thinking about the large sum of money they were carrying from the train robbery.

"We've got a teeny bit of time before we've got to get started with fixin' supper," Darlene suggested. "Maybe you've got a hankerin' to see the inside of my cabin." She favored him with a warm smile that easily conveyed her intent.

Will answered her with a faint smile of his own and said, "Maybe later on, if I stay a few days. I need to go take a look at my horses now. They've been rode hard the last couple of days, and I think that bay might have a loose shoe."

Darlene looked disappointed, displaying a playful pout for his benefit. "I guarantee you it would be more fun visitin' with me than it would be with your horses."

"I don't doubt that for a minute," Will said. "And it's a mighty tempting offer, but a man in my line of business never knows when he might have to leave someplace in a hurry. So I expect I'd better make sure that what I'm plannin' to ride is ready to take me where I need to go." Her obvious disappointment caused him to try to soften his rejection. "Tell you what, though. Why don't I give you a little advance payment to reserve a visit with you when I'm ready?" His suggestion confused her, but she brightened a moment later when he peeled off five dollar bills and handed them to her.

"You just let me know," she said cheerfully, having been paid more than she had planned to charge.

"I'll do that," Will said. He had no interest in coupling with the coarse woman at any time, at any price, giving the money with the sole purpose of further conveying the notion that he was flush with cash. He could see from the expressions of the others and the way that the older man's eyes lit up, that his ruse was working. He picked up his rifle and his saddlebags and started toward the door. "Well, I'd best go take a look at my horses."

"You need any help?" Pop asked, and gave Slim a wink. "I expect you're gonna wanna put some of them packs inside the cabin."

"I reckon not," Will replied. "It ain't that much to carry."

"Suit yourself," Pop said, then turned to Slim. "I expect we'd best split some more firewood and build up the fire in our cabin. Maybe we'll get up a little card game before supper."

Overhearing his remark, Elmira said, "If you're lookin' to have anything to eat after tonight's supper, I expect you're gonna have to go ahead and butcher another one of those cows."

"Yessum, Miss Elmira," Pop replied with a hint of sarcasm. "We'll butcher another one. Sure seems like we et up that last one mighty quick."

"You're the ones doin' the eatin'," she returned. "If I had some more payin' customers like those two boys that showed up a couple of days ago, I'd go buy some pigs and raise my own bacon. If you'll go ahead and kill a cow, we might as well have some fresh meat for supper. I reckon the weather's cool enough now so the rest of the meat will keep for a few days. I'll smoke what we don't cook right away."

Accustomed to hearing Elmira complain about the lack of money from the three of them, Pop sighed and said to Coy, "Come on, you and Slim give me a hand. We'll go butcher a steer." After Will left them to tend to his packs, Pop remarked, "He sure is particular about them packs, ain't he?"

"I noticed that myself," Slim replied. "I wonder what he's got on that packhorse."

"I wonder what he's packin' in those saddlebags," Coy said. "He don't never take his eyes off 'em."

"He's in a helluva hurry to get on up in Kansas," Pop mused aloud, then looked at Eddie. "You said he told you he had to get up that way pretty quick. Did he say why, or where up that way he was headin'?"

Eddie shrugged. "Nah, he just said he had to move on pretty quick before winter sets in." His answer did little to curb the three petty outlaws' curiosity.

Outside, out of Elmira's son's hearing, Pop was quick to comment. "That feller's got somethin' he don't wanna talk about, and I sure would like to find out what it is."

"Yep," Coy agreed. "And he's in a mighty big hurry to get outta the Nations, like somebody's after him. Maybe he's got the law on his tail."

"That, or maybe he's run off with more'n his share of a mine holdup or somethin', and it ain't the law that's after him," Slim speculated.

"Look, comin' yonder," Slim said. He stood upright and stepped away from the fire he was in the process of laying out portions of the half-butchered carcass over. Since there was only speculation that the weather may or may not get cold enough to keep the meat from spoiling, a good bit of the carcass had to be smoked over the flames. Pop and Coy looked in the direction he indicated to see the two riders passing through the horses grazing near the creek.

"The packhorse is gone, but they still got that sorrel. It ain't got the fancy saddle on it no more, though," Coy commented. "They musta done some tradin' with ol' Scully. Reckon Scully didn't want the sorrel."

"Looks that way, don't it?" Pop observed. "I'll bet Scully give 'em about half what everythin' was worth." Both Slim and Coy grunted in agreement, having dealt with the hard-bargaining owner of the trading post on the Arkansas River. The three of them paused in their butchering to watch the two men ride up.

"Howdy, boys," Ben Trout said as he and Larsen pulled up before them. "Looks like we're gonna have some fresh beef for supper."

"That's a fact," Pop replied. "Looks like you been doin' some tradin'. Did ol' Scully treat you right?" He smiled in anticipation of hearing that Scully had got the better end of the deal.

Ben smirked. "He didn't want to at first, did he, Brock? But we had him take a closer look, and he decided it was all worth more'n he thought."

Brock chuckled mischievously. "Yeah, he got a little more generous when we explained who he was tryin' to cheat." He nodded back toward the horses. "Where'd that buckskin come from?"

"Some stranger rode in this afternoon," Pop answered. "That bay's his'n, too."

"A stranger?" Ben was immediately cautious. "You

know who he is?" he asked, in spite of the fact that Pop had called him a stranger.

"Nope," Pop replied. "Said his name is Walker, rode in from Colorado Territory."

Ben looked at Brock and repeated the name. "Walker. You ever hear of anybody named Walker?" Brock shook his head. "Where is he?" Ben asked.

Pop shrugged, so Coy answered. "He's puttin' his possibles in the cabin. At least that's what he said he was gonna do." He grinned and added, "We offered to help him tote his stuff inside the cabin, but he said he didn't need no help. I don't think he wants anybody messin' around with his packs."

"You sure he ain't a lawman?" Brock asked.

"I ain't sure of nothin'," Pop replied. "But if he is, he'll be the first lawman to come to supper at Sartain's."

"He ain't a damn lawman," Ben informed his partner. "What would a lawman be doin' showin' up here at Sartain's by hisself?" He looked quickly back at Pop. "You did say he was alone, right?" When Pop said he did, Ben continued. "He'd be a damn fool. Besides, we know for a fact that the last deputy marshal that come up this way ain't likely to be showin' up nowhere no more." When Brock responded with a grin, Ben suggested, "Let's go say howdy to Mr. Walker."

Will stood by the lone window in the front of the cabin, watching the five men talking around the beef carcass some fifty yards away. Even though he had never seen them and really had no description of them, there was little doubt in his mind that the two on horseback were the men he sought, Ben Trout and Brock Larsen. It was difficult at this moment not to think of Ed Pine, lying back in Walking Bird's tipi with two bullet holes in his body. The odds that Ed was still alive were not good. And the temptation to rest the forearm of the Winchester on the windowsill and squeeze off two quick rounds was almost overpowering. Justice could be served in a matter of moments. He picked the rifle up and held it, testing its weight, knowing that at fifty yards, he couldn't miss. After a moment, he propped the rifle against the wall again. What if the two were not the men he thought they were? *Damn it*, he cursed silently, *I've got to make sure.* The sorrel one of them led looked like the horse Ed Pine rode, but a lot of sorrels looked like that. He reminded himself of the plan he had decided upon, to lure the two murderers away from the camp to arrest them. That way, no one at Sartain's would know that the cabins had been discovered by the law. It would make it easier to find other fugitives who sought to hide out in this part of the Nations, now that he knew where the cabins were. He glanced at his rifle again and cursed softly, knowing he had to attempt to place the two outlaws under arrest. And he was going to have to draw them away from the camp to do it. The two riders started toward the cabin then, so he tested the Colt on his hip to make sure it was riding free and easy in the holster, in case he was given no option to carry out his plan. Then he went over to the door.

Brock and Ben rode up to face the door of the cabin and remained in the saddle when Will opened the door. Not a word was spoken for a brief moment while the two outlaws exchanged intense stares with the stranger in the doorway. "Something I can do for you boys?" Will finally asked.

"Pop back there said your name was Walker," Ben said. "Is that your real name?"

"Does it make any difference to you?" Will came back.

"Huh," Ben scoffed. "It don't make a gnat's worth of difference to me what your name is. I just like to know who I'm talkin' to. I ain't never heard nothin' 'bout anybody named Walker."

"Is that so?" Will responded. "Well, I reckon that's a good thing for me, ain't it?" He shifted his gaze from the powerfully built man doing all the talking to the more rangy man on the horse beside him. He decided the one doing the talking was probably the stud horse. The other one had not said a word, but was obviously enjoying the confrontation, judging by the grin on his face. Will nodded toward Coy and Pop, who had walked over to join them by then. "They said you told 'em your name was Brown," Will said. "Is that your real name, Brown? That's the color of shit, ain't it?" His intention was to get them riled up to the point where they might respond in anger. He was successful.

"Why you smart-mouth son of a bitch!" Ben bellowed. "You lookin' to get your back broke? You ain't got no idea who you're talkin' to. If you'd spent any time in Texas, or Kansas, you'd know it don't pay to cross Ben Trout."

There it was! There was no longer any need to worry about going after the wrong two men. He had been 99 percent certain before Ben's angry confession, but now all doubt was eliminated. The next step in his plan might be a hell of a lot harder to pull off. "So you're Ben Trout. Then I reckon you're Brock Larsen," he said, nodding toward his partner. "You're the two men that held up the train in Muskogee and killed the train guard."

"That's right, smart mouth," Brock boasted, "and shot the damn deputy marshal that didn't have no better sense than to try to arrest us!"

Ben aimed a heavy frown in Brock's direction, but it was already too late. The stunned expressions on Coy's and Pop's faces were evidence enough of the folly in revealing their true identity. Sartain's was supposed to be a haven for those operating outside the law, but there was no guarantee that the two-bit outlaws holed up there would not sell them out, looking for reward money. He had a fair idea of the character of the three cattle rustlers. He and Brock could take care of them easily enough, but now he had to find out if Walker was dangerous. Something else occurred to him then. "They said you rode in from Colorado Territory. How the hell did you know about the train job in Muskogee?"

Will realized that he might have slipped up there, so he had no choice other than bluffing. "Word gets around," he said. "They were talkin' about that holdup in Wichita a couple of days ago—said you boys got away with a helluva lot of money."

"Maybe we did and maybe we didn't," Ben said. "That ain't nobody's business but me and Brock's."

"Maybe you're thinkin' about makin' it some of yourn," Brock snarled, and dropped his hand to rest on the handle of the .44 he wore.

"No, sir," Will quickly replied. "You're right, that ain't nobody's business but yours. I got my own business to tend to, and I sure ain't lookin' for no trouble. We got off on the wrong foot. I didn't know who you were till you told me, so I'll just mind my own business."

Satisfied that Walker was showing a proper streak of fear now that he knew who he was dealing with, Ben was curious to find out what the stranger's game was. Pop Strawbridge had said that Walker was mighty secretive about what he was carrying in his packs, and he seemed damned anxious to get up to Kansas with it. "Mister, I'm wantin' to know what your business is. I heard you're mighty particular about keepin' an eye on your packs."

"Oh? Who told you that? Well, that ain't anything that would interest a man like you," Will said, giving his best impression of an overly cautious man.

"Is that so?" Ben replied, and gave Brock a knowing glance. "Well, I reckon we'll all just tend to our own business then, won't we?" *I'll have a look in those packs before I'm done with you,* he thought.

"Yes sir," Will answered right away.

With a sneer of contempt on his face, Ben locked

his gaze on Will's eyes for a long moment before glancing at his partner. "Come on, Brock, let's go take care of these horses before supper." He turned his horse away then and headed for Darlene's cabin, where they would leave their saddles before turning the horses out to graze.

Silent, but fascinated witnesses to the initial confrontation between the stranger called Walker and the two train robbers, Pop and Coy hesitated for only a moment longer before returning to the fire where Slim was still tending the meat. "I was startin' to wonder if you was gonna let me finish this butcherin' by myself," Slim complained. When his remark failed to inspire the sarcastic comeback he expected, he noticed the blank expressions on both faces. "What's eatin' you two?"

"Them fellers ain't brothers, a-tall," Pop said. "And their names ain't Brown. They're Ben Trout and Brock Larsen, outta Kansas, and all that big talk they've been doin' ain't just hot air. They held up the Katy over in Muskogee and killed a train guard and a U.S. Deputy Marshal that was after 'em."

"I swear . . ." Slim responded. Like his partners, he was properly impressed. After a long moment, he came out with the thought they were all thinking. "I wonder how much money they got away with?"

"I was wonderin' that myself," Pop said.

"For a minute there, I thought Ben and Brock was fixin' to throw down on ol' Walker," Coy said. "He had his backbone raised up there till he found out who they really are, didn't he, Pop? Then he found his proper manners right quick."

Pop nodded while he thought about the confrontation. "You know, boys, Ben and Brock are holdin' a helluva lot of money. And Walker is mighty mysterious about what he's tryin' to keep secret. It seems to me like we're suckin' hind tit, us havin' to rustle a few cows just so Elmira don't throw us out. Maybe we oughta be figurin' out some way we can cut ourselves a piece of the pot."

"Yeah?" Slim responded. "Whaddaya got in mind? 'Cause if you're thinkin' about takin' on Brock and Ben, I ain't sure the three of us are enough to handle that job."

"What about Walker?" Coy asked. "The three of us oughta be able to take care of one man, specially if we jump him when he ain't lookin'."

"The trouble is, we ain't sure if Walker's got anything or not," Slim said. "We might end up with nothin' but two extra horses and some campin' supplies. We know those other two are settin' on a whole sack of money."

"The way Walker's been so free and easy with his money sure looks to me like he's got plenty to spare," Coy said.

"You know somethin'?" Pop interjected then. "We can't jump Walker as long as he's here. We might have more'n Brock and Ben after us if we gun him down while he's at Sartain's. There's rules among outlaws, and we might have to answer for goin' against another outlaw where he's supposed to be in a safe hideout."

"You might be right," Coy said. "It wouldn't do for word to get around that we jumped a man at Sartain's. But he's been sayin' he ain't gonna be here long, so there ain't no reason we can't follow him and take care of him away from this place."

"I got a feelin' we ain't the only ones thinkin' about tailin' Mr. Walker," Pop said. "I'm thinkin' the best thing for us to do is talk to Brock and Ben. Maybe we could join up with them on this deal. We might end up ridin' with them on some other jobs." No one had a better suggestion, so they decided that it wouldn't hurt to present their proposition. They had little to lose, for their prospects were pretty slim at the present time.

It was no coincidence that Ben Trout and Brock Larsen were talking about the stranger calling himself Walker at the same time the three cattle rustlers were. They agreed with Pop and the others when they figured a man that mysterious about what he was carrying on his packhorse must have something he couldn't afford to lose. As far as Brock was concerned, simple curiosity was reason enough to shoot the son of a bitch and see if he really was carrying cash from a mine holdup. This was what Pop suspected Walker was into, and told them so when he and his two partners approached them at Darlene's cabin.

"If you're lookin' for Darlene, she ain't here," Brock called out when they knocked on the door of her cabin. "She's helpin' Elmira fix supper, and she's gonna be busy for the rest of the evenin' after supper." He had already reserved her services for the entire night.

"We ain't lookin' for Darlene, we're wantin' to talk to you and Ben," Pop called back.

In a few moments, the door opened and Ben stood in the doorway. "Whaddaya wanna talk about?" he asked.

"Me and the boys have been lookin' for somebody to join up with, and we were thinkin' maybe you and Brock might be takin' on some extra guns," Pop said.

"What for?" Ben replied. "We don't need nobody to help us."

"We ain't sayin' you do," Pop came back quickly, "but with five, instead of just two of you, we could take on some bigger jobs with less risk." He went on to extol the talents of Slim and Coy and his own long experience in operating outside of the law. "We been workin' this territory and parts of Kansas, too, and there ain't been nobody come close to catchin' us."

Ben looked at him and grinned. "Maybe ain't nobody been lookin' for you," he said. "Don't look to me like you boys got anythin' goin' for you but a few stray cows that wandered offa somebody's range." Pop was about to reply when they were interrupted by Darlene at Elmira's cabin, beating on a triangle dinner bell with an iron striker.

"Damn, I've been waitin' for that," Brock exclaimed. "Let's go eat while it's hot."

"I'm right behind you," Ben said. "We ain't et

nothin' since sunup this mornin', and right now I could et the south end of a northbound mule." Aware of the frustration in the faces of the three would-be gang members because of his apparent lack of interest, he said, "Let's go eat, and we can talk about it after supper."

Disappointed, but trying not to show it, Pop replied. "Sure, Ben, let's go eat, then we'll talk about an idea or two me and the boys have about makin' some money."

Will could hardly miss the outright curiosity displayed on the faces of the five outlaws seated at the table when he walked in. Making an effort to do so casually, he pulled a chair back, placed his saddlebags beside it, and laid his rifle across them before he sat down. "Something smells good," he offered in Elmira's direction.

"Somethin' smells kinda fishy, too," Ben Trout piped up. "You don't even go to the outhouse unless you're totin' those saddlebags with you."

Will shrugged. "Just a habit, I reckon."

"You ain't never been here before, so I reckon you don't know that ain't nobody gonna bother you at Sartain's," Brock said. "If they did, their life wouldn't be worth a plug nickel after that. Ain't that right, Elmira?"

"That's the way it's been ever since Elmer Sartain built the first cabin," Elmira replied.

"And that's the way it oughta be," Will said,

making an obvious attempt to change the subject. "Pass me that bowl of beans."

Darlene picked up the bowl and walked it down to Will's end of the table, but Brock wasn't content to let the issue pass. "Just what the hell are you totin' in them saddlebags?" he demanded. "You'd think they're full of gold."

"I wish they were," Will responded immediately. "There ain't nothin' in 'em that would interest anybody but me. It ain't worth anybody else's time to talk about it, so why don't we just enjoy this fine supper and forget about my saddlebags?"

Brock wasn't ready to drop it, and he was about to insist on seeing the contents of the bags, but Ben interrupted. "He's right, Brock, it ain't nobody's business but his'n, so let the man eat in peace." His furrowed brow and the faint smile on his face were signal enough to let Brock know they would take care of it later. Although reluctant, Brock nevertheless took his partner's cue and turned his attention back to his supper. Will, fully aware of the silent signals between the two, was satisfied that the seeds of curiosity were successfully planted. The only real concern now was whether or not they could restrain that curiosity until he had left the camp.

When he finished his supper, he complimented the women on a fine meal. "I've got to take a quick trip up toward Coffeeville, over the line in Kansas," he said to Elmira. "Then maybe I'll be back to stay a spell." He gave Darlene a smile and said, "I'll have a little more time to collect on that money I gave you then. I'm gonna turn in early tonight, 'cause I wanna get an early start in the mornin'." None of the five outlaws said anything, but there were five pairs of eyes focused intensely upon him as he picked up his rifle and saddlebags and headed for the door. Before closing the door behind him, he glanced at Pop and said, "I'll go fetch some more wood for the fire before I turn in. It's liable to be a cold one tonight."

"Yeah, much obliged," Pop replied, and shot a quizzical look at Coy. After the door was closed, he remarked, "That jasper is sure keepin' his cards close to the vest—makes me wanna know what he's holdin'."

Outside the door, Will paused for a moment to listen, but the talk was subdued. So he couldn't hear what was being said, but he felt sure he was the topic of the conversation. He couldn't help thinking that he might be playing a foolish game. *One man in an outlaw camp, against five outlaws, two of them confirmed murderers, I must be crazy*, he thought. *Well, I'm the one who dealt this hand, so I guess I've got no choice now but to play it out.* One thought that stuck in his mind was the urgency to get out of the camp before they worked themselves up to attack him. He knew his odds were a great deal better if he was out in the open, away from this cluster of cabins and free to pick his place to fight. The only way he was going to be able to do that would be to leave tonight, because he doubted he would be allowed to sleep through the night. So he wasted no more time trying to listen at the door.

He was counting on his announced intent to cut

more firewood to discourage any questions they might have, should one of them happen to see him moving about outside the cabin. He was also counting on the five of them to linger at the table to decide what to do about him. He needed that time to make his escape. There was the possibility that they would join up to come after him, but he seriously doubted Trout and Larsen would be willing to split any gains with Pop and his two partners. They likely would see no need to.

After threatening for most of the day, a light snow began to fall, which added to his concern for a moment, before he realized it would most likely help him in leaving a trail. Hustling to get away before anyone knew he was gone, Will ran to the cabin and picked up his saddle and a couple of the packs he had brought inside. He headed for the back of the hill at a trot, the best he could do with the load he was carrying, and whistled softly when he reached the horses. Hearing his whistle, Buster came to meet him, the bay following close behind. He saddled Buster and tied the packs on the bay, then tied both horses to a tree limb to make sure they didn't wander while he ran back to the cabin to get the balance of his packs.

He had just reached the cabin door when he was startled by a voice from the darkness on the other side of Elmira's cabin. "You need a hand with that wood?" Eddie called out.

"No, thanks, Eddie, I'm about done," Will called back. "I've got one more armload back there, and that'll do it for the night." He went inside the cabin and closed the door, then he went quickly to the window. While he watched, Elmira's young son emerged from the darkness, casually walked to his mother's cabin, and went inside, having answered nature's call. Will immediately picked up the rest of his packs and headed out the door, well aware of the fact that, had he been a few seconds later, Eddie would have seen him. He hurried to his horses and quickly tied the remaining packs in place. Halfway amazed that no one was onto him yet, he stepped up into the saddle and turned the buckskin toward the creek.

Chapter 6

"What are we gonna do about that jasper?" Brock wanted to know.

"I've been thinkin' about that," Ben replied. "He's done got my curiosity up now, so I'm gonna have to see what he's up to. I think we'll pay him a little visit tonight." He glanced up when Eddie came in the door. "Before you set yourself down again, how 'bout takin' a look at that cabin across the creek and see if ol' Walker went to bed like he said?"

"I just saw him outside a minute ago," Eddie said. "He's been totin' wood in for the fireplace. He said he's goin' after one more load before he's done."

"Sounds like he's fixin' to crawl in his bedroll, like he said, and leave outta here early in the mornin'," Brock said. "Why don't we give him time to get to sleep, then pay him a little visit?"

"Hell," Ben replied, "we might as well go pay him a visit right now. Ain't no need to wait."

"What's the hurry?" Brock protested. "He ain't goin' nowhere till mornin', and if we let him go to sleep, he won't have a chance to use that Winchester he's always got in his hand." Truthfully, Brock was not particularly worried about Will's skill with a rifle. Darlene was the principal reason he wanted to wait until later to attack the stranger. He had been anticipating a visit with her ever since he and Ben had returned from Clem Scully's trading post on the Arkansas. He had his mind set on hustling her next door to her cabin as soon as she had finishing helping Elmira clean up the supper dishes. "Besides," he added, "it would be downright impolite not to finish up this jar of corn whiskey Pop brought to supper."

Fully aware of the real reason behind his partner's preference to wait, for Brock had talked about very little else all the way back from Scully's, Ben couldn't help but grin. Brock always fancied himself a favorite with the ladies. "I reckon there ain't no real hurry. Anyway, you ain't much good till after you've cured your itch. Hell, I might have a little go-round with her myself." He turned to favor Darlene with a smile. She responded with a fabricated smile of her own. "That settles it, then," Ben said. "Pass me that jar down here."

Silently listening up to that point, Pop decided it was time to enter the conversation. "That's what we was talkin' about before supper, don'tcha know? Me and Coy and Slim was fixin' to see what Walker was up to before you boys got back from Scully's. But we figured we'd wait to see if you wanted to join in with us—seemed like the decent thing to do. I got a feelin' he might be carryin' enough to give us all a good payday. And he wouldn't have no chance to do much about it with five of us against him."

Ben's dark eyebrows lowered in a heavy frown. "I don't see as how me and Brock need any help in handlin' that coyote. I expect we'll skin him and hang him up to dry before he even knows what's happenin'."

This was the reaction that Pop had hoped not to hear. One thing that he, Slim, and Coy had in common was a reluctance to butt heads with men known for savage violence, like Ben Trout and Brock Larsen. Of the three, Coy was the most likely to throw his weight around in the right situation, but this was not the right situation. Like Pop, Coy knew he couldn't stand up to Ben Trout, but he was reluctant to give in to the two gunmen. "That may be right," he said in response to Ben's statement. "But me and Pop and Slim wouldn't have no trouble handlin' Walker, either, and we was fixin' to do that very thing. But we figured it'd be the right thing if we was to cut you boys in on the deal. Now you're talkin' 'bout cuttin' us out. That ain't the right thing to do."

"Is that so?" Brock started before being interrupted by Elmira.

"I've been listenin' to all your talk about jumpin' Walker," she said. "Maybe you've done forgot about the reason this place has lasted for so many years. Anybody on the run can come here without anybody botherin' 'em. If word gets around about what you fellers are talkin' about doin', it's liable to put me outta business. If you're gonna do it, then wait till he leaves my place. Don't do it here."

"Hell, old lady," Brock snarled, "I don't give a damn about your business. That ol' boy might be carryin' a sackful of money, and I don't see no sense in chasin' him out on the prairie to get it when it's right under our noses."

"That's right," Pop was quick to agree. "And we might as well all go in together on this deal. We're stayin' in the same cabin, so he won't think nothin' about it when the three of us come in later on. If you and Ben come in, he's liable to have that rifle ready for you."

"Not if we wait for him to get to sleep," Brock said.

"All right," Ben decided, tiring of the argument. "We'll all be in on it, cut the money five ways."

"Six ways," Elmira piped up then, since it seemed they weren't planning to do their dirty business away from Sartain's. "You're takin' money that right-fully belongs to me."

"How the hell you figure that?" Ben asked.

"You heard him say he was plannin' on comin' back here to stay for a while," she replied. "So he'da been spendin' some of that money with me." She looked around the table, meeting every eye. "That's money I've got comin'."

"Seven ways," Darlene interjected then, not to be left out of the split. "He's already given me money down to guarantee he'd be givin' me a lot more."

"All right, damn it," Ben finally blurted. "We'll

go in together on it. He better have as much as everybody thinks he does. We'll split it, but his horses and saddle belong to me and Brock." He gave Elmira a sharp glance. "And seven ways is all. Eddie will share your cut with you. Now pass that jar back up here."

Knowing it would be risky to push the issue any further, Pop settled back with everyone else while they sharpened their enthusiasm with corn whiskey and waited for Will to go to sleep. That is, all but Brock and Darlene, who retired to her cabin for a crude carnal tussle.

The object of the discussion around the supper table slow-walked his horses through the horse herd, so as not to create any disturbance among them that might alert their owners. Will knew he had been extremely fortunate to have been able to ride out while all five of the outlaws lingered around Elmira's table. When he made his plan to leave that night, he had anticipated no more than a few minutes head start before someone realized what he was up to. In fact, he expected them to be in the saddle and after him in about twenty minutes. But he had figured that was all he would need, hoping to be able to disguise his trail enough to cause them to fall even farther behind him. He thought he might need the extra time to find a good place to wait for them, while they looked around to pick up his trail. But now, as he nudged Buster with his heels, and the big buckskin increased his pace to a gentle lope, there was still no indication that he had been missed. A big yellow moon was resting in the tree-tops on a faraway hill before him. With the clouds now breaking up, there was a good chance it would light up the prairie in a short while, and it should make it easy to follow his tracks.

When there was still no activity outside the cabins, now half a mile behind him, the head start he already had gave him plenty of time to find a suitable place to wait for them. Looking back over the way he had come, he could see that his trail was almost as plain as day in the lightly scattered snow. His goal now was to find a good spot to prepare a little welcome party for his pursuers, so he scanned the rolling prairie before him. The only place he could see that might give him the cover he wanted was the line of low hills that the moon was now rising above, so he guided Buster straight toward them.

After a ride of approximately a mile and a half, he approached the dark forms of the slopes, none of which rose more than a hundred feet above the prairie floor. The hills were sparsely covered with patches of gnarled post oaks, giving them a ragged profile against the night sky. He turned Buster and rode along the base of the hills, hoping to find a stream, although he knew that patches of blackjack and post oak were often found where there was none. Luckily, however, he was rewarded when he came to a narrow ravine with a tiny stream running down the middle. Little more than a trickle this late in the year, it would at least be enough to give his horses a drink, so he rode up the ravine, looking for a place to make his camp.

Following the ravine up the hill, he dismounted when he came to a grassy shelf and left his horses there while he continued to the top on foot. Looking back over the moonlit way he had come, he could see no sign of anyone following him. Satisfied that he still had plenty of time to set up his camp, he went back down to the shelf and the horses. He pulled the saddle off Buster, then unloaded the bay. After picking up an armload of dead limbs, he built a fire and unrolled his bedroll nearby. When the fire was burning steadily, he paused to decide whether or not to risk making a pot of coffee. He might soon become too busy to drink any of it. The need for coffee was paramount, however, so he got his coffeepot out of the packs and a handful of the coffee he had ground at Jack Burns's store. He filled the small pot from the stream, although the water looked a little dusty in the moonlight. *A little rust from off these rocks*, he thought. *It'll boil off.* He set the pot in the edge of the fire to boil while he hurried back up the hill to see if he was going to have any company before he could drink it.

There was still no sign of any riders on the open prairie, causing him to wonder if they were going to wait until daylight before coming after him. Maybe he had not been convincing in his charade after all and had not convinced them that he was in possession of a great deal of money. As soon as he thought it, he shook his head. *No*, he decided, *they bought it.* At any rate, he was going to have to assume they did, and would be coming after him as soon as they discovered he was gone.

It was his guess that he would be dealing with only Ben Trout and Brock Larsen. He couldn't imagine the two outlaws cutting Pop Strawbridge and his two saddle bums in on what they figured to be a lucrative deal. As he thought about it, he reached in his pocket, took out his badge, and pinned it back on his vest. He went back down the hill then to pour himself a cup of coffee to warm his insides while he maintained the watch for his pursuers.

Will had been gone no more than half an hour before Ben Trout became bored with the company sitting around the supper table. Not really listening to Pop Strawbridge ramble on about what a good team the five of them would make if they joined up, he stared blankly at the empty whiskey jar on the table. The longer he sat there, the more impatient he became, and he decided that as soon as Brock returned from his tussle with Darlene, they would pay Walker a visit. *Why did I let them talk me into waiting until Walker was asleep?* he asked himself. *I don't give a damn if he's awake or asleep,* he thought. Brock was really the reason he was sitting around waiting. Brock couldn't delay his lust for the gangly prostitute. He was the one who said they should wait until Walker was asleep.

Sensing the gruff outlaw's impatience, Pop suggested, "Why don't me and the boys go on back to the cabin? If he's asleep, we'll take care of him quick enough. If he ain't, then he won't think nothin' of it, since it'd be just us comin' to bed. Then one of us could let you and Brock know to come on, or wait a little longer."

"Ah, to hell with it," Ben said, not willing to trust the three rustlers. "I'm goin' to see what that jasper's holdin' right now. If he's asleep, that's fine—if he ain't, I'll put him to sleep right quick."

"Ain't you gonna wait for Brock to get back?" Slim asked.

"No," Ben replied. "I don't need no help to take care of one man."

"That's a fact," Pop said, "and we'll be right there to make sure you don't have any trouble." He said it to remind Ben that they were all in on the deal together.

The big man pushed his chair back from the table and stood up. As a matter of habit, he hefted his gun belt to make sure his .44 was riding comfortably on his hip, and then he headed for the door. Pop and his partners scrambled to their feet and followed him. When Eddie started after them, Elmira caught him by the arm. "It's best you stay right here," she said. "I got a feelin' if that feller ain't asleep, there's gonna be some shootin', and he's gonna give as good as he gets. Ain't no sense in you takin' a chance of gettin' hit with a stray bullet. Maybe we'll be lucky and he'll get one or two of 'em before they kill him, and we won't have to split whatever he's got so many ways."

Having formed somewhat the same opinion of

Walker as had Elmira, Pop made sure he was the last in the line following Ben as he crossed the narrow footbridge over the creek. He was content to let Coy and Slim hurry along behind the impatient brute. Walker had not impressed him as being a careless man, so Trout might have a surprise awaiting him when he went bursting in the door. At any rate, it always paid to be careful, a trait that had certainly contributed to Pop's longevity in the occupation he had chosen. And being a cautious man, he was the only one who noticed that there was not much smoke coming out of the chimney—odd for a man who left the supper table early to build up the fire. Young Eddie had told them that Walker was chopping wood for the fire, but Pop didn't see any wood stacked up by the cabin door. *Come to think of it,* he thought, *I don't remember hearing anyone swinging an ax while we were sitting around the table drinking.* He was certain then that Ben was going to charge into an empty cabin. Walker had gone. A moment later, he heard his confirmation.

"What the hell?" Ben roared. "He ain't here!" He turned to Slim, who was right behind him, and demanded, "Where is the son of a bitch?"

"I don't know," Slim stammered, flustered by the assumption that he might be responsible for Walker's absence. "He said he was goin' to bed," he offered weakly.

"He took off, all right," Pop said as he looked around the cabin. "His saddle, packs, everything's gone—while we was just settin' around jawin'." He might have expressed some humor in the fact that

Walker had put one over on them, if it hadn't so obviously angered Trout. "Whaddaya wanna do, Ben?" he asked.

Trout didn't answer at once. Ignoring the questioning faces of all three, he stormed back out of the cabin, looking right and left, as if searching for the missing man. He glared up at the moon, now climbing higher in the sky of broken clouds, its light reflecting from the light blanket of snow. "We oughta be able to track him, if we find his trail outta here," he said. "Oughta be easy with this snow." He turned to face Pop. "You boys look around over by the horses. See if you can find his tracks. I'm goin' to get Brock." Assuming they would follow his orders, he hurried back across the footbridge, and headed toward the cabin next to Elmira's.

In a few minutes, Ben returned with his saddle on his shoulder and a complaining Brock following, still tucking his shirttail in and buckling his belt while trying to drag his saddle behind him. "You coulda given me a little more time," Brock grumbled.

"I told you," Ben shot back, "we've set around here twittlin' our thumbs while that Walker feller up and rode off."

"Well, there ain't nothin' we can do about it till mornin'," Brock said, still complaining.

"The hell there ain't," Ben shot back. "If we wait till mornin', we might lose him for good. He'll play hell tryin' to hide his tracks in this snow." They heard a shout from the bank of the creek beyond the side of the hill. When they looked that way, they saw Slim waving his arm. Ben knew that was a signal that meant they had found Walker's trail. "Come on," he said to Brock. "Pick up your saddle and get ready to ride."

"This here's where he lit out, all right," Pop announced, and pointed to the fresh tracks Will's horses had left in the snow on the bank. "Headin' straight north."

"Reckon where he's headin'?" Brock wondered. "What's up that way?"

"Nothin' much," Pop said. "If he keeps goin' the way he started out, he'll strike the Arkansas River in about twenty miles. And there ain't nothin' but wild prairie north of the Arkansas. He was always talkin' 'bout needin' to get up to Kansas Territory, and it's a good fifty miles from the Arkansas to the Kansas border. I expect he's plannin' to change directions one way or another—go west to hit Arkansas City, or east to strike Coffeeville. Both of them towns are right on the border."

"He said he was goin' up to Coffeeville," Slim reminded him.

"He said a lot things," Pop replied. "Trouble is, how many of 'em is true?"

"Sounds to me like we've got plenty of time to catch up with him, if we quit lollygaggin' around here," Ben said, looking up at the broken clouds. "And with that moon shinin' up there, there won't be any trouble followin' his trail. If we're lucky, he might stop somewhere tonight to get a little shut-eye." He started toward the horses then. "All right, me and Brock are fixin' to ride. Anybody thinkin' 'bout goin' with us, better get saddled up, 'cause I ain't waitin' for nobody."

As Ben had anticipated, it was an easy task to follow the ribbon of fresh tracks out across the prairie with the lightly scattered snow—so easy, in fact, that it brought a faint smile of amusement to his harsh face. *Ain't he gonna be glad to see us*, he thought. He glanced back over his shoulder briefly at the three small-time scoundrels who had invited themselves to join the party. He told himself that it was probably a mistake to have let them talk him into joining up with him and Brock. Maybe they might come in handy, but he could not imagine that Walker would be any trouble for him and Brock. Thinking of Pop and his two cohorts again, he decided their fate rested in large part on the size of the jackpot they found on Walker. If it turned out to be too small to provide a decent share, Ben had no qualms about reducing the number of shares by three. When he thought about it a minute longer, he decided that the same rule might apply in the event the shares were much greater than expected. Further speculation was interrupted when Brock's horse pulled up even with his. "What?" Ben asked when he didn't understand Brock's comment.

In response, Brock pointed toward a line of hills ahead. "Smoke," he said.

"Where?" Ben asked, and pulled his horse to a stop. The other three men pulled up beside them, and Ben said, "Brock says he sees smoke, but I don't see no smoke."

They all stared in the direction Brock pointed out, and after a few moments, Slim exclaimed, "I see it!" He pointed to the same ravine that Brock had. Soon, they all spotted the thin gray column of smoke drifting up from the top of the ravine, barely defined in the moonlight. "Whaddaya reckon that is?" Slim asked.

"It's a campfire!" Ben answered him. "He's done stopped to camp!" He couldn't believe his luck. "He thinks he's hid up in that ravine. This is gonna be easier than I figured, but we gotta be careful now and make sure he don't hear us comin'."

"The way that smoke's risin' up outta that ravine, I'd say his camp is about halfway to the top of that ridge," Pop speculated. "That ravine ain't very wide. We'd have to ride damn near single file up it, and that idea don't sound too good with him layin' up there with that Winchester rifle."

"I wasn't figurin' on ridin' up that ravine," Ben informed him sarcastically. "I ain't that big a fool. We need to circle around to the east side of them hills, so we come up on him where he can't see us. That ravine's so narrow, he won't have no place to hide."

"There's five of us," Pop pointed out. "Instead of all of us climbin' up behind him on that ridge, we could fan out and cover him from both sides."

"And one of us could set up at the bottom of that

ridge, in case he tries to run out the front," Coy added.

"That's what I was fixin' to tell you," Ben said, although the notion had not occurred to him. "We need to surround him, hit him from both sides and from the top of that ravine, too. But the first thing we gotta do is to get around to the other side of that ridge, so he don't see us comin'." He turned his horse to head toward the lower end of the line of hills, and the others followed.

When they reached the point behind the lowest in the line of hills, they rode up to the top of it where they dismounted, tied the horses on the branches of the oaks, and went on foot to the top of the next hill in the line. "That ravine he's camped in is on the other side of this ridge," Brock said. "We oughta be able to see down in there if we can get down to where it runs out at the top."

"Mind where you're walkin'," Ben cautioned. "We don't wanna kick some of this loose gravel over the side and wake him up." They worked their way down through a small pocket of dead trees, apparently the result of a lightning strike at some point in time, until coming to a rock outcropping at the head of the ravine. "Stay here," Ben said to Pop. "Me and Brock'll slip down to the edge of them rocks and take a look." So the three rustlers remained in the dead trees while Brock and Ben moved carefully out on a rock shelf some fifty feet above the pocket where Will had made his camp.

"Well, now, ain't that a peaceful sight?" Ben said softly. "Sleepin' like a baby."

"Maybe, maybe not," Brock whispered. He was not as sure as his partner that the scene below them was as peaceful as it appeared. Walker had made his camp on a level shelf halfway up the ravine. There appeared to be a body rolled up in a blanket close to the fire. Walker's two horses were tied away from the fire, closer to the top of the ravine. It looked like a perfect setup—the sleeping man an easy target, and his horses out of the line of fire—too perfect, Brock was thinking. "I think we'd best be damn careful," he said. "That ol' boy might be smarter than we think. He might be tryin' to make us fall for one of the oldest tricks in the book. Maybe he thinks we're that dumb."

"Hell," Ben scoffed, "he ain't that smart. He just thinks ain't nobody likely to come after him till daylight, and he'll be long gone from Sartain's by the time anybody starts after him. Probably thinks he's hid his camp pretty good and won't nobody know he's back up in this ravine. He didn't count on anybody seeing smoke from his campfire comin' up outta there."

"I don't know, Ben," Brock said, still not convinced. "We been starin' at whatever's wrapped up in that blanket down there for about five minutes, and it ain't ever give so much as a twitch."

Impatient to get on with the business of killing Walker and seeing what was in those packs, Ben groused, "Hell, he's asleep. If he was twitchin' and turnin', he'd be awake. Let's get on with it." Indicating an end to the discussion, he turned and signaled Pop and the other two to come on down.

"What if he ain't in that blanket?" Brock insisted, still suspecting an ambush.

Annoyed by his partner's caution, Ben growled, "Well, what if he ain't? It won't do him much good, 'cause I'm fixin' to kill him wherever he's hidin'. He ain't goin' no place without his horses. And if he's tryin' to ambush us, he didn't count on us climbin' up the back of this hill, so I know he ain't behind us." He glared at Brock, angry now at his apparent hesitation. "He's in that blanket," he grumbled low as the other three joined them. "Take a look," he said to Pop. "He's sleepin' like a baby down there by the fire."

"Ain't that handy?" Pop replied as he edged closer to see for himself.

"Looks too easy, don't it?" Slim mused.

Coy moved up close beside Pop and brought his rifle up, ready to fire. "Hold your horses!" Ben cautioned. "Remember what I said. We got to make sure this ain't no setup." He glanced briefly at Brock. "We're gonna surround that camp and make sure he ain't hidin' someplace away from that fire."

"Makes sense," Pop said. "How you wanna do it?"

"One of you work your way down the side of this ravine, even with his camp," Ben said. "One of you go down the other side." He nodded to Coy and Pop. "One of you go back down the hill and circle around to come up on the bottom of the ravine—just in case he tries to run out that way. Me and Brock will stay up here where we can make sure he don't get to his horses." If there were any objections to the two of them remaining in the choice position, no one had the boldness to say so. "We'll give everybody time to get in place, and when I fire the first shot, everybody cut loose and fill that blanket full of holes." The three rustlers responded right away and started for their assigned positions. "And don't shoot at them horses," Ben called softly after them. "They're worth somethin'."

After the three went back to get their horses, Brock and Ben readied themselves to start the assault. As he stared down at the helpless form by the fire, Ben's anticipation of a large score grew and grew until he was certain Walker was transporting a sizable treasure. If he wasn't, why would he slip off in the middle of the night? As the treasure grew in his mind, he also had second thoughts about the shares he had agreed to. Why should he and Brock share it with anyone—especially the likes of the three small-time thieves riding with them? He looked at Brock and grinned.

"You reckon they've had time to find 'em a spot?" Brock asked, his eyes steadily focused upon the motionless form by the fire. "It's been a good while."

"Maybe a little bit longer," Ben said. "We'd best give Slim a little more time to get around to the mouth of the ravine." They waited awhile longer before Ben could restrain his eagerness no more. "All right," he said. "Let's put some holes in that blanket."

They fired almost simultaneously, triggering a constant hail of rifle fire, as Coy and Pop joined in from the sides of the ravine. Fast and furious, the four rifles rained shot after shot down upon the unsuspecting form by the fire. Those shots that missed plowed into the snow nearby; some kicked up sparks and pieces of wood from the fire, sending them flying. The almost constant rain of rifle fire, combined with the frightened screaming of the horses, created a storm of merciless slaughter as it echoed up from the narrow confines of the ravine. As Ben cranked out shot after shot at the riddled form by the fire, he caught sight of Coy when he moved up closer to the edge of the ravine. Without hesitation, Ben brought his rifle around to bear on the heavyset rustler. A moment later, Coy doubled over when the bullet struck him in the stomach. A second shot finished him off when it struck him in the back, causing him to fall over the edge of the ravine and slide halfway down the slope.

"What the hell . . . ?" Brock muttered, just then aware of Ben's actions.

Ben grinned at him. "Too bad he caught a stray bullet," he said. "I reckon that's one less share of what's in them packs."

Brock nodded and grinned back at him. Then he immediately shifted his rifle around to see if he could spot Pop on the other side of the ravine. Unfortunately for the assassin, Pop had found concealment in the darkness of the trees, and all Brock could find to shoot at were the muzzle flashes when Pop had fired. Nevertheless, he cranked out a series of rounds at that spot, in hopes of a lucky shot. Ben joined in to send a rain of lead toward the target.

Finally pausing to reload once again, they watched the spot carefully for any signs of life. There were none, and there were no more muzzle flashes from that area. "Think we got him?" Brock asked.

"We threw a helluva lot of lead on that little bunch of trees he was hidin' in," Ben said. "I don't see how he coulda helped catchin' some of it. He ain't fired no more, that's for sure." He took another look down at the camp, silent now, as the quiet little ravine recovered from the sudden storm of gunfire. "I'd say we done a pretty good job of takin' care of business."

"What about Slim?" Brock asked, thinking he had heard no shots fired from the mouth of the ravine.

"I almost forgot about him," Ben admitted. "I reckon he'll come in when we go down to that camp. We'll send him to hell with his partners when he shows up." Satisfied that the only living things left in the ravine were the two horses in the narrow part, the two assassins moved back from the ledge and returned to get their horses. They figured that, if the camp had been set up as an ambush, there would have been return fire from somewhere. "Now, I'm ready to see if that jasper was worth all the cartridges we spent on him," Ben said.

Long minutes after the relentless hailstorm of lead ceased, Pop Strawbridge lay still behind a log that had been literally chewed up by the barrage of rifle fire from the top of the ravine. He waited a few minutes longer before risking his head above the safety of the log. It had only taken him a few seconds to dive for the log after he saw Coy's body slide over the side of the ravine. He cursed himself for trusting the two evil gunmen to honor their agreement. He should have known they wouldn't hesitate to murder Coy, Slim, and him to eliminate the necessity of sharing Walker's fortune. He counted himself lucky to have taken some precautions purely as a matter of common sense. And that was when he went back to get his horse, instead of simply scrambling down the side of the ravine on foot. And he had advised Coy to do the same. *Poor Coy*, he thought, *he just wasn't lucky*. He realized, too, that it was also pure luck that they hadn't shot at him first, otherwise, he'd be the one lying halfway down the slope, and Coy would be hugging the ground behind a log.

Reasonably sure the firing was over and Brock and Ben were probably on their way back to their horses, Pop rose to his hands and knees. Once he was assured that he could not be seen in the darkness, he got to his feet and hurried down the side of the hill to get to his horse. There was no thought of retaliation against the two murderers. He knew his salvation was to run, since he would have very little chance in a confrontation with the hardened killers. When he reached his horse, he led it down through the trees until the slope leveled out near the bottom, and he could ride. There was a moment's hesitation when he thought about Slim—to run, or to alert him? He had heard no shots coming from the mouth of the ravine, where Slim was supposed to be waiting in ambush to prevent Walker from escaping. There was no doubt that Slim was next on the list of the assassinations Ben and Brock planned. Pop figured he owed Slim a warning. To hell with the idea of riding with the notorious pair of train robbers. He and Slim should get back to stealing cattle before they came to the same fate as Coy. The healthiest course of action for them now was to put this place behind them. So he stepped up into the saddle and galloped around the foot of the hill toward the mouth of the ravine.

Having taken cover in a deep gully, Slim had waited nervously through what sounded to be a thunderstorm of shooting. His eyes glued to the mouth of the ravine before him, he held his Henry rifle ready, the barrel resting on the edge of the gully. *If Walker comes hightailing it out of there*, he told himself, *I won't hesitate to shoot him.* It was not the first time he had assured himself of that since he had been sitting in ambush, even though he had never shot a man before. He wished, however, that Pop or Coy had taken this position at the foot of the hill. He would have preferred to be closer to the others. *But I will shoot the son of a bitch*, he told himself again, even though he had willingly taken this position because he knew there was little likelihood Walker would have a chance to run.

Now the silence that hung over the ravine seemed almost as ominous as the gunfire had been. At this point, he struggled with the decision on whether or not he should leave his gully and ride on up to the camp. His partners might even now be sorting through Walker's packs, and he wanted to be there for that. That was enough to make him decide to get his horse.

There was no time to think! The horse and rider charged around the foot of the hill at a gallop, catching Slim halfway out of the gully. Terrified, he raised his rifle and fired, knocking the rider out of the saddle. Still startled, and trembling with excitement, he cranked another cartridge into the chamber and held the Henry ready to fire again. But the rider lay still on the ground.

Slim waited for a minute or two before leaving the gully, until he was certain there would be no return fire, then he moved cautiously toward the body. It was the first man he had ever killed, but that thought would not sink in until later. For now, he wanted to make sure Walker was not playing possum. He was still twenty yards from the body when he recognized him. *Pop!* The horrible realization of what he had just done staggered him, almost dropping him to his knees. He ran to the body and dropped to the ground beside it, frantic in his efforts to will his friend to live. "Pop," he pleaded. "I didn't know it was you!" He looked around him, as if begging for help from some quarter. "Talk to me, Pop. You're gonna be all right, ain'tcha?" But there was no response from the gray-haired little man, seeming now to look older and smaller than he had in life. Slim rocked back from his kneeling position to sit down heavily on the ground, dazed by the realization of what he had done. Lost without the one person who had always told him what to do, he clasped his arms around his knees and rocked back and forth while he tried to understand what had just happened. Looking at Pop's cold face, he suddenly knew that he didn't want Coy to find out. Pop was probably just coming to get him and tell him that Walker was dead. In a panic to put this place and everything that had suddenly happened here behind him, he cursed himself for being led into a job with two gunmen like Ben Trout and Brock Larsen. He thought of Pop again, and the picture of him coming around the foot of the hill. He had come at a gallop, as if something was wrong. What if he was really coming to warn him that something *had* gone wrong? There had been so many shots fired. A strong feeling struck him then that maybe Coy was dead, too. "I've gotta get outta here," he blurted, and got to his feet. Taking one more long look at his late partner, he said, "I didn't go to do it, Pop. I'da never done it if I'd knowed it was you on that horse. I hope you know that." He started to turn away, but hesitated, then pulled Pop's gun belt from around him, searched his pockets, and said, "Hope there ain't no hard feelin's, but you ain't got no use for 'em anymore." He grabbed the reins of Pop's horse and led it to the clump of trees where his horse was tied. After tying Pop's horse to a lead rope, he was in the saddle, not sure where he was going, just so it was far removed from this ravine and the two murdering outlaws.

CHAPTER 7

"There ain't much doubt about ol' Coy, down there," Ben said, looking at the body lying halfway down the side of the ravine. "But I expect we'd best make sure we hit Pop." They started to withdraw from the rocky ledge when they heard the shot from below the camp, sounding as if from the bottom of the hill. It caused them both to stop to listen for more, but there was only the single shot.

"What the hell was that?" Brock wondered. "That had to come from the mouth of the ravine. You reckon that was Slim?" The only explanation he could think of was that Walker had somehow survived the attack and made a run for it on foot—and Slim shot him.

Thinking the same as his partner, Ben said, "It sounded like that Henry rifle Slim carries. If that was Walker he shot, then Walker sure as hell wasn't in those blankets we just shot up. Never mind Pop, we'd best get down to the bottom of this ravine and make sure Slim shot Walker, and not the other way around." They hurried up the hill where their horses were tied.

Down the back of the hill, they descended as fast as the slope would allow until reaching the bottom. Then following the same trail that Pop had, they galloped along the base of the hills until they reached the one with the ravine. In the lead, Brock reined his horse back as soon as he rounded the corner of the ravine and spotted the body lying on the ground. "Whoa!" he exclaimed as Ben pulled up beside him, leading Coy's horse by the reins.

"Careful!" Ben cautioned. They both scanned the entrance to the ravine, back and forth, looking for anyone waiting in ambush. When there was no sign of Slim, they pulled their rifles and nudged their horses forward, walking slowly toward the body. A few feet from it, they were surprised to see that the dead man was not Walker or Slim. It was Pop. "Well, how the hell did he get here?" Ben blurted. "Where's his horse?"

"Walker musta got away," Brock said.

"On foot?" Ben asked, not so sure.

"Maybe he took Pop's and Slim's horses," Brock offered, every bit as confused as Ben and still wondering how Pop ended up lying on the cold ground in the mouth of the ravine. "If we look around, maybe we can find which way he lit out, and most likely find Slim's body not far away."

"Unless Slim's done rode up to that camp," Ben said. "I think we'd do good to get up there ourselves before he digs into any of them packs."

With the odd occurrences of the last half hour, which were still not explainable, there was no need for either of them to caution the other. Each of them cradling his rifle across one arm, they guided their horses up into the ravine, constantly scanning the steep sides of the gulch for any signs of ambush. When they reached the point where the ravine formed an almost level shelf, they dismounted. Taking no chances, they held their horses by their bridles, and walking between them for cover, led them up onto the shelf. All was quiet except for a whinny from one of the horses tied in the narrow part of the defile, and the answering whinny from Brock's sorrel. After a long moment with no sign of anyone else in the camp, Ben said, "I don't know what happened down at the foot of the hill, but there sure ain't nobody in this camp now." He released his hold on his horse's bridle and walked over to the rolled blankets, riddled with bullet holes. "He mighta had an idea about ambushin' us, but I reckon when we peppered this gulch with all that lead, he decided it wasn't good for his health."

"I don't know, Ben," Brock said, still not ready to step out from between the horses. "It don't seem likely that he'd just cut and run, and leave everything he had for the takin'. I ain't sure he ain't settin' up above us somewhere with that Winchester he's always totin'."

"Well, if he is, what's he waitin' for, a special invitation? As long as I've been standin' out in the open, if he was lookin' to pick us off, he woulda already been shootin'.'" He looked over at Will's horses then and the stack of packs next to them. "Let's go take a look in them packs, and see if it was worth our trouble." Eager to see for himself, Brock finally left the protection provided by the two horses and followed Ben to the neck of the ravine.

They paused only a moment to look at the horses tied there by the tiny stream that found its way through a narrow opening in the rocks above. "I'll say this for him," Brock said, "he was ridin' a fine-lookin' pair of horses."

Ben grunted an acknowledgment, but he was more interested in opening the packs, as he was eager to see the jackpot he had built up in his mind. Spotting one that appeared to be bulky, he picked it up. When he did, it produced a clinking sound, like that of metal against metal. With a gleam of anticipation, he winked at Brock and hefted the pack a couple of times. "It's got some weight, too," he announced. "I knew that ol' boy was carryin' something valuable."

"Well, open it and let's see what it is," Brock said, even as Ben was untying the flap.

"What the hell . . . ?" Ben muttered, confused by what he found. He pulled out one end of a bracelet linked to a chain before he realized what the treasure was. "Handcuffs," he declared, astonished.

"That's a fact," a voice behind them confirmed. "And they're just your size." Both men froze, taken completely by surprise. "I'm arrestin' you for train robbery and murder. Drop those rifles on the ground and unbuckle your gun belts and let 'em drop." Stunned, both men remained frozen for another moment. Finally, first Brock, then Ben released his rifle to fall on the ground. "Now the belts," Will ordered.

Regaining his wits somewhat, Ben was not inclined to surrender so easily. "I knew there was somethin' fishy about you. So whaddaya gonna do if we don't drop 'em," he asked, "shoot us in the back?"

"I expect so," was the calm reply.

"You can't do that!" Brock blurted. "Are you a U.S. Marshal? There's rules you gotta follow!"

"I don't hold myself to many rules at all," Will replied. "I reckon I'm kinda like you two. Now drop 'em and turn around real slow."

Still stalling for time, in hopes of somehow getting the jump on the lawman, Ben countered. "What if we don't drop 'em and both of us turn around at the same time? Me and Brock are pretty quick with a .44. You might get one of us, but I'll guarantee you one of us will get you before you can crank another cartridge in the chamber."

"Is that a fact?" Will replied. "Well, in that case, you boys better decide which one gets shot, and I'll be sure to cut that one down. Who's it gonna be?"

Brock had heard enough to know he wasn't willing to risk being the sacrifice. Ben was talking crazy talk, when a man was standing behind them with a cocked Winchester. "Hold on!" he exclaimed. "I'm droppin' my belt." He unbuckled his gun belt and let it drop, then he held his hands in the air and slowly turned around to face Will.

"Damn, Brock," Ben complained. "We coulda took this bastard. You threw our trump card away. I reckon you ain't left me no choice. I gotta give up, too." He started unbuckling his gun belt. Wary of the deceitful gunman's intentions, Will took two steps to the side while Ben made a show of pulling the belt off with his left hand before suddenly making his move. He yanked his .44 from the holster as it dropped to the ground, and spun around to fire.

It was over in a fraction of a second. Will's shot slammed into Ben's chest before the unfortunate man could raise his pistol waist high to aim at the spot where Will was no longer standing. Just as quickly as the fatal shot was fired, a new cartridge was chambered, and the Winchester aimed at Brock's chest. Stunned, Brock cried out when the rifle spoke and Ben stumbled backward a few steps before crumbling to the ground. He started to go to his partner's side, but hesitated to see if the next bullet was to be his. "Go ahead," Will said. "Just be real careful."

Will positioned himself a few yards away from them where he could see everything that passed between them. It had been his intention to take both of them back to Fort Smith to hang, if at all possible, but he had been given no choice. His concern now was the Colt .44 lying several feet away from Ben's feet. So he walked over to pick it up before Brock might have a sudden impulse to avenge his killing. Will watched the final moments between the two murderers while he emptied the cartridges out of

Ben's gun and tossed it over with the other weapons on the ground. Seeing the genuine look of vengeance on Brock's face, Will couldn't help thinking it fateful justice for Brock to experience the loss that he and Ben had brought to innocent people. He thought of Ed Pine, especially, left for dead by the two outlaws, and for a brief moment, he was tempted to do the same to Brock. But he told himself that he was going to do his job and take him back to be tried.

When Brock finally accepted the fact that Ben was dead, he turned to gaze at the deputy marshal watching him, his rifle ready to fire if necessary. "You killed him," Brock said in angry accusation. "You murdered him!"

"I didn't murder him," Will answered calmly. "He committed suicide."

"Damn you, you son of a bitch," Brock spat. "Are you gonna shoot me now?"

"If you do something stupid like he did," Will replied. "It was my intention to take the two of you back to Fort Smith for trial. I kinda expected one of you to make a dumb move, and the same thing is gonna happen if you're thinkin' about tryin' to be as dumb, too. Like I told you, you're under arrest, but if you behave yourself and don't give me any trouble, I won't be hard on you. I've got a little shovel with my packs. I'll even let you dig a grave and bury him if you want to. Or we can just leave him for the buzzards, like you did with Ed Pine."

"Who the hell's Ed Pine?" Brock growled.

"He's that deputy marshal you bushwhacked west of Muskogee."

"Oh," Brock responded simply, then blurted, "Who said we killed that son of a bitch? We never killed no marshal."

"Sorry, Brock," Will said. "There was a witness to the murder, a young Creek boy saw you do it. Besides, there ain't no need to lie about it. I expect you'll hang for killin' that train guard in Muskogee, anyway. There were witnesses on that job, too."

"I didn't kill nobody," Brock said, realizing he was bound to be hanged. "Ben did the shootin'. I never shot at anybody. You've got no cause to arrest me."

"Is that a fact?" Will replied. "Well, maybe the judge will just give you a little jail time for associatin' with the wrong people. It doesn't make a lot of difference to me. My job is to escort you back for trial, then it's up to the judge and the witnesses." He shrugged then and concluded, "So, you wanna dig a grave for Trout, or not? I figure we've got about a hundred and fifty miles or so from here to Fort Smith, and I'm aimin' to get started at first light. That don't give you much time."

"I don't think Ben gives a damn if I bury him or not," Brock decided, having no inclination to dig a hole big enough for Ben's huge body.

"Right," Will said. "I expect he doesn't. After I get you settled down real comfortable, I'll drag his body away from the creek, so when he starts to rot, it won't run down in the stream and ruin the drinkin' water."

He ordered Brock to get to his feet then and marched him back to a tree close to the fire. After he fitted him with a pair of the handcuffs Ben had discovered in the packs, he attached a short length of chain from the same pack and secured Brock to the tree. Then he dropped the blanket over him that he had used as a decoy by the fire. "This blanket's got a lot of holes in it," he said, "but I think there's enough of it left to keep you from gettin' too cold." Satisfied that his prisoner was not going anywhere, he collected the weapons they had dropped and checked to be sure they were unloaded before leaving them with his packs. After he had taken care of the horses, he unrolled his bedroll, and using his saddle for a pillow, closed his eyes for a couple of hours' sleep.

Will opened his eyes with the first rays of light that found the ravine. He looked at once toward the tree to make sure his prisoner was still secured. Brock was still sleeping. After having a difficult time adjusting to his new sleeping arrangement, he had finally succumbed to fatigue and drifted off barely an hour before dawn. Content to let him sleep while he broke camp, Will saddled the horses, including Ben's and Coy's, and loaded his packhorse. When he was ready to ride, he walked over and kicked the bottom of Brock's boot. "Let's go," he said. "We're burnin' daylight."

Brock snorted, still groggy from lack of sleep, and started to scramble up on his feet, only to be jerked back by the chain attached to the tree. Back on his rear end again, he scowled as he came to his senses and realized where he was. "Take these things offa me," he demanded. "I need to take a leak, and I can't do nothin' chained to a tree."

Will removed the chain from Brock's handcuffs, but left the handcuffs on. Brock protested that he needed his hands free to take care of his business. "You're gonna find out that you can do most anything with those handcuffs on. So you go right ahead and take a leak. As soon as you're done, you can step up in that saddle, and we'll get started."

"What about breakfast?" Brock asked.

"We'll stop for breakfast when we have to rest the horses," Will said.

Brock proceeded to perform his toilet while Will stood a few yards away with his Winchester trained on him. Finishing up, a question occurred to Brock that he hadn't thought about till just that moment. "Where the hell were you hidin' when we rode up here last night?"

"I wasn't hidin'," Will replied. "I was just sittin' on that rock over there, waitin' for you boys to show up."

"The hell you were," Brock growled after looking at the rock Will had motioned toward. "We'da seen you if you was."

"You were just too anxious to see what I was carryin' in my packs to notice anything else." It was partly true—he had been at the large outcropping of rock, some fifteen yards from the fire. He was not sitting on it, however. When the shooting started, the bullets were flying so thick and fast from the top of the ravine, he had been flat on his belly, trying his best to crawl up under the rocks. He had remained there until the shooting finally stopped, regretting the fact that he had not found a better place. He saw no reason to confess this to his prisoner. "I believe I saw you come ridin' by me on that sorrel when I was sittin' on that rock, so suppose you climb up on him, and we'll get started."

Will rode out of the ravine with Brock on the sorrel behind him, his reins tied to a lead rope tied to Will's saddle. Behind Brock, Ben Trout's roan, the sorrel Coy had ridden, and Will's bay packhorse followed. His prisoner had very little to say, having already learned that his complaints had no influence upon his jailor. And he had made no request to say a final word to his late partner.

Starting out on a course that he guessed was more or less in the direction of Fort Gibson, Will figured to strike that fort after about a day and a half. He had given a great deal of thought to the matter of Ed Pine. He knew he had to get back to see if Ed had survived his wounds. He had promised Ed that he would. If he had, then Will felt it his responsibility to take him back to Fort Smith as soon as he was able to ride. The problem was, Ed's recovery might take some time yet, and Will had a prisoner on his hands that he needed to transport to Fort Smith as soon as possible. He couldn't wait for Ed to get well enough to travel. Even if he was well enough to stay on a horse now, it might prove to be considerably difficult to try to deliver a prisoner at the same time. Then it occurred to him that he could take Ed to the army hospital at Fort Gibson and the doctors there. *I should have done that in the first place*, he thought. It would still depend on whether or not Ed was even well enough to take the ride to Fort Gibson. It was only a distance of about twenty-five or thirty miles. There was nothing left but to wait and see how well Ed was after Walking Bird's care. Thinking again of his prisoner, he decided the best thing to do was to take Brock to Fort Gibson first. He was sure the soldiers would let him leave him in the guardhouse while he went to get Ed.

After a ride of about twelve miles, Will saw a line of trees snaking across the flat white prairie, which surely indicated water. He decided he would stop there to rest the horses and rustle up some breakfast for his prisoner and himself. There were a few snow flurries when they first left the low line of hills where he had captured Brock, but they had not been in the saddle long before there was a break in the clouds and the sun peeked through again. Will looked back at the sullen man behind him, and said, "We'll stop up there by that creek and rest these horses. Then I'll feed you."

"It's about time," Brock grumbled, his first words since leaving the ravine.

They rode for almost another half hour before actually reaching the narrow creek, bordered on both sides by cottonwoods. Will pulled up near the bank and stepped down, his rifle in one hand, and stood beside the sorrel waiting for Brock to dismount. He watched patiently while Brock threw one leg over and lowered himself to the ground, his handcuffed hands holding on to the saddle horn. Based on his experience in transporting felons, Will figured this would probably be the time when his prisoner tested him. Brock didn't disappoint him.

"Somethin's wrong," Brock started. "My hands are caught on the saddle horn."

"Is that right?" Will replied, and stepped closer as if to take a look. When he did, Brock swung his bound hands around, using the weight of the heavy manacles like a bludgeon, aiming at Will's head. Ready for just such a move, Will ducked and countered with a sharp blow to Brock's ribs with the butt of his rifle. Brock dropped to the ground in pain, the wind knocked from him by the blow. Unable to move for a few moments while he struggled to regain his breathing, he was rendered helpless. "I thought I made myself clear when I told you if you behaved yourself, I wouldn't go too hard on you. Looks like you already forgot that." He left him there to recover while he led the horses to water. He was still on the ground, having struggled up on one knee when Will walked back up from the creek carrying the length of chain he had used before.

"Damn you," Brock said, wincing with pain. "I think you broke my ribs."

"I might have," Will responded. "You didn't give me much time to pick a spot that wasn't so tender. Hold up your hands." Brock did as he was told, and Will attached the length of chain to his handcuffs. "Now let's see if we can get you on your feet." Over Brock's protest, Will pulled him up to stand on his feet. Brock remained stooped over, however, since his ribs hurt too badly when he tried to straighten up. With Will leading him with the chain, Brock walked slowly over to a large cottonwood with a low-hanging limb. Will hooked the end of the chain around the limb. With his prisoner chained to the tree, Will proceeded to gather wood to build a fire and prepared to cook some breakfast.

After a breakfast of nothing more than coffee and bacon, Brock's condition improved to the point where he decided his ribs were probably bruised, but not broken. Convinced that he was not seriously injured, after all, he regained his contemptuous manner. He stared with intense defiance into Will's eyes when Will emptied the last of the coffeepot into their cups. "What the hell is your name?" Brock suddenly blurted. "I know it ain't Walker."

"That's a fact," Will replied. "The name's Will Tanner. I'm a deputy marshal outta Fort Smith, same as that deputy you and your partner gunned down."

"Tanner, huh? I shoulda known you were a lawman the first time I saw you," he said. "You had that look about you that a man can't trust." Will didn't reply, his only response a wry smile, so Brock went on. "Me and Ben always figured any man's a damn fool to ride for the law. How much they pay you for comin' after us?"

"Not enough," Will answered, and got to his feet to pick up his coffeepot and frying pan.

"If you had any sense, you'd throw that badge in the creek and make some real money," Brock said, raising his voice to call after Will's back, as he continued walking to the creek to rinse the coffeepot and pan in the creek. "That money you found in our saddlebags is just a little bit of the money that's waitin' out there—easy as pickin' berries offa bush. You oughta think about that. Course you'd need a partner, one that knows how to get things done. You can't tell me the thought ain't ever crossed your mind. I know what you might be thinkin'—I mean about Ben and all. But I wouldn't hold no hard feelin's about that. Hell, he drew on you. You didn't have no choice."

Will came back up from the creek and paused to look at the deceitful man, scarcely able to believe that he was making a pitch to join him in crime. He found it impossible not to reply sarcastically. "That sure is a temptin' idea," he said. "But I reckon if I decide to go over to the other side of the law, I'd want a partner with a little more brains than to wind up chained to a tree with his ribs stove up. Now, get off your backside and let's get movin'. The horses are rested enough."

"Damn you," Brock cursed, defiant again. "It's a long way from here to Fort Smith. There's a lot can happen before we get there."

"You might be right," Will said. "That's why I'm fixin' to let you visit the army for a spell while I go see if that deputy you shot is still alive."

"I told you," Brock protested, "I never shot nobody. Ben did all the killin'." He didn't like the idea of being turned over to the army, thinking his chances of escape might be worse in an army guardhouse. "Besides, ain't no use goin' back to look for that feller. He was dead when we rode outta that gulch. We might as well keep on ridin' to Fort Smith."

"Well, that ain't exactly true," Will said. "Ed Pine is a little bit tougher to put under than you and Trout thought. I'm figuring on Ed ridin' to Fort Smith with us, and I'm thinkin' he's most likely gonna want his boots back. Too bad you didn't bring along an extra pair when you came after me."

Brock was visibly stunned by the remark, having forgotten that he was wearing Ed's boots. "What . . . ?" he sputtered. "His boots? I ain't got his boots."

"When you and Ben left Ed to die, you stole his boots, and if I remember correctly, they look just like that pair you're wearin'."

"Somebody else stole his boots," Brock insisted. "I bought these boots in Kansas City."

"Is that a fact?" Will responded. "Well, I reckon they won't have Ed's initials scratched inside 'em, then." He had no idea if Ed scratched his initials inside his boots or not, but he felt his hunch was a correct one when Brock couldn't help taking a quick look inside the top of his boot. With cuffed hands, he hooked his thumbs inside the top of his other boot before he glanced up to see Will watching him, an accusing smile upon his face. Realizing then that he had been played, he claimed, "I bought these boots. I don't know nothin' about that deputy's boots."

"Right," Will said. "I'll let you wear 'em till I pick Ed up. Then I expect you'll be goin' barefoot." The prospect of going without boots was not welcome news to Brock, and he thought of his old boots left with the packs back at Sartain's.

CHAPTER 8

After another camp that night, they struck the Arkansas River and followed it for half a day before reaching Fort Gibson. The fort was built on the Neosho River, also known as the Grand, three miles upstream from the confluence of the Arkansas, Verdigris, and Neosho rivers. Located on a wide ledge of shelving rock on the east bank of the river, it would seem a natural boat landing. Will had never been to the fort, but was well aware of its location and how it happened to be there. At one time, it had been taken over by the Cherokees, but the Union army had reclaimed it after the Civil War. And now it was a key post in the army's control of the various Indian tribes in the territory. He could see signs of continuing development as he led his prisoner toward the stockade. There were a few stone buildings, as well as the original log structures, and more stone buildings under construction. The fort looked busy, with soldiers coming and going in all directions, but none seemed to pay much attention to the man leading a handcuffed prisoner across the parade ground. So he guided Buster toward what he guessed might be the headquarters building, a stone structure on the far side of the parade ground. There was a hitching rail in front of the building, so he pulled the horses up there and tied them. He didn't miss the faint gleam of hope in Brock's eyes while he was looping the reins over the rail. "You wanna get down, or are you gonna sit there?" Will asked him.

"I'll just set right where I am," Brock said, his mind already working on the possible opportunity for escape when Will went inside.

"Suit yourself," Will said. He went to his pack-horse and pulled the length of chain out of one of the packs.

"Ah hell, no," Brock protested at once. "There ain't no call for that."

Ignoring his objections, Will locked the chain around Brock's cuffed hands and locked the other end around the hitching rail. "Just in case that horse decides to take off, I wanna be sure you stay here." His remark was met with a sour scowl from his prisoner, which he also ignored.

He opened the door partway and looked in before entering since he was not sure he was in the right place. Two soldiers were seated at desks in the front room. Noticing that one of them was wearing sergeant's stripes, he pushed on inside. The sudden appearance of the tall, rangy civilian in the doorway caused both men to stare in bored puzzlement. They remained silent, waiting for Will to state his business. Will walked over and stood before the sergeant's desk. "Something I can do for you, mister?" the sergeant finally asked.

"I hope so, Sergeant," Will replied. "I'm U.S. Deputy Marshal Will Tanner, ridin' outta Fort Smith."

"Right, Deputy," the sergeant responded, the expression of irritation disappearing when Will identified himself as a marshal. "I'm Sergeant Williams. What brings you to Fort Gibson?"

"I've got a prisoner out front that I'm hopin' to leave in your guardhouse for a spell while I go down to Muskogee to fetch the deputy him and his partner shot."

Williams wasn't sure what the protocol was for a request such as that. "You've got a prisoner out front?" he asked.

"That's right," Will said. "Him and another man held up the MKT in Muskogee, killed a train guard, and shot a deputy marshal that came after them."

"We heard about the train robbery," Williams said, seeming now to respond to the deputy's request. "Let me get Major Vancil. Wait right here." He got up from his desk and walked down the hall to an open door, where he knocked and then entered. In a few minutes, he returned with an officer following.

"I'm Major Vancil," he said. "Sergeant Williams tells me you want to leave a prisoner here."

"Yes, sir," Will replied. "I expect it wouldn't be for much longer'n a couple of days. I've got a wounded deputy laid up in an old Creek woman's tipi a little way west of Muskogee. I'd like to go see if I can bring him back here—thought maybe the army might let him rest up here in your hospital—that is, if he's still alive when I get there. When I saw him last, he didn't look like he could make it if I tried to take him all the way back to Fort Smith—especially while I'm transportin' a prisoner at the same time and trailin' extra horses."

"I see," Major Williams said. "What was your name again?" Will told him, and the major continued. "Well, Tanner, we've certainly held civilian prisoners for the Marshals Service to pick up before, so I see no problem with that." He walked over to the window to take a look out at the prisoner. "What did you say you arrested him for?"

"He's one of the two fellers that held up the train in Muskogee," Will explained again. "They killed a train guard and mighta killed a deputy marshal. I won't know for sure till I get back down there to check on the deputy, but he was in bad shape when I left him." He repeated the request he had made of Sergeant Williams. "I was hopin' your doctors could tend to the deputy," he concluded.

"Yes, I think we certainly can," Vancil replied at once, "especially for a U.S. Deputy Marshal. From what you tell me, though, it sounds like you might need an ambulance to pick your man up. Are you sure he can ride?"

"To be honest with you," Will said, "I ain't sure he'll even be alive by the time I get back there. But Ed Pine's a mighty determined man, and I know that old Creek woman's doin' the best she can for him. I reckon I can rig up a travois to pull him on, if he can't stay on a horse."

"We'll send a detail back with you, driving an ambulance to pick your man up," Vancil decided. He turned to the sergeant and told him to detail a couple of men to hitch up an ambulance to accompany Will. "They'll be leaving right after breakfast in the morning." He glanced at Will. "They won't have time to drive an ambulance down there before dark, so you might as well stay here tonight." Will nodded agreement and Vancil looked back at Williams. "Better have them take three days' rations with them in case that Creek woman's tipi is farther than he remembers." Then he turned back to the corporal seated at the other desk. "Miller, take Deputy Tanner to the guardhouse and tell Sergeant Gossage to take his prisoner off his hands. Tell him he's a dangerous man, so be careful with him."

"Much obliged," Will said to Vancil. "I hadn't counted on an ambulance. That'll sure make it a sight easier on ol' Ed."

"The army's glad to help," Vancil said. "You can come back here after you drop your prisoner off. Maybe we can find an empty bunk in the barracks for you tonight."

"I appreciate it, sir" Will said. "But if it's all the same to you, I'll just ride up the river a piece and make a camp. That'll make it easier for me to take care of my horses—get 'em watered and grazed."

"Suit yourself," Vancil said, "but you might as well be here in time to get breakfast with the troops."

Will thanked him again, then followed Miller out to escort Brock to the guardhouse.

After turning over a sulking Brock Larsen to Sergeant Gossage, Will had another chore in mind before he made his camp for the night. He asked Miller where the sutler's store was located. Then, after thanking Miller, he led his string of horses over to the building pointed out to him.

"Howdy, neighbor," Weldon Dean greeted Will when he walked inside. "What can I do for you?"

"I was thinkin' you just might have what I'm lookin' for," Will replied, scanning the long counter briefly. "I was hopin' you might have a pair of Indian moccasins for sale." Not seeing any right away, he said, "I reckon you don't sell anything like that."

"Then you'd be wrong," Weldon said. "I've got a whole passel of Injun handiwork for sale. Look on that table down at the end of the counter. Beaded shirts, breast plates—you say you're lookin' for moccasins? There's several pairs, some of 'em with some mighty fancy stitchin' and beads. Is that what you're lookin' for?"

"I'll take the plainest ones you got," Will said. He walked down to the table and started sorting through the moccasins. There were more than the several Weldon had claimed. "These oughta do," he said, holding up a pair of moccasins with simple stitching and no decorative bead work. He paid Weldon, went back to his horse, and returned to the guardhouse with his purchase.

Sergeant Gossage looked up from his desk when Will walked in. "I thought you'd gone for the night, Deputy—you forget something?"

"Yeah, I did," Will said. "I need to get that pair of boots my prisoner's wearin'. They ain't his."

"They ain't?" Gossage replied. "Whose are they?"

"He took 'em offa the man he left for dead," Will answered. "And I reckon he'll want 'em back."

"Huh," Gossage snorted, amused. "Well, come on and we'll get 'em." He got up from his desk and led Will into the cellblock. "Open up, Cecil," he said to a guard, who promptly unlocked the door, then stood aside while Will and Gossage went in.

Stretched out on a bunk, Larsen made no effort to sit up, raising his head only slightly when he saw Will following the sergeant. "You come to tuck me in?" he mocked.

"Nope," Will said. "I brought you a present." He tossed the new pair of moccasins at Larsen, causing him to flinch when they landed on his belly. Will then grabbed one of his boots by the heel and jerked it off before Larsen realized what was happening.

An amused Sergeant Gossage took hold of the other boot before Larsen could try to react. He chuckled as he handed it to Will. "It came off awful easy. I believe they're a little too big for him."

"He ain't nowhere near man enough to fill this pair of boots," Will said.

"Hey, what the hell?" Larsen finally blurted. "I

can't wear no Injun moccasins—not and ride no horse!"

"Indians do it," Will said, turned, and followed Gossage out of the cellblock. "Much obliged, Sergeant."

Ready to call it a day, Will led his string of horses along the bank of the Neosho until he found a suitable spot to camp. Sheltered by a stand of cottonwoods with grass prairie beyond, it offered a peaceful place to spend the night without the scowling presence of Larsen. Hearing voices that sounded a short distance beyond the trees, he walked up the river until he could see past the cottonwoods. He was surprised to discover a mill of some sort with a large waterwheel. He remembered having heard of a corn mill at Fort Gibson, then, one of the first in the territory. If he remembered correctly, it was Ed Pine who had told him about it. According to Ed, settlers in the area could take their corn to the mill, where the river turned the wheel that drove the stones that ground the corn into meal. He also thought Ed had said you could buy ground meal from the army. *I'll bet Walking Bird would be tickled to get a sack of corn meal,* he thought.

Early the next morning, Will turned his extra horses out to graze with the cavalry's mounts. He figured the ambulance could carry any supplies he needed for the short trip. After a breakfast with the men of Company B of the Fifth Infantry, he met Corporal Lucas Ware and Private James Blunt in front of the headquarters building. They were driving a team of horses hitched to the ambulance. It was a welcome sight for Will because two horses would move the light wagon at a reasonable pace. Sergeant Williams gave the two men their simple orders, to go with Will and bring a wounded man back to the post hospital. That done, Will stepped up into the saddle and led the ambulance off the post, heading for the ferry across the Arkansas.

Once across the river, Will turned Buster's head toward the southwest, on a course he figured would take them north of Muskogee, instead of following the wagon road to the town. There was little more than gently rolling prairie, thick with grass before them, so he was sure the wagon could handle it very easily. This route would be much more direct to the distinct line of low hills where he had left Ed Pine.

The team of horses easily made close to ten miles before they needed a rest. Will reined Buster to a stop when they came to a narrow stream that looked to be ideal for the purpose. He waited for the wagon to pull up beside him and suggested a spot to park it. Then while he pulled his saddle off Buster and Private Ware unhitched the team, Corporal Blunt started gathering wood for a fire.

Giving the horses a good rest, the three men sat around a healthy campfire, eating their noon meal, which in the soldiers' case was coffee, hardtack, and bacon. Will contributed more of his coffee supply as well as some additional salt pork. It was the first opportunity to know the two soldiers assigned to the detail, both of whom were comfortable with the duty. As Private Blunt put it, it was a couple of days' vacation from the army routine of the fort and required nothing more than driving a wagon. Of the two, he was obviously much older than the corporal. During the casual conversation around the fire, which was mostly between the two soldiers, Will learned that Blunt had served since the beginning of the Civil War. He had risen to the rank of sergeant, but was busted back to the rank of private. When Will asked why, Blunt laughed and said he had been found passed-out drunk while on duty as sergeant of the guard. "I don't drink as much as I did then," he said. "My stomach can't seem to handle it now like it did back when I was as young as Corporal Ware, here."

Will figured the corporal not to be many years older than he, so he evidently worked harder at soldiering than Blunt had. "I'd like to know what calls a man to the Marshals Service," Blunt asked when he grew tired of talking about himself.

"Lack of sense, I reckon," Will replied.

His answer didn't satisfy the talkative soldier. "Seems to me, ridin' after outlaws in Injun country ain't the best way to guarantee dyin' of old age."

"Maybe not," Will said. "Maybe dyin' of old age ain't the best way to cash in, either."

"It sure as hell beats gettin' bushwhacked by some murderin' skunk while you're ridin' through Injun country," Blunt said. The high mortality rate for lawmen working in Indian Territory was no secret.

"I reckon," Will conceded. Blunt's remark brought to mind the image of Ed Pine when he had last seen him. He looked near death then, causing Will to wonder once more if they might find nothing more than a corpse when they arrived at Walking Bird's camp. He got to his feet then and went to check on his horse, having tired of hearing the soldiers' idle conversation.

"That was tactful as hell," Corporal Ware commented after Will walked away.

"I was just tellin' him the truth," Blunt said. "I expect it ain't nothin' he don't know already."

When the horses were rested, the party got under way again. After a few miles, Will guided Buster toward the low line of hills now rising faintly on the horizon. They reached the northernmost slopes of the range in the late afternoon, amid a light flurry of snow, and rode south along the line until reaching the stream Will looked for. "This is it," he announced when they pulled up beside him. "You can't drive that ambulance up this stream, so you might as well go ahead and make your camp here for the night. I reckon I'll leave my horse here, too. It ain't that far to walk. And it wouldn't hurt to be kinda quiet approaching the camp, in case Walkin' Bird's grandson gets a little touchy with that bow."

"Should we go with you?" Ware asked. "You're

gonna need us to carry your man back down, aren't you?" He looked around him then and reconsidered. "Or should one of us stay here to watch the horses?"

"That's always a good idea in this country," Will said. "Ain't no need for either one of you to go with me right now, though. We ain't headin' back till mornin', so there's no use haulin' Ed down here. He might as well sleep one more night where he is."

"And that'll give us more room to sleep in the ambulance," Blunt said, always thinking of personal comfort.

"What if he's dead?" Ware asked.

"Then I reckon he won't care whether we bring him down tonight or in the mornin'," Will answered. He left them to unhitch the horses while he started up the pathway beside the stream.

He had climbed only halfway up to the clearing where Walking Bird's tipi was standing when he heard his name called. "Will Tanner," Walter Strong Bow pronounced softly as he stepped out from behind a tree and relaxed the string on his bow.

"Walter," Will acknowledged, hiding his annoyance at having been surprised.

"I heard the horses and the wagon down at the foot of the hill," Walter said. "I wasn't sure it was you."

"It's me, all right," Will said. "What you heard was a couple of soldiers with an ambulance to carry Ed Pine to Fort Gibson. I'm hopin' they didn't make the trip for nothin'." He paused, waiting for Walter to speak, but the boy said nothing. "Is Ed still alive?" Will had to ask.

"Yes," Walter said.

When it was obvious the Creek boy was not prone to embellish, Will said, "Well, let's go see him." Walter nodded, turned, and led Will up the path to the clearing. When they reached the tipi, they found Walking Bird standing outside, watching. She had heard the horses and the voices of the men below, too. Like her grandson, she had been concerned that it might be the outlaws looking for Ed again. "Walking Bird," Will called out when he saw the old woman.

"Will Tanner," Walking Bird greeted him. "I am glad it is you."

"How's your patient?" Will asked.

"He lives," she replied. "I think he is a little better, but the bullet in his chest makes him very sick." She held the tipi flap open for him to go inside.

Will bent over and entered the tipi, where he found Ed Pine lying awake on a bed of blankets. "Will," he greeted him, his voice weak, but steady.

"How you makin' it, Ed?" Will asked. "You ready to take a little trip? I brought a couple of soldiers and an ambulance with me to take you to the hospital at Fort Gibson in fine style."

Ed's eyes opened a bit wider in response, the news evidently bringing him a ray of hope. "I'm ready to go," he said. He knew that the bullet was going to have to be removed from his chest, or he was going under for certain. And he wasn't enthusiastic about having Walking Bird attempt it. "Walking Bird and Strong Bow have took real good care of me, but I expect they'll be glad to get rid of me," he said.

"I figured they would," Will said, and smiled at the old Creek woman standing behind him. "First thing in the mornin', we'll start back to Fort Gibson. One day's ride oughta do it."

"Did you catch up with those two that bushwhacked me?" Ed wanted to know.

"Yep. One of 'em's dead. He didn't wanna go peacefully. The other one's in the guardhouse at Fort Gibson. I expect I'll take him back to Fort Smith while you're layin' up in the hospital. When you're well enough to sit a horse, I'll see about gettin' you home."

Ed exhaled heavily and nodded his head. It was the news he wanted to hear. "I'm much obliged," he muttered. It was a simple thank-you, but Will could well imagine how Ed had lain suffering and uncertain about ever seeing the young deputy again—fearing he might be left to die in this lonely tipi.

"You rest up," Will said. "I brought your boots with me. They're down in the ambulance with the soldiers. I'm gonna go back down to help them set up our camp." He didn't tell him that he half expected to find him dead, but he had been determined to bury him with his boots on. Walking Bird followed him out of the tipi. Outside, Will turned to her. "I can't thank you and Strong Bow enough for takin' care of Ed. How are your food supplies holdin' up?"

"I still have a little of the food you left me," Walking Bird replied. "He does not eat much."

Will was somewhat surprised; he had expected they would already be running out of basic supplies. "And neither do you, I think. I brought you some more beans, salt pork, coffee, sugar, salt, lard, and flour." Her expression told him that it was a welcome surprise. "I also brought you a sack of cornmeal from that mill at Fort Gibson—thought maybe that was something you don't get too often." Her delighted smile told him he had guessed right. Turning to Walter then, he said, "Maybe I can get Strong Bow, here, to come with me and help carry some of that stuff up the hill." The young boy stepped forward eagerly, causing Will to think he had been right in his initial assumption. Walking Bird and Strong Bow had been limiting their eating to be sure Ed would have the food he needed.

Early the next morning, they carried Ed Pine down the path by the creek and made him as comfortable as possible in the ambulance. As a parting gift, Walking Bird brought Will and the soldiers some corn cakes she had made early that morning. After Ed had expressed his appreciation to her and her grandson, the party prepared to get under way. Walking Bird walked over beside Will's horse when he was about to step up into the saddle. "You are a good man, Will Tanner," she said to him. "You be careful chasing those bad men."

"I will," he said, and thanked her again for taking care of Ed. With a nod to Walter Strong Bow, he

said, "Take care of your grandmother." Walter
nodded in return.

Will turned Buster toward the northern end of
the hills, and the big buckskin gelding led the
ambulance bearing Ed Pine back the way they
had come. As they reached the northernmost hill
in the range and struck a more easterly course,
Will couldn't help wondering how much longer
the old woman could continue to live in her iso-
lated tipi with no one but her grandson to sup-
port her.

As they had on the ride down to the hills, they
traveled over the open prairie until it was time to
stop and rest the horses. Ed seemed to be comfortable enough in the ambulance, actually sleeping for
a good part of the time, causing a wisecrack from
Private Blunt. "Hell, he don't mind this wagon ride
a-tall. How 'bout swappin' off some? Let him drive
these horses, and I'll take a turn in the back."

Under way again, they made good time. The
weather was cool, but with no snowfall to amount to
much, allowing the ambulance to travel easily. They
arrived at Fort Gibson at around four-thirty in the
afternoon, just as the bugler sounded "Stable Call."
The sound of the bugle caused Blunt and Corporal
Ware to encourage the horses, since "Mess Call"
would follow thirty minutes later. In their haste to
make it to the mess hall in time, they drove the ambulance straight to the post hospital and lost no
time carrying Ed Pine in the door. They were met
by a hospital orderly named Johnson, who was reluctant to admit the patient without some form of

authorization, for Ed was clearly not a soldier. In the midst of a hurried attempt to explain, Corporal Ware was saved by the arrival of Captain John Welch.

"Is this the wounded deputy marshal?" Welch, a surgeon, asked. When Ware said that it was, Welch turned to the orderly and said, "Find him a bed, Johnson. Major Vancil told me we were getting a gunshot marshal, if he was still alive. I'll have a look at him before I go to supper."

Standing, silently watching during Ed's admittance, Will stepped forward to speak to him before leaving him in the army's hands. "Well, I reckon I'll be seein' you sometime after they fix you all up. Don't give the doctor no trouble, and if they don't do a good job, I'll come getcha and take you back to see old Walkin' Bird." Ed made an effort to give him a grin.

Will left the hospital, feeling that he had done what he could for Ed. His thoughts were now concentrated on Brock Larsen, so he went directly to the guardhouse. He caught Sergeant Gossage just as he was about to go to supper. "I see you made it back," Gossage said when Will reined Buster up before the door. "How 'bout your man, did he make it back all right?" Will said that he had and he was already in the hospital. "Well, that's good," Gossage went on. "You come to get your prisoner now?"

"No," Will replied. "If it's all the same to you, I'd like to leave him with you one more night and pick him up in the mornin'."

"Fine with me," Gossage said. "I was afraid you

wanted me to release him right now when I was fixin' to go to supper. Why don't you tie your horse on the porch post, and we'll go get something to eat? Have a little supper courtesy of the U.S. army."

"That sounds to my likin'," Will said. "I believe I will." They walked across the parade ground to the mess hall, after Will promised Buster he'd see that he got a full ration of oats when he got back. After supper, Will thanked Gossage for the army's hospitality, then rode Buster to the stables to get his other horses. All four, their bridles still on, were bunched together in a corner of the corral. After helping himself to a portion of oats for each horse, he collected his saddlebags and his packs, loaded his horses, and led them back to the spot near the corn mill where he had camped before. He could have left the horses in the corral overnight, but he preferred to camp with his horses. He had an idea it would be better to avoid the early routine around the stables of an army post waking up in the morning. Unloading the horses once again by the river, he settled in for what he anticipated to be at least one more peaceful night before picking up his prisoner. As he kindled a fire in the ashes of the one he had built when he was there before, he thought about the ride ahead of him. Fort Smith would be a hard day's ride from where he now was, a distance of over sixty miles. It was a ride he could make, if it was only him and Buster, but it would be hard on the buckskin. Even as anxious as he was to get Brock Larsen off his hands, he was going to have to make it a two-day ride back to Fort Smith. Since that would give him plenty of time, he decided he might as well let Larsen eat breakfast at the army's expense before they started.

"Well, if it ain't my old friend Will Tanner," Brock Larsen snarled. "I was hopin' you'd fell offa that buckskin of yours and broke your neck." He held his wrists out for Will to put the handcuffs on him while Sergeant Gossage stood watching.

"He's a beaut, ain't he?" Gossage commented. "He's been doin' some big talkin' to the other prisoners—said he'd bet any of 'em that you'll never get him all the way to Fort Smith."

"Is that so?" Will replied, not really concerned with Larsen's boastful threats. "He might be right— I might shoot the son of a bitch before we get back to Fort Smith." His response brought a few chuckles from the prisoners in the lockup behind Larsen.

"You heard him, Sergeant," Larsen charged. "Anything happens to me, it'll be because he went loco again, like he did when he shot my partner— cold-blooded murder. Ain't there somethin' you soldiers can do to keep me here? My life ain't worth a plug nickel the minute I set foot outta this fort with this hired killer." He had decided that he might have more opportunity to escape from the guard-house than he would with Will Tanner.

"That is pretty serious business," Gossage said, making no effort to hide his sarcasm. "I'll tell Major

Vancil to wire President Grant and see if he can get you a pardon."

"I expect you can go to hell, too," Larsen grumbled.

With an air of indifference, Will ignored the banter between the sergeant and his prisoner while he locked the cuffs securely. Turning to Gossage, he thanked him for letting him leave Larsen there while he went to get Ed Pine. Back to Larsen then, he said, "Let's get movin', we've got a ways to go today."

Gossage and a guard walked outside with Will and Larsen and stood by while they climbed into the saddle. "Well," Gossage said, "he's all yours. Come back and see us, Deputy—without your friend next time." He and the guard stepped back then and watched as Will started out, leading Larsen behind him, and three horses on a line behind Larsen.

CHAPTER 9

After a short stop to rest the horses, Will pushed on, planning to stop for the night at Sallisaw Creek, a wide creek that journeyed down out of the hills to join the Arkansas River. Through most of the day, he was spared the complaints normally expected from his sullen prisoner. He might have been led to believe that Larsen had finally accepted his fate had it not been for his constant watchful eye, as if alert for any opportunity to escape.

They arrived on the tree-covered banks of Sallisaw Creek in the middle of the afternoon. With plenty of daylight left to make camp, he decided to lead the horses south along the creek, looking for an easier crossing for them. Rounding a sharp bend, he was surprised to come upon a covered farm wagon on the opposite bank, halfway out of the water. Pulled by one old horse that appeared to have had better days, the wagon's front wheels had managed to gain the creek bank, while the rear wheels were submerged. Holding on to the horse's bridle, a woman was pleading with the helpless horse to try harder to free the wagon. Beside her, a small boy pulled on one corner of the front wagon box, trying to help the horse in its task. Will reined Buster to a halt while he stared, astonished by the scene. There was no sign of a man anywhere, only the woman and the boy. "Would you look at that?" Will heard Larsen mutter behind him, the first words he had spoken in more than an hour. After a few moments more, Will nudged Buster to proceed.

"Curse you, Caesar," Annabel Downing cried in utter frustration, "you can't leave us stranded here! I've got everything I own in this wagon." She pulled on the bridle as hard as she could, but the horse could not pull the wagon up the bank, even though it made an effort to hunker down and strain against the harness.

"The back wheels must be hung on somethin', Mama," her son, Bobby, offered.

"The front wheels made it to the bank," his mother said. "I don't understand why Caesar can't pull the back wheels up, too." She paused for a moment to take a breath, thinking about her cooking staples and their bedding and clothes, which were dangerously close to getting wet. The rear of the wagon box was almost sitting in the water already. She feared that if the horse didn't continue to pull, the wagon might roll backward and water would seep into the bed.

"What are we gonna do?" Bobby asked. "I don't think Caesar can do it."

Annabel drew out a long sigh. "God has gotten us this far. I'm sure he won't leave us here at this creek." She only wished she believed it as she reached up to push a strand of hair from her forehead. Only then did she discover the two men and the horses standing still on the other side of the creek. At once alarmed, she instinctively drew her son to her side. When she and Bobby had jumped from the wagon, there had been no thought of grabbing the shotgun under the seat. Feeling helpless to defend Bobby and herself, if it came to that, she could only stand and watch as the men started across, guiding their horses into the water. Before they reached the bank where she stood, she could see that one of the men was leading the other's horse. A lawman? She hoped so. There was nothing she could do but stand and wait. She attempted to assume a bearing of confidence and a lack of fear.

"Looks like you're havin' yourself a little trouble," Will called out as he approached the wagon. "Maybe I can lend a hand." He made a point then of looking right and left before asking, "You and the boy ain't alone, are you? Where's your husband?"

Annabel didn't answer at once, still staring at the smiling face of Brock Larsen, who was openly appraising her. When she did respond, it was with a question. "Are you a lawman?"

"Yes, ma'am," Will replied. "I'm a deputy marshal."

"And he's a prisoner?" she asked, noticing that Brock's hands were in irons.

"That's right," Will said. "I'm takin' him to Fort Smith to stand trial. But you ain't told me what you're doin' out here—just you and the boy. Where's your husband?"

"Oh, he should be back any minute now," Annabel said.

"Ma?" the boy started, but she quickly shushed him, telling him not to interrupt the grown-ups. Her reaction did not go unnoticed by Will.

"Maybe we can give you a hand. I expect you'd like to get your wagon outta the creek before he gets back," Will said.

"That would be a godsend," Annabel said at once. "I know Robert will surely appreciate your help."

Will turned Buster's head and led the horses a few yards away before pulling his rifle from the saddle sling and dismounting. "Get down and we'll see if we can get the lady's wagon on dry land," he said to Larsen. He lowered his voice then and said, "Don't think I won't shoot you down if you try anything funny."

"I'm already about to freeze from crossin' that creek," Larsen complained. "I ain't gonna get in that water, if that's what you're thinkin'." They were both wet from the knees down because of the depth of the creek.

"I think the back wheels are caught on somethin'," the boy suggested.

"Might be," Will said. "I reckon we'll find out. I expect you mighta found a hole in the bottom of the creek for the back end to sink like that." He noticed that the wagon was loaded fairly heavy.

Then Larsen blurted what Will was thinking. "More likely your horse is too poor to pull it outta the hole."

"He might be right," Will said. "We'll give him a little help. He looks like he could use it." He glanced over at Larsen. "First we'll find you a seat where you can be nice and comfortable while you watch."

"Ah no," Larsen complained when Will got the length of chain from the pack. "You don't need to put that damn leg iron on me again. It's so tight it's about to cut through my leg."

"Your new shoes are supposed to make it easier on you. You just figure this chain is your lifesaver," Will said. "It'll keep me from shootin' you if you take a notion to run for it." He pointed to a young oak. "Walk on over to that tree."

Annabel watched while Will secured Larsen to the tree, then took a coil of rope from one of the saddles. Before tying it onto the front axle, he waded partway into the creek to take a look at the back wagon wheels. Reluctant to getting wet over his boots if it wasn't necessary, he decided to go ahead and tie the rope on and see if Buster could pull the wagon out. He figured if the wheels really had gotten hung up on some roots or something, Buster would snap the rope. Then he'd go in the water, if that happened, so he proceeded to tie the rope and hope Buster could do it without help from the other horses.

Not sure what to say up to that point, Annabel finally expressed her appreciation. "I'm glad you came along when you did, sir. My husband will be sorry he missed you. He would certainly have helped you get the wagon out." She looked around as if expecting to see him. "I don't know what's keeping him."

Busy testing the knot, Will paused and asked, "Where did he go?"

"Uh . . ." she stammered, trying to think quickly, ". . . looking for some help."

Will started toward his horse, stringing the rope out behind him. When he reached her he paused. "Ma'am, I ain't got no idea why you're out here in Cherokee country all by yourself, but there ain't no husband comin' back to help you. You've got no need to worry about me and my prisoner. I'm just gonna try to help you if I can."

She flushed slightly, embarrassed by having been caught in what she realized was a pathetic attempt to deceive him. "I'm sorry," she said. "I guess it's pretty obvious that Bobby and I are traveling alone. But I do truly thank you for helping us." She glanced at Brock Larsen, chained to the tree. "Your prisoner, what did he do?"

"Oh, he's done a lotta bad things," Will said, not wishing to alarm her, "enough to earn him a day in court." He started toward his horse again. "But before you go to thankin' me, let's see if Buster can get your wagon outta that hole."

Once he had secured the end of his rope to the saddle, he took Buster's bridle in hand and led him until the slack was out. "All right," he said, "get your horse to start pullin' again." The old horse gave his all once more. At Will's command, Buster hunkered down and the wagon resisted for a brief moment, then rolled up over the creek bank, pulling one end of a fair-sized oak root with it. Bobby cheered and his mother smiled, relieved. Will untied his rope and coiled it. He gave Bobby a pat on the head and said, "Looks like you figured right, son, it was hung on a root," even though he knew the root had little to do with holding the wagon back. He was a little surprised that the front wheels managed somehow to avoid the hole. He assumed that the back end of the wagon must have somehow shifted sideways when the lady's horse was straining against the load.

"I am so very grateful for your help," Annabel said. "I don't know what I would have done if you hadn't happened along." She extended her hand. "I guess I should at least introduce myself. I'm Annabel Downing, and this is my son, Bobby."

"Pleased to meetcha, ma'am. My name's Will Tanner. I'm glad I could help."

She paused for an awkward moment before announcing, "Well, I guess Bobby and I can be on our way."

"I wouldn't recommend you goin' anywhere right now," Will said. "That horse of yours is pretty much wore out. He's gonna need some rest." He nodded toward the sun lying low on the horizon. "There ain't much daylight left, so you might as well make camp for the night. That's what I was plannin' to do when I came up on you, and this spot looks as good as any."

She hesitated again. "I suppose you're right," she

said. "I guess I wasn't thinking about poor Caesar—
he must be tired."

He studied her face for a moment, while he considered whether or not to concern himself further.
"If you don't mind me askin', where is it you're
goin'?"

Looking suddenly tired, she replied, "I'm trying
to get to Fort Smith."

"You got family there?"

She nodded. "Yes, I have a sister and her husband
there."

"Do they know you're comin'?"

"No, but I'm sure they'll take Bobby and me in."
Even as she said it, she hoped that would be the
case. She actually wasn't sure Helen and Wallace still
lived there. It had been two years since she and
Robert stayed with them on their way to the farm
Robert had bought north of Tahlequah. Bobby was
only three then. Just thinking about it caused
her mind to bring forth the last miserable years
of her marriage to Robert Downing. In one sense,
she dreaded going back to Helen's home in Fort
Smith. Helen and Wallace had tried to talk her out
of going to Tahlequah, thinking it another of Robert's
poor decisions in a long list of moneymaking schemes.
Unfortunately, they had been right, and she was not
looking forward to telling them the rest of the story,
even though they would no doubt say she was better
off without Robert. Although she would rather keep
it to herself, she knew she would have to tell Helen
of the note he left under his pillow when he rode
into town, supposedly to buy seed. She stifled a

bitter smirk as she recalled his farewell, along with some simple directions back to Fort Smith. *Drive the wagon south until you reach the Arkansas, follow it to Fort Smith. Good luck to you and Bobby. It's better for both of us this way.*

Noticing the sudden weariness in the woman's eyes, Will knew he was faced with a decision he had just as soon not have to make. At the same time, he knew that he could not abandon the lady to make her way to Fort Smith alone. He didn't know the story behind her situation, but it was already obvious to him that she was not the kind of woman who took bold undertakings by her own choice. In fact, she seemed more of a fragile nature. *Damn,* he thought, *I figured on getting to Fort Smith tomorrow. That wagon, especially with that worn-out horse pulling it, will take two, maybe three days to make Fort Smith.* He could hitch one of his horses to the wagon and cut the time to two days possibly. "Well," he finally said. "I expect it would be best if we rode along with you to Fort Smith. I'll admit we ain't the best company for a lady and her child, but you won't have anything to fear."

She was at once relieved. He seemed like a decent man, and he was a deputy marshal. "That is very kind of you, Mr. Tanner. I greatly appreciate it."

"No trouble a-tall, ma'am," Will lied. "I'll build us a good fire as soon as I take care of the horses, and we'll see about findin' us something to eat."

"Why don't you let me build the fire," Annabel said. "And I'll cook supper for us. That's the least I can do for your trouble. If they didn't turn over in the wagon, I've got a pot of beans soaking. I usually like to let them simmer all day, but I'll just boil them for supper, and maybe they'll still be fit to eat. I've got coffee and some salt pork and I'll make some biscuits."

"That sounds like a real feast," Will said. "But I don't wanna eat up all your provisions."

"Never you mind," she said. "Provisions are the one thing I do have."

"If you're sure about that," he said. "I reckon I can repay you for some of your supplies when we get to Fort Smith." He got up then. "Why don't you build your fire right here?" he suggested, and indicated a spot not too far from the tree where his prisoner was chained.

While she watched over her pot of beans, she couldn't help sneaking sidelong glances at the sullen man chained to the tree. She wondered what crime he had committed. He didn't look like such a bad man. In fact, he seemed to be a rather nice-looking man when she imagined what he might look like without the growth of whiskers he wore. The deputy had said that his prisoner had done a lot of bad things. It struck her that Robert might have been just such a character under different circumstances. She turned to watch him when the deputy unlocked his chain and walked him into the woods—to relieve himself, she supposed. After several minutes, they returned. "Supper's ready," she sang out. "Better hurry before Bobby eats it all up." She reached over and playfully ruffled her son's hair.

"Yes, ma'am," Will responded. He walked Larsen back to his tree and clamped the leg iron around his ankle. "I'm gonna let you eat without your handcuffs as long as you behave yourself in front of the lady and her son," he said to Larsen. He was feeling no sympathy for his prisoner's situation, but he thought it might be less disturbing to Annabel and Bobby. The youngster was already nearly bug-eyed from staring at Larsen. He felt it necessary to caution Annabel to keep her distance from the prisoner, however, telling her that he preferred to take Larsen his plate and cup.

Annabel did as she was told, but she could not help feeling compassion for the poor man, chained to a tree like a dog. At Will's request, she instructed Bobby to stay away from Larsen. "And for goodness' sake, stop staring at the poor man, or your eyes are gonna fall out." Sneaking a sideways glance at him, herself, she was prompted to ask Will, "What is your prisoner's name?"

About to take another gulp of hot coffee, Will paused. "His name's Larsen, ma'am, Brock Larsen."

"Is he such a dangerous man that you have to keep him chained like that?" Annabel asked.

"Yes, ma'am, he is, and I expect it's best if you and your son don't get to feeling sorry for him," Will said. "It's my job to take him to court, and if I don't keep him chained up, he'll sure as shootin' run away." He hoped that he had repeated the warning enough for the lady to take it to heart.

"I could sure use another cup of that coffee, if it would be all right," Larsen announced. His polite request amazed Will. He was hard put to believe Larsen capable of minding his manners. Maybe it was a good thing Annabel and her son had joined them. Maybe Larsen was going to be a lot less troublesome to travel with. As soon as he thought it, he realized the odds against that. More likely, Larsen was up to something.

"Why, of course you may have another cup of coffee," Annabel replied to Larsen's request, and started to get to her feet.

Will was quicker. "I'll get him his coffee," he said to her, and picked up the pot.

Larsen held out his cup when Will brought the pot. "I'da lot druther had that little honey bring me my coffee," he said, keeping his voice low enough that Annabel could not hear—"instead of a big ol' ugly deputy." In response, Will splashed a little hot coffee on his hand. "Ow!" Larsen yelled as if in great pain. "You poured it on my hand. What did you do that for? I didn't do nothin'." He glanced toward the fire to see Annabel's reaction, pleased when he saw her frown.

"Whatever you got workin' in that rotten mind of yours, you might as well forget it," Will said. "There ain't nothin' that woman can do to help you."

"I'm just tryin' to watch my manners around a lady," Larsen claimed. "That's all I'm tryin' to do."

"The minute you forget to watch 'em, I expect I'll tie you up and gag you," Will told him.

As the sun sank low on the western horizon,

Annabel gathered up the pot and pans and the dishes she and Bobby had used and took them down to the creek to wash. With Larsen attached securely to the tree by his chain and leg iron, Will decided to gather the horses back up closer to the camp for the night. "Whaddaya say, Bobby," he asked the boy, "you wanna help me round up the horses?" He thought it might be better to have him tag along than risk the chance he might decide to visit with Larsen. As he suspected, Bobby was eager to help him with the horses. He seemed like a nice enough kid. Will wondered how he happened to be without a father.

Down by the creek, Annabel made short work of cleaning the dishes. Gathering them up in her apron, she started back to the wagon, pausing briefly to watch her son skipping along beside the tall, sandy-haired lawman. It was a scene she could not remember ever having seen with the boy's father. She felt a pang of dire regret for being so naive as to believe in Robert Downing's hollow promises. Her sister was right—she was so damn gullible. Helen had always been the pretty one. She had more choices between the young men who came courting in Little Rock. She never knew how desperate her plain sister had been to find someone genuinely interested in her. Her thoughts were suddenly interrupted by a word from the prisoner.

"Ma'am," Larsen called out softly.

Startled, Annabel looked quickly toward Will and Bobby, who were now too far away to overhear. She looked at Larsen then, not sure if she should acknowledge or not. The deputy had warned her not to. "Yes?" she finally answered, too gentle to be unkind, even to a criminal.

"I just wanna say thank you for the fine supper you cooked for us," Larsen said, raising his voice just enough so only she could hear. "It's the first real food I've had ever since Tanner arrested me."

Perplexed as to whether or not she should respond to his gratitude or ignore it, she could not bring herself to be rude. She could at least accept a simple thank-you. "You're welcome, although it really wasn't a very fancy supper." She started to hurry to her wagon, thinking it best not to engage the man in further conversation, as Will had advised. However, she paused again when Larsen quickly replied.

"I beg to differ, ma'am," he insisted. "It was a fine supper. I know it was special for me because Tanner don't believe in wastin' food on a prisoner."

Curious now, in spite of herself, she had to ask, "But he does feed you, isn't that so? You mean he's just not a very good cook."

"Oh no, ma'am," Larsen hastened to reply. "Most times, he don't give me nothin' to eat at all—says if I'm real hungry, I can eat grass like the horses. He likes to let me watch him eat, though."

"My goodness!" Annabel exclaimed. "That's cruel."

"I reckon so," Larsen said. "But please, ma'am, don't let on to Tanner that I told you this. I shouldn'ta said anythin'. Tanner gets pretty riled up if I complain about anythin', and I sure don't want another whippin' like the one I got last time I asked him for some coffee. I just wanted to let you know I appreciate you fixin' food for me. It'd be bad manners and disrespectful of a lady if I didn't." The deep frown of distress on her face told him that she was at least uncertain about her initial impressions of the deputy. He was sure that he had guessed right when he figured she was a compassionate woman. And that kind was easier to sway than the kind he most often had occasion to meet in a saloon or bawdy house. Given a little more time out of Tanner's earshot, he felt he might convert her sympathies to favor him. The real problem facing him was the short time it was going to take to reach Fort Smith.

Annabel was stunned by Larsen's claims of abuse at the hands of the soft-spoken deputy. He had not impressed her as a cruel man. Perhaps he was just on his best behavior because of her and Bobby's presence. She didn't know how to respond to what Larsen had just told her, or if she should respond at all. Already, she had had more words with him than she had intended, but she couldn't bring herself to simply ignore him and walk away. "No one should be treated that way," she said, "if what you say is true."

"I don't blame you if you think I'm lyin'," he said in his most contrite manner. "Ain't nobody believed me yet. I guess most folks don't wanna believe a down-and-out cowboy just lookin' to find honest work." He studied her face for her reaction, encouraged by what he read there. After a quick glance to see where Will was, he continued to appeal to her sense of justice. "I reckon I was just in the wrong place at the wrong time," he said. "It was an unlucky time for me when I rode into Muskogee that day and ran into a feller named Ben Trout. He seemed like a right nice feller— bought me a drink. It wasn't an hour after that that he up and robbed the MKT train and killed a guard. I've been tryin' to tell Deputy Tanner ever since that I was in the saloon when all that happened. But somebody told him me and Trout was drinkin' together before the robbery. So I can't convince Tanner that I didn't even know the man. I can't even talk him into goin' to the saloon to ask the bartender if I was there when it all happened." He paused again to judge her uncertainty. "He coulda asked Ben Trout if I was a friend of his, and maybe Trout woulda set him straight. But he couldn't hardly do that since he shot and killed Trout before he had a chance to say anythin'. Now I reckon he thinks he's gotta have somebody to take back to the hangin' judge in Fort Smith, and I'm the unlucky one he picked. Don't matter if I had anythin' to do with it or not."

Annabel was appalled to hear Larsen's story. If true, it would be a cruel miscarriage of justice and a sin against all that was righteous under the eyes of God. Could she believe him, however? At this moment, she did not know. Overwhelmed by his passionate appeal for empathy, she immediately wished she had not ventured close enough to have heard his plea. But what if it was true, and she turned her back, just as he claimed the deputy had? It was too much for her to handle, so the only recourse she had was to flee to her wagon and try not to think about the conversation that had just passed. Larsen grinned as he watched the enlightened woman scurry away, satisfied that he had stirred her sense of right and wrong into utter bewilderment. *I can still sweet-talk the ladies*, he thought. It might profit him nothing, but it wouldn't hurt to have the woman's sympathies riding with him. Given a little more time to work on her, he might be able to count on her help if Tanner should happen to get careless. Smug in that thought, he settled back against the tree and relaxed while Will and Bobby came walking back up the creek, driving the horses before them.

CHAPTER 10

The next morning they awoke to find a light covering of snow on the ground. Anticipating the possibility, Will had provided an oilskin ground cloth for Larsen to use for cover. It made an adequate tent to protect him from the snow. Will made his bed under the wagon, since he had only the one ground cloth. Before getting the horses saddled and loaded, he took Larsen back down the creek far enough to permit him to take care of nature's call.

"Be a helluva lot easier if you'd take these cuffs off my hands," Larsen complained. "I ain't hardly gonna try nothin' with you holdin' that Winchester on me."

"I expect you can manage," Will said, "just like you've been doin' all along."

Larsen snorted in reply as he took a few steps closer to a sizable oak tree. After he finished his business, he turned and appeared to lose his footing, lurching awkwardly against the tree trunk. Much to Will's astonishment, Larsen banged his forehead on the rough bark of the oak, resulting in a large scrape above his eye that brought blood. "Damn it," Larsen cursed. "It's havin' to walk draggin' that damn chain on my ankle."

"I reckon your luck's just run out," Will commented, his tone dry and without sympathy, for it looked to him like an unusually clumsy accident. "You wanna walk on down to the water and wash that blood off?"

"Nah," Larsen snorted. "To hell with it."

"Suit yourself," Will said.

While Will hitched one of the extra horses up to the wagon, Larsen stood as close to it as the chain would let him, following Annabel's every movement with his eyes until she finally turned to look at him. When she did, he affected the most pitiful expression he could manage. Satisfied to see the instant concern written on her face, he gazed forlornly at her for a long moment before hanging his head as if ashamed. It was hard to keep from smiling as he thought how easily he could work the woman's emotions. As an added effect, he spoke to Will when he led the sorrel up for him to ride. "I learned my lesson, Deputy. I won't drag my feet next time you take me to the bushes."

"All right," Will replied after a pause, puzzled by the odd remark.

It was too much for Annabel, having put two and two together and come up with the erroneous conclusion that Larsen implied. "Let me at least get a cloth and clean the blood from his forehead," she demanded in disgust for the deputy's apparent lack of compassion. Without waiting for Will's permission, she picked up a cloth and took it to the water's edge to wet it.

When she brushed back by him, Will said, "I'd rather you didn't get too close to my prisoner. Besides, I already asked him if he wanted to clean it up when he bumped his head on that tree, and he said he didn't." Ignoring him, she pushed on to render her assistance to the injured man, leaving Will even more perplexed by her actions. He couldn't help wondering if he was going to have to tie her to the wagon to keep her from showering her compassion on his prisoner. *One more night and a short day*, he told himself, *and I'll be rid of her*. It would certainly be a relief.

"Bumped his head on a tree," Annabel huffed loudly as she began cleaning the blood from Larsen's forehead. There was no excuse for treating the man brutally, even if he was guilty of robbing a train. Her impression of the deputy was considerably less favorable than before. Lowering her voice to a whisper, she asked, "Did he do this to you?"

"I'd druther not say, ma'am," Larsen whispered his reply. "It'll just make it worse on me." Then raising his voice, he said, "I reckon I'd better be more careful where I'm walkin'. Thank you, ma'am, for your kindness."

Will permitted her to tend to Larsen's wound, since his prisoner was making such a big show out of being so respectful. But he wasn't fooled by Larsen's pathetic performance to gain the woman's sympathy. It evidently amused the conscienceless

murderer, but Will couldn't see that it was going to
help his predicament—he was still going to jail.
After a moment or two more, he decided the patient had had enough attention. "All right, we've got
a ways to ride today, so let's get movin'." After hitching Coy Trainer's sorrel to the wagon, he picked
Bobby up and lifted him up on the seat of the wagon.
Then he turned to Annabel. "Ma'am," he said, and
offered his hand to help her up, which she point-
edly ignored. With an indifferent shrug, he went to
unlock Larsen's chain from the tree, never giving
Annabel's sudden coolness toward him a second
thought. Sometimes it was just plain hard to figure
women out. After unlocking the other end of the
chain from Larsen's handcuffs, he stood back while
Larsen grabbed the saddle horn and stepped up
into the saddle. "We'll stop after a while to rest the
horses and take time to eat," he informed them.
Then he climbed into the saddle and led his little
caravan east—Larsen's sorrel tied onto Buster's
saddle, Annabel driving the wagon behind them,
with Will's packhorse and Ben Trout's roan tied
onto the back of the wagon. Annabel's horse, Caesar,
was left to follow them at his own pace. Will figured
the tired old horse would more than likely trail the
others without having to be tied to the wagon.

Their line of travel was more or less the same as
Annabel's husband had advised her to follow in the
farewell note he left her. Will planned to continue
southeast until they struck the Arkansas River, then
follow it to Fort Smith. Since he figured they were
only about thirty miles from Fort Smith, he planned

to do it in two short days. Annabel's wagon was loaded fairly heavily, however, and even with the change of horses, the going was pretty slow. It occurred to him that her horse Caesar's near-foundering state might possibly have been somewhat caused by being driven beyond a sensible distance without rest. That, combined with the fact that the horse looked to be as old as the original Roman it was named for, was cause enough for the horse's condition. Much to Will's annoyance, the sorrel pulling the wagon showed signs of fatigue after about eight miles. So he stopped short of the ten miles he had planned to cover before stopping to eat and rest the horses at a small stream.

"Pull the wagon up under the trees there, ma'am," he called back to Annabel as he reined the buckskin back to wait for her to catch up to him.

"Are we going to stop here long enough to fix something to eat?" she asked as she drew up beside him and Larsen.

"Yes, ma'am," he answered.

"I'm worried about my horse," she said. "I've lost sight of him. He's been dropping farther and farther back all morning, and now I don't see him at all. I'm afraid he's gotten lost."

"He's just slowed down in his old age," Will said. "Maybe he'll come wanderin' in after a bit." He had been unconcerned about the horse and had paid no attention to its progress, figuring it could keep up with the wagon.

"I hope you're right," she said. "Caesar's not just any horse, he's part of my family. He was my father's horse for years before he gave him to my husband and me when we got married. I can't bear to think he may have gotten lost. He was going to be Bobby's horse when Bobby gets big enough to ride."

Damn, lady, Will thought, *how long do you think that horse is going to live?* He caught the amused grin on Larsen's face out of the corner of his eye. "I doubt he's lost," Will said. "He's just slow—takin' his time, I reckon—he oughta be able to follow these horses all right."

"Maybe so," she allowed reluctantly, and drove her wagon under the trees where Will had indicated. If he had read the determination in her eyes, he would have seen that she had no intention of driving a step farther until Caesar showed up.

While Will picked out a tree and chained his prisoner, Annabel put Bobby to work gathering wood for her cook fire. The youngster seemed to be doing an adequate job, so Will unharnessed the sorrel, unsaddled the other horses, and left them to drink at the stream. When he returned, Annabel had a fire going and her cast-iron pot filled with beans on the ground beside it. They had been soaking since leaving Sallisaw Creek. "I'm afraid it's going to be pretty simple fare again," she warned, "since I don't have the time to fix a proper meal."

"Anything you cook will be appreciated," Will said.

"It'll just be boiled beans and salt pork again," Annabel said. "But there's plenty of coffee and I'll mix up some slapjack to go with it." Will had never eaten slapjack, but he had heard of it. So, out of curiosity, he paid attention to the preparation of it in case it was something he might make sometime. He watched as Annabel mixed up some flour, sugar, water, and a little yeast until she had a stiff paste. She formed it into patties to fry in grease. When he tried one of the cakes later, he decided they weren't bad, kind of like fritters. He figured if he ever tried to make them, they would have to be without the yeast. He couldn't recall ever using yeast in anything he tried to cook.

When the meal had been eaten and washed down with the last of the coffee, Annabel took her cooking utensils to the creek to wash. Will watched her as she got to her feet when she had finished and stood a long time gazing back along the path they had traveled. *Looking for that danged old nag*, he thought, for there was still no sign of Caesar. It looked as if the horse was going to be a problem, one he didn't need. He was within twenty or so miles of Fort Smith, and he was ready to get under way again. He figured he'd give it a try. "Well, that was a mighty fine meal, ma'am," he said when she walked back to the wagon. "The horses are rested up now, so I expect we'd best get goin'. We need to make a few more miles, so we can have a short day tomorrow."

"I can't go anywhere until Caesar shows up," Annabel stated. There was no mistaking the stern resolve in her tone.

"Ma'am, I'm afraid I'm gonna have to insist that we get movin' again," Will stated in as official a voice as he could affect. "I've got a prisoner on my hands and I'm bound to get him to Fort Smith as soon as I can."

"You can insist all you want," Annabel replied. "I'm not going anywhere until Caesar shows up. If you have to go so bad, then go. I'll stay here until I get my horse back."

"Ma'am . . . Miz Downin' . . ." he started, but she stopped him with a shake of her head. Larsen looked on in silent amusement at the deputy's obvious frustration. The stubborn woman had created a virtual impasse that Will was too much a gentleman to charge through. Seeing no way around it, he had no choice but to yield to her stubbornness. He considered leaving her, as she had demanded. But he could not, even this close to Fort Smith, with no protection, and no horse to pull her wagon. He could leave the sorrel with her, but she and the boy would still be alone. If some harm came to them, he could never live with his conscience. He finally decided there was only one thing to do, and that was to backtrail and find the horse. Otherwise, they might be sitting here waiting who knew how long for the broken-down nag to show. He wasn't comfortable with the thought of leaving the woman and her child alone with a callous murderer like Brock Larsen. But chained securely to the tree, there was little harm he could do them other than making noise.

"All right," he said to Annabel. "I'll go back and see if I can find your horse." He glanced at the smiling face of his prisoner and continued. "I want you and Bobby to stay on the other side of the wagon.

And promise me you won't have nothin' to do with my prisoner." He went to his packhorse and pulled the .44 out of the holster that had belonged to Ben Trout, checked to make sure it was loaded, then handed it to her. "You know how to use this?" She nodded. "Good. The hammer's restin' on an empty chamber, so you'll have to cock it to shoot it." She nodded again. "That's for your protection just in case, but there ain't no way he can get loose from that chain. You and Bobby just stay away from him." Still uncomfortable with the situation, he nevertheless climbed aboard the buckskin and started back.

Aware that the lady's lagging horse might not be far behind, Larsen knew he couldn't count on much time to make his break for freedom. "I surely hate to trouble you, ma'am," he called out, "but I've got a powerful thirst. I'd be most grateful if you or the boy could bring me a dipper of water." He was fairly confident that she wouldn't send Bobby.

She had every intention of following the deputy's orders and staying away from his prisoner, but she found it difficult to ignore his request for water. To do so would fly in the face of her Christian upbringing. Still, she struggled with her emotions for a few moments more before finally surrendering to her conscience and answering him. "Very well, Mr. Larsen, I can certainly give you a drink of water." She got the dipper from her bucket and gave it to her son to fill at the stream. "Bring it back to me," she said. "Then I want you to stay here behind the wagon while I take it to Mr. Larsen."

"Ahh, thank you, ma'am," Larsen said in contrived

appreciation. "I declare, I don't know why my throat is so parched." She turned when he handed the dipper back, starting to return to her wagon, but he stopped her when he spoke again. "I surely hope Tanner finds your horse all right. I know how attached to a horse a person can get. I learned to ride on my daddy's horse, just like you were plannin' for little Bobby. I reckon Tanner don't think about things like that. He's a hard man. I've been tryin' to get him to take me back to Muskogee, so the bartender in that saloon could tell him right off that I didn't have nothin' to do with that train robbery." Pleased by the obvious frown of concern on her forehead, he continued. "But don't you worry none about me. I won't be the first innocent man hung by that hangin' judge at Fort Smith."

Perplexed by the man's distress, she could not deny that his plea of innocence had a profound effect upon her. The thought of a man being hanged who had nothing to do with the crime was indeed a most horrible sin. "I believe you when you say you are innocent," she finally said, after a long moment of thought. "I would help you if I could. I don't have a key to unlock your chains, but I will talk to Mr. Tanner on your behalf when he comes back. Maybe he will relent and take you to Muskogee to prove your innocence."

"Oh, I knew you were an angel when we first came up on you," Larsen said. He glanced in the direction Will had ridden, hoping to see no sign of his return. When there was none, he resumed his play upon her conscience. "There is one thing you

could do to make it a little easier on me. I asked
Tanner to do it, but he told me he didn't care if I
was in pain or not, so I quit askin' him."

"What is it?" she asked. "I'll help you if I can."

"When he arrested me, he kicked me pretty hard
on my knee, and it's got kinda stiff and painful ever
since. I ain't sure that he didn't break it. I don't
know if you've took notice or not, but I kinda limp
when I have to walk." She replied that she hadn't.
He went on. "Anyway, I asked Tanner if I could cut
me a limb to use like a walkin' stick to take some of
the strain offa my knee. I reckon he was afraid I was
gonna try to hit him with it or somethin'. It sure
would make it a little easier on me." He paused for
a moment to make sure he had all of her sympathy.
He pointed to a small limb about the size of a hoe
handle above his head. "If I could borrow that ax on
the side of your wagon for just a minute, I could
chop that limb off and trim me up a walkin' stick
in a jiffy."

Hesitant, she thought of Will's warning to stay
away from Larsen. It was certainly not wise to put
an ax in a criminal's hands—*if he was a criminal.* The
trouble was she believed him to be innocent, as he
so fervently pleaded. She tried to think of the possible harm he could do with the ax. He couldn't cut
the chain with the ax. The blade would break before
the chain did. In the worst case, if he was evil, he
might have notions of attacking her with the ax, but
that would still leave him chained to the tree.

He watched her patiently for a few moments, as
she struggled with it in her mind, then tried to ease

her dismay. He reached up and took hold of the limb and made a show of bending it down as if testing it. "I was thinkin' about breakin' it off, but it's a little too stout." He looked back at her and gave her an innocent smile. "If it wasn't stout, it wouldn't make much of a walkin' stick, would it? I could make short work of it with that ax, though."

"All right," she finally decided. "I'll get the ax, if you'll promise me you'll give it right back as soon as you cut that limb off."

"Oh yes, ma'am," he replied at once. "I'll promise on my dead mother's grave, and there ain't no promise more sacred to me than that." She searched his eyes intently, looking for sincerity. "And I know my poor old mother is lookin' down from Heaven and blessin' you for your kindness," he added, knowing that his mother was still alive and could care less if he lived or died.

She promptly turned on her heel and went to the wagon to fetch the ax. He watched her as she left, a smug grin on his face, scarcely able to believe how easily she was manipulated. Then he shifted his eyes to the hills along their back trail, looking for Will. *Hurry up, woman,* he thought, even though there was still no sign of the deputy. It took only a minute before she returned from the wagon and handed the ax to him. He took the handle in his handcuffed hands. Although awkward, he managed to hold it firmly.

She stepped back to watch him cut off the limb. Moments later, she was shocked to see him attack the trunk of the tree, violently chopping with all the strength he could muster. "What are you doing?" she cried. "You're not cutting the limb!"

"I need a bigger walkin' stick," he cracked, without pausing, and already breathing hard. Rendered helpless, she could not speak. "When's the last time you sharpened this damn ax?" he grunted between blows against the trunk, his voice no longer hinting the humbleness he had contrived before.

"You promised me!" she wailed when she was able to speak again.

"I've promised a lot of women a lot of things," he huffed, never pausing in his eagerness to chop the tree down. Even though the trunk was no more than about nine inches in diameter, it was taking a little longer because of the dullness of the ax. But the tree had to surrender to his relentless attack, and soon it began to lean over until at last it fell. Frantic and confused, Annabel finally realized what he had in mind, and remembering the pistol that Will had left for her, she turned and ran to the wagon. Larsen paid her no mind, instead hacking away at the split part of the trunk that remained attached to the stump. He chopped the last of the trunk away and pulled the chain up over the stump just as Annabel came running back with the .44 in her hand.

"I trusted you," she admonished him sternly, sick with the realization that she had once again been deceived by a man, this time putting her and her son in danger. She pointed the pistol at him.

Busy trying to decide what he could do about his chain, for it was still locked to his cuffs, he ignored the gun aimed at him by the frantic woman. He decided that the first order of business was to get away before Will returned, and find a way to free himself later. He turned to Annabel then. "What are you gonna do, shoot me?" he taunted, feeling confident that she didn't have the nerve to do it.

"I want you to sit down on the ground and don't move until Mr. Tanner gets back," she directed as sternly as she could.

Certain that he had correctly judged her likelihood to act, he said, "I'd oblige you, lady, but right now I've got things to do." Throwing his chain over his shoulder, he walked past her, heading for the horses, still standing, saddled, and packed. Since time was critical, he looked quickly through Will's packs until he found his gun belt, as well as the empty holster that had belonged to Ben Trout. He hung his gun belt over the saddle horn on his sorrel, since he couldn't put the belt on with his hands cuffed together. After that, he pulled his Winchester rifle from the straps of the pack saddle and replaced it in the empty scabbard on his saddle. Then, working clumsily with his cuffed hands, he managed to tie Will's packhorse to his saddle. When he was ready to ride, he turned around to find Annabel facing him, her pistol aimed at his face.

"You're not going anywhere," she warned. "I'll shoot you."

"No, you won't, lady, you ain't got the guts," he scoffed, and walked past her to untie Trout's roan from the tailgate of the wagon. She tried to follow him, but he suddenly stepped to the side and whipped his chain around her, pinning her arms to her sides as he pulled the end of the chain tight. Trapping her hard up against his body, he kept pulling the chain tighter and tighter until she cried out in pain. "Drop the gun," he ordered, "or I'll cut you in two." She had no choice but to drop it. "There you go," he smirked, loosening the chain just a little. "You know, you're kinda homely, but you feel pretty good. I'd take you with me, but you'd be too much trouble right now, and I'm in a hurry." He released her then and threw her to the ground. "Crawl on back to the wagon and take care of your brat." He picked up the pistol and made one futile effort to chase the roan away, but the horse would run only a few yards before stopping again. Aware that his time was running out, he finally gave it up and climbed into the saddle. Dazed and bruised on her arms where the chain had pinched them, Annabel sat on the ground watching him ride off up the stream. The horrible mistake she had made was resounding in her brain, and she was at a loss as to how she could possibly explain her actions to the deputy. She couldn't help wondering if she was going to be arrested now for helping his prisoner escape. In that event, what would become of Bobby? Resigned to her fate, whatever it was, she got up from the ground and walked back to her wagon.

Her son was peeking over the wagon seat, afraid to make a sound after he had seen his mother thrown to the ground.

After backtracking for approximately two miles, there was still no sign of the wayward horse, and Will was just about ready to end the search. The old nag had evidently wandered off in a different direction. He didn't look forward to telling Annabel that Caesar was gone for good, but he couldn't take the time to search the whole Cherokee Nation for him. He turned Buster back toward the wagon and nudged him into a gentle lope. Ten minutes later, he spotted Caesar standing in a patch of pines off to his right. "Well, I'll be . . ." Will muttered. He had to have missed him when he rode by in the opposite direction. *Thank the Lord,* was his next thought, for he was concerned that he might have had to hog-tie Annabel and haul her to Fort Smith had he returned without her beloved Caesar.

The old horse stood motionless, its head hanging low with drooping ears. It did not even respond to Buster's greeting nicker. It was the perfect picture of a horse totally used up, Will thought. A bullet to the brain would be the kindest thing he could do for the horse, but he didn't care to try to convince Annabel of that. So he rode Buster up beside the unresisting horse, slipped a noose over its head, and started back, leading Caesar behind him.

When still fifty yards short of the stream where he

had left the wagon, Will reined Buster back to a
halt, alarmed by what he saw. Larsen's horse and the
packhorse were gone! He looked at once toward
the tree where he had left his prisoner, only to find
the tree no longer standing and no sign of Larsen.
"Dammit, dammit, dammit," he muttered, not willing to believe his eyes. Larsen had escaped. That
much was blatantly apparent, and the next thought
that leaped to his mind was the safety of Annabel
and the boy. Brock Larsen would not hesitate to kill
them both if they stood in his way. He drew the Winchester from his saddle scabbard and cocked it,
alert for the possibility of an ambush awaiting him.
A movement in the trees below the camp caught his
eye, causing him to jerk the rifle to his shoulder,
prepared to fire. But it was only the roan that had
belonged to Ben Trout, somehow free from the
wagon. Returning his gaze to the wagon, he spotted
Annabel, with her son beside her, seated on a blanket by the remains of the campfire. *Thank goodness
for that,* he thought, and continued to scan the clearing in search of a possible hiding spot for a sniper.
He decided that Larsen had chosen flight instead of
fight.

When she caught sight of him, Annabel got to her
feet and walked to the edge of the stream to meet
him. She didn't wait for him to dismount before she
starting apologizing. "I'm so sorry I misjudged you,"
she said, pleading for his understanding. "It's all my
fault, all of it, and I feel so miserable." She felt some

relief in seeing that he had found Caesar, but she was fearful to even mention it.

"How long ago?" he asked, with no trace of emotion. When she appeared not to understand, he asked, "How long has he been gone?"

His cold lack of expression frightened her more than had he reacted in violent anger. She trembled as she answered, her words halting and stumbling. "He's been gone over an hour, I think."

Her answer was disappointing. Larsen had an hour's start on him. It was too much for a chase. Now it was a matter of tracking him. "Which way did he go?" he repeated.

She pointed toward the north. "He rode up the stream." She hesitated. "In the water."

Although his face wore a blank facade, there was a fury growing inside him that he fought to control. He looked toward the tree then. "How did he chop the tree down?"

"With an ax," Annabel answered.

"Where did he get an ax?" Will asked calmly.

"I gave it to him," she murmured fearfully, and pulled Bobby close to her as if to protect him from the violent storm certain to come.

"You gave it to him," he repeated, as if giving it a lot of thought. That was all he said for a long moment as he played the scene in his mind. His mind immediately flashed back to recall Larsen's theatric attempts to gain Annabel's sympathy, even to the extent of banging his head against a tree. *She bought every bit of it*, he thought, thinking then of the cold remarks she had made to him—that baffled him at the time. It was damn near impossible to understand how she could be so gullible.

"He said he only wanted to chop off a small limb to make a walking stick," she offered in her defense.

"A walkin' stick," he repeated, his voice still calm, his face still a blank while he refrained from asking what in blue blazes did the man want a walking stick for. *He stole my packhorse, too,* he thought then, which added fuel to the fire already burning inside him. He glanced at Caesar. *That damn horse,* he cursed silently, thinking he should have shot it back at Sallisaw Creek. Without another word, he left her and walked over to the felled tree as if to take a look at the stump. The real reason was to take a few minutes to think, to decide what to do. His inclination was to jump on Buster and go after Larsen—and tell Annabel she could drive her wagon on in to Fort Smith by herself. There was another option: he could tell her to wait right there while he went after Larsen. He considered that for a moment, then rejected it because she would still be sitting in Indian Territory alone. The fact that she had made it to this point without being harmed did not count. She had been lucky, but now it was up to him to see that she reached Fort Smith still unharmed. He could not escape the thought that, along with his job to catch outlaws, it was his duty to protect the citizens of the territory.

It frustrated him to do so, but in the end, he knew what he had to do. He turned abruptly and walked back to the wagon. "You and Bobby get in the wagon. We're headin' out." He did not offer his assistance this time, nor did she wait for it, but scrambled up on the wagon seat immediately. He stepped up into the saddle and rode over to the roan still standing in the trees, took hold of its reins, and led it back to tie onto the wagon again. This time, he tied Caesar onto the tailgate as well. Ready to get under way then, he turned Buster toward Fort Smith. His plan was simple—make as many more miles on this day as possible before having to rest the horses, then one more camp and a short ride into town tomorrow.

CHAPTER 11

Will led Annabel's wagon onto the ferry and they crossed the Arkansas River at Fort Smith close to midday. Once across, he led them up to the head of Garrison Avenue before pulling to a halt. She watched him solemnly as he went around to the tailgate and untied the roan. There had not been much conversation between them since leaving their camp of the night before. But when she gave it some thought, she recalled that he had wasted very few words even before she set his prisoner free. Had she known him better, she would have realized that he was not a man to dwell on misfortune. He was angry when first finding out what part she had played in Larsen's escape. But in a little while, he looked upon it as simply an unfortunate delay in the chase, much as a horse going lame, or a heavy snowfall to slow him down.

He paused a moment to look at Caesar. The tired old horse had made it to Fort Smith, but Will wouldn't have guaranteed the horse to make it all the way to Annabel's sister's place. He walked back to the front of the wagon. "You sure you're gonna make it all right?" he asked her.

"Yes," she answered. "I know where I am now. It's only a mile or so to my sister's house." He nodded and started to turn away, but she stopped him. "Please, Mr. Tanner . . ." she started.

"Will," he interrupted.

She smiled. "Will, then," she continued. "I'm so sorry to have caused you so much trouble. Are you going to go back after that man right away?"

"I expect so," he said, although he was still undecided whether to leave at once or wait until morning.

"I was afraid you were going to arrest me for helping him escape," she confessed.

"I thought about it," he said, halfway serious. He figured that he was going to be a long time tracking Larsen after this delay. But he should at least report in to Marshal Stone, even though he didn't look forward to informing him that he was within twenty miles of Fort Smith when his prisoner escaped. He was sure Stone had expected him a day or two sooner, since he had telegraphed before he left Fort Gibson.

"Well," Annabel said, "I know it's not much, but I wish you a successful and a safe journey. And I thank you again for seeing that Bobby and I reached Fort Smith safely. I pray I haven't cost you too much time. I'll see about returning your horse to you if you'll just tell me where to take him."

You have no idea how much you've cost me, he thought, *not only time, but that sorrel, money, and supplies, not to mention my damn packhorse.* To her, he replied, "You'd better just keep that horse. I don't think Caesar's gonna be able to pull that wagon anymore. I hope all goes well for you and your son, and you find your sister in good health." He nudged Buster and rode off toward the courthouse, relieved to be free of Annabel Downing.

"Hello, Will." Dan Stone looked up from his desk in surprise. "I've been lookin' for you to show up. You turn Brock Larsen over to Sid down at the jail?"

"Nope," Will answered. "I didn't bring Larsen back with me."

Confused, Stone asked, "You didn't? Why not?"

"Because he got away about twenty miles back," Will said. Then he went on to tell Stone the whole story, explaining his reasons for the decisions he had made. "I'm fixin' to go back to find him," he said in conclusion. "But I've gotta pick up some supplies and some more cartridges. He took that bay packhorse of mine with damn near everything I need on it."

After Will turned over the stolen money he had recovered, Stone listened to his report without commenting, confining his reactions to an occasional shake of his head until Will had finished with a shrug of his shoulders for final punctuation. "Well, if that ain't the damnedest thing," Stone said. "Sweet-talked the lady into givin' him an ax." He shook his head again, then said, "You did the right thing, though. I mean, escortin' the lady and her child back here."

"It don't make me feel any better about losing my prisoner," Will said. "And I'm goin' after him, if I have to chase him to California."

"I expect you'll consider takin' a posse rider and a wagon with you," Stone said, figuring it was going to take a long time to track Larsen down this time. He should have known better.

"I reckon not, Dan," Will replied. "I need to move fast. I don't wanna mess with a cook and a wagon. I can travel better by myself."

Although he halfway expected Will's response, it still brought a frown to Stone's face. "Damn it, Will," Stone reproached, "I can't afford to lose another deputy. With Ed Pine laid up in the hospital at Fort Gibson, we're short of men as it is. I don't want you to go gettin' yourself shot because you ain't got anybody watchin' your back."

"I ain't plannin' on gettin' shot," Will answered matter-of-factly.

Stone knew it was useless to complain. Will was the best deputy riding for him, but it was just a matter of time before an outlaw got the jump on him. Exasperated, he settled for a mild warning. "Just be sure you don't get careless."

"I won't," Will said.

After leaving Stone's office, he took his horses to the stable, where he met Vern Tuttle cleaning out a stall. "Howdy, Will," Tuttle greeted him. "I was wonderin' when you'd be back."

"Vern," Will returned. "I ain't gonna be here

long. I need to leave again in the mornin', so I'd like a portion of oats for both of these horses tonight, all right?"

"Sure," Vern replied, looking the roan over. "What happened to the bay you've been using as a packhorse?"

"He's one of the reasons I'm ridin' out again in the mornin'," Will said, "him and the man who stole him."

"That's a fine-lookin' double-rigged saddle on him," Vern commented. "The previous owner musta been a cowhand."

"I doubt that," Will said, picturing Brock Larsen in his mind. "I expect the feller he stole it from mighta worked cattle." The double-rigged saddle was better than a single-rigged for roping cattle. "I'm fixin' to leave it here and throw a pack saddle on the horse."

"I don't reckon you'll be wantin' to keep two saddles," Vern speculated. "You might be wantin' to sell that one."

"I might at that," Will said, not surprised by Vern's interest, since he was always in the market to pick up a bargain. And Will was well aware that he usually came out on the short end of most trades with the wily stable owner. "We'll talk about it when I come back."

"What if you don't come back?" Vern asked. The short lifespan of the average deputy in Oklahoma Territory was a well-known fact. "No offense," he quickly added.

"None taken," Will said. "But if I don't, then I reckon you've got yourself a saddle."

"I druther pay you somethin' for it," Vern said, and meant it. In the short time since Will had signed on as a deputy marshal, Vern had come to like the young lawman.

"You can be thinkin' about what it's worth, and we'll talk about it when I come back from this trip," Will said. "I've gotta get some supplies and be ready to leave first thing in the mornin'." With that, he left the stable and headed for Floyd Meeks's general merchandise store. After that, he planned to have supper at the Bennett House and sleep in his own bed that night.

"Is Garth calling on you tonight?" Ruth Bennett asked her daughter.

"I don't know," Sophie replied. "I wouldn't be surprised. Why?"

"I was just wondering if we should set a place for him," Ruth said. Her daughter's suitor had been showing up quite frequently in the last week, and usually in time for supper.

"He didn't say anything about it," Sophie said. "I'd kinda like to see if he's shaved off that skinny little mustache he's tried so hard to grow. I've been trying to get him to get rid of it. It looks like somebody dipped a pen in an ink bottle and drew a line on his upper lip." She laughed at the image. "If he shows up, we'll get him a plate then."

"If you don't mind, you can set one out for me."

Startled, for neither of the women had noticed the tall figure standing in the kitchen doorway, Sophie exclaimed, "Will!" Her first thought after her initial surprise was, had he overheard her remarks about Garth Pearson's mustache?

Sophie's outburst caused her mother to start as well. "Goodness' sakes, Will, you gave me a fright."

"Where did you come from?" Sophie asked. Then, without waiting for his answer, she implored, "Did you hear what we were talking about?"

"Maybe . . . some of it," he said. "There wasn't anybody in the parlor, so I thought I'd best come back here and tell you I plan to take supper here tonight."

Still slightly flushed, Sophie said, "We're gonna have to hang a cowbell around your neck, if you're gonna keep moving around here like a ghost."

"Pay no attention to her, Will," Ruth said, laughing at her daughter's embarrassment. "Don't worry, we'll set a place for you. I'm glad to see you back safe and sound."

"Thank you, ma'am," Will said. "I'm lookin' forward to one of your fine suppers, and that's a fact. I'll just be here for tonight." He turned about-face and headed for the stairs with the hint of a smile on his face, like Ruth, amused by Sophie's embarrassment. It faded away before he reached the top of the stairs, however, with the return of an anxious thought of Brock Larsen vanishing into the hills. It seemed a sin to be wasting time here in Fort Smith while Larsen was getting farther and farther away. So he had to tell himself again that his horses needed to rest, and he had had to prepare for another hunting trip with new supplies and ammunition. And another night was not going to make that much difference. It was likely to be a long hunt.

In the kitchen behind him, Ruth couldn't resist asking, "Did he say he was just going to be here for tonight?" When her daughter said that was so, Ruth commented, "My goodness, I would certainly feel sorry for any girl he might take for a wife—gone for so much of the time, and never sure to come home at all." Sophie made no response while she continued to set the table for supper, knowing that her mother was going to continue making comments like that until she saw her daughter successfully married to Garth Pearson.

As no surprise to any of the regular boarders at Bennett House, Garth showed up to call on his fiancée just at suppertime. He graciously accepted Ruth's invitation to join them, and Sophie set a place for him at the opposite end of the table from Will. Having become familiar with all the boarders at the house by now, Garth exchanged friendly greetings with them all and offered Will a polite nod. Will returned it with little enthusiasm, for he still held a feeling of resentment toward the handsome young man. He almost smiled when he noticed that the thin mustache was still gracing his upper lip.

After supper, Ruth insisted that Sophie should entertain Garth in the parlor, saying that she would clear the dishes away and clean up the kitchen. Since the evening was still young, Will decided he would take a walk down to the Morning Glory Saloon. For a reason he cared not to admit, he decided he would like a glass of beer. That would be better than sitting in his room all evening.

"Well, look who's here," Gus Johnson sang out when Will walked in. "Where you been, partner? I thought you'd took up drinkin' at some other saloon."

"Hello, Gus," Will replied. "I've been outta town for a while."

"What's your poison?" Gus asked. "Whiskey?"

"No, I think I'll just have a glass of beer," Will said. "I ain't in a drinkin' mood tonight—gotta get up early in the mornin'." He watched while Gus filled a glass from a keg behind the bar, then set it on the bar before him.

"Where you been, Will?" Gus asked.

"Nowhere in particular," Will answered, not really interested in sharing the details of his failed arrest attempt. "Just lookin' for some fellers over in the Nations." He felt someone rub up against his elbow and turned to find Lucy Tyler standing close beside him.

"Hello, stranger," Lucy greeted him. "Where you been keeping yourself?"

"Evenin', Lucy," Will said. "You want a drink?"

In response, she nodded to Gus, and he reached under the bar for a glass and filled it from a bottle of whiskey. "Thanks," she said to Will, and proceeded to toss the shot back. Then she cozied up closer to him and asked, "You wanna go upstairs and visit a little while, honey?"

"I reckon not tonight, Lucy. I need to get on back to the house. I've gotta get up early in the mornin'. I just thought I'd like a glass of beer before I turn in for the night."

She affected a pretty little pout for him. "That's what you always say. When are you gonna come upstairs with me?"

On Sophie's wedding night, probably, he thought. To Lucy, he said, "Oh, I don't know. I wouldn't be no good for you tonight, anyway. Got too many things on my mind." It was not just a lame excuse like those he usually came up with to decline Lucy's invitations. He was still smoldering over his unfortunate encounter with Annabel Downing.

Lucy gave him a tired sigh and thanked him for the drink. Then she went back to a table in the corner where two of the town's bachelors were involved in killing a bottle of Gus's rye whiskey. She had been assisting them in their efforts before Will walked in. She still had hopes of luring one or both of them upstairs when they got drunk enough.

"Draw you another'n?" Gus asked when Will set his empty glass on the bar.

"Reckon not," Will answered. "I ain't as thirsty as I thought I was." He paid for his beer and Lucy's shot, then headed for the door.

Walking back to the boardinghouse, he saw Sophie and Garth sitting in the porch swing, both bundled up against the cold night air. Will guessed that two of the boarders, Leonard Dickens and Ron Sample, were probably playing cards in the parlor, and the two young people retreated to the cold of the porch for privacy. He decided he'd best announce his presence, since they might not notice him approaching in the dark. "Hello, the porch," he called out when still a dozen yards away.

"Hello, yourself," Sophie called back, knowing why he had warned them and resenting the fact that he thought it necessary. She freed her hand from Garth's as Will walked up the steps, but not before he noticed it.

"Kinda chilly to be sittin' out here on the swing," Will commented as he stepped up on the porch.

"Not if you're wearing plenty of clothes," Sophie informed him.

"Reckon not," Will said, and went inside.

It was early afternoon when Will arrived at the site of Brock Larsen's escape and the start of a search that he hoped wouldn't be as long as he feared. He had to rest Buster and the roan pack-horse. They had already covered twenty miles since leaving Fort Smith early that morning. While they rested, he built a fire and boiled some coffee to wash down some fried bacon, and tried to think like Larsen would have. He had no way of knowing where the outlaw would head. Back to Sartain's? Probably not. He could have gone in any direction, up in Kansas, or back south to Texas, or maybe northwest to Osage country. But first, he would have had to free himself from his handcuffs and the chain around his ankle. That brought to mind Plum Creek and Zach Goodson. Zach was a blacksmith as well as a trader, so he had the tools to free Larsen. The question was, did Larsen know about Zach's trading post? Maybe he could pick up Larsen's trail away from here to find out. Zach's place was on Sallisaw Creek, about twenty miles north of the spot where Will had come upon Annabel Downing. According to her, when he made his escape, Larsen had ridden up the stream where they had stopped to rest the horses after leaving Sallisaw Creek.

Just to be sure, he scouted the area around the place where her wagon was parked when he had gone back to look for Caesar. Annabel was somewhat in a state of bewilderment when he had returned with her old horse, so it was possible she may have been confused. When he could find no tracks leading into the stream in a southerly direction, he decided she had been right. That was confirmed when he saw tracks leading upstream into the water. When the horses were rested, he rode north along the stream, watching for any tracks leading out of it. After approximately forty or forty-five yards, the stream split around a large rock, creating two narrow gullies, so Larsen was obliged to take to the bank, leaving the tracks Will was looking for. They continued to follow the stream north. Whether or not Larsen knew about Goodson's place, he was going to strike it if he continued on this course.

* * *

Zach Goodson looked toward the path leading down to his forge when a whinny from one of his horses told him a strange horse was approaching. It was getting along toward sundown, and Zach's eyes weren't as sharp as they used to be, so he squinted in an effort to identify the rider. A muscular man, Zach wore nothing but a heavy blacksmith's apron over his long handles, even though the evening was chilly. He took one more look at the red-hot horseshoe he had just hammered out, dropped it into a half barrel filled with water beside his anvil. Pulling a dirty rag from a pocket in the apron, he mopped the sweat from the top of his bald head before walking out to meet his visitor. When he recognized the rider, he wasn't surprised, in spite of the fact that it had been some time since he had last seen him. "Deputy Will Tanner," Zach announced when Will rode up to his shop and dismounted.

"Howdy, Zach," Will came back.

"I was wonderin' if one of you boys was gonna show up here pretty quick," Zach said.

That was what Will wanted to hear. "Sounds like you mighta seen a fellow I'm lookin' for."

"I expect I have," Zach said. "Day before yesterday I took these handcuffs and a chain off of him." He walked over to a barrel in the corner of his shop and held the cuffs up for Will to see. "You might want these cuffs back, but they ain't much good after I got through with 'em."

Will took a look at the mangled cuffs. "I expect you're right."

"Ain't nothin' wrong with the chain," Zach went on. "I took that off his ankle—he was wearin' Injun moccasins—said I could keep the chain as payment, on account he didn't have no money." He wiped his head again to remove the sweat that continued to form. "He was leadin' a packhorse that looked like it was carryin' a good bit of stuff, but he said he didn't have nothin' he wanted to trade as payment, either. I mighta held out for a better deal, but he was holdin' a Colt .44 on me the whole time we was negotiatin' the price. He said if I did a proper job, I could have the chain and my life. At the time, that didn't seem like a bad deal, so I said, 'Fine by me,' and that was that." He paused finally to hear what Will had to say.

"Sounds like you met Brock Larsen, all right," Will said. "And you're right, you got a pretty good deal. Larsen doesn't mind killin' instead of payin'. I don't reckon you've got any idea where he was headin' when he left here."

"Not for a fact," Zach said. "He asked me how far it was to the territory line. I told him it wasn't but about seven miles east of here to the Arkansas line. But he said, 'Hell, I don't wanna go to Arkansas. How far is it to Kansas?' I told him it was about eighty-five miles to Baxter Springs, if he rode due north." He paused to let Will think about that. "What's he wanted for?"

"Held up the Katy over in Muskogee and killed

a guard," Will replied, "plus, he shot Ed Pine up pretty bad."

"Well, I ain't surprised," Zach said. "I didn't figure you was chasin' him for stealin' handcuffs." He shook his head. "Ed Pine, huh? How bad is he?"

"Like I said, pretty bad. Larsen left him for dead, but Ed is still hangin' on. He's over in the hospital at Fort Gibson. Did you see which way Larsen rode outta here? Did he go north to Kansas?"

"That would be my guess," Zach replied. "Couldn't say for sure, but when he rode up the path to the trail by the creek, he cut to the north. Don't know if he stuck to it after he got outta sight. Tell you the truth, I didn't care a helluva lot which way he went. I was just as happy to see him go."

"Well, I expect I'll head out that way and see if I can catch up with him somewhere," Will said. He would have thought Larsen would have headed for the wild country west of the five Indian nations, looking for a remote place to hide out. But maybe his plan was to return to Kansas, since he had asked about the distance to Baxter Springs.

"You ain't thinkin' about headin' out tonight, are you?" Zach asked. "You ain't gonna be able to do much trackin' in the dark." He nodded toward the sun settling down on the horizon, in case Will had failed to notice.

"No," Will replied. "It's a little too late tonight. I'll camp tonight and start first thing in the mornin'. My horses have already had a full day, so I reckon I'd better give 'em a good rest, and I expect they'd appreciate a portion of grain, too, if you've got some to sell."

"Sure do," Zach said. "Anything else you need?"

"Have you got any yeast?" Will asked, suddenly recalling Annabel Downing's recipe for slapjack.

"Yeast?" Zach echoed. "Nah, I ain't never carried nothin' like that. Whaddaya want it for?"

Will shrugged. "Ah, nothin' really, just something I was gonna try."

Zach matched Will's shrug with one of his own. "Why don't you make your camp right here next to the creek and take supper with me tonight? I've got a hindquarter of deer meat hangin' in my smoke-house. I'll cut a couple of slabs offen it and we'll roast it over the fire. I'd admire havin' somebody to swap lies with for a change. It gets pretty lonesome around here ever since my woman run off."

"How come she ran off?" Will asked, aware then that there was no sign of the Cherokee woman in the cabin next to the store.

"I don't know," Zach replied, scratching his head as if puzzled himself. "I been tryin' to figure that out myself. I give 'er a lickin' one night about a week ago for knockin' over a fruit jar full of good corn likker. I reckon that got her back up a little, 'cause I woke up the next mornin' and she was gone. Women are a funny breed, hard to figure out some-times." He shook his head as if still puzzled. "Just as well, I reckon. She couldn't cook worth a flip, anyway."

"That's mighty generous of you," Will said, not

eager to get into a long discussion about women since his recent encounter with Annabel Downing. "Smoked deer meat sounds pretty good right now. I'll take care of my horses, then I'll make us some coffee to go with it."

"Ain't no need," Zach said, and pointed toward a large gray pot sitting on the edge of the forge. "There's still plenty in that pot I made fresh this mornin'."

Will tried to keep from cringing. He had sampled a cup of Zach's coffee on one occasion before, and he swore he would never drink another one. "If it's all the same to you, I'll make us another pot. I've got this new coffeepot I had to buy when Brock Larsen ran off with my packhorse, and I wanna see what kinda job it does. While I'm at it, I'll buy a sack of coffee beans from you, if you've got some." *Never hurts to have some extra*, he thought.

"Suit yourself," Zach said. "Always glad to sell some coffee beans, and I'll run 'em through my grinder for you. Seems a shame to waste half a pot of good coffee, though." He shrugged. "I can set it on the fire in the mornin'. It'll still be good."

"Let me unsaddle my horses," Will said. "I'll let 'em graze for a while before I put 'em in the corral with yours."

"Fine and dandy," Zach replied. "I'll fetch the meat, then I'll grind you up some coffee beans."

Will went down close to the creek, took Buster's saddle off, then unloaded the packhorse. He took his bedroll off, but didn't unroll it, thinking there was no reason to give any critters an invitation to move in. When he got back to the shop, Zach had a spit set up right over the forge and was in the process of spearing two large portions of venison on it. "There's your coffee right there," he said, pointing toward a sack sitting on a stool in the corner. "I always like to have a little snort before supper. How 'bout it?" He reached down beside his foot and picked up a fruit jar filled with moonshine. "I won't tell you where I got this, so you won't have to worry about goin' to arrest some honest bootlegger."

Will couldn't help laughing at the remark. "I reckon I could use a drink at that."

Zach poured into two cups he had set out on his anvil. He tossed the whiskey down, then followed it with a loud snort, dipped his cup in the barrel of water beside the anvil, and gulped that down. "It's a fair batch of whiskey, but it needs a chaser." There was no telling how many horseshoes, wagon wheel rims, and other items had been cooled in that half barrel of water. That was evident by the dark scale floating on the top. And Will felt sure the water was never replaced, only added to when needed. So he took his shot of whiskey without the chaser. Guessing that Will was reluctant to dip in the barrel for water, Zach commented, "A little iron won't hurtcha, might even be good for what ails you."

"Maybe so," Will replied when he could talk again. He picked up his coffeepot and went to the creek to fill it.

* * *

They talked a long while after they had finished supper, with Zach doing most of the talking. Knowing the blacksmith was enjoying an opportunity to visit, Will stuck with it for a good bit longer than he desired. When he thought he'd had enough, he announced that he had to get started early in the morning and was ready to crawl into his bedroll for the night. Zach was disappointed, but got to his feet when Will did and volunteered to help him put his horses in the corral. Will declined an invitation to have breakfast with him, saying he planned to hold off on breakfast until he had to stop to rest his horses. "All right," Zach said. "But remember there's still half a pot of coffee left in my pot. I'll let it sit in the coals in my forge. They'll keep it hot, if you want a cup of coffee before you start out."

"Much obliged," Will said while doubting he was man enough to handle a cup of that coffee.

Chapter 12

Brock Larsen pushed his horses hard, making no efforts toward hiding his trail. If he had judged Will Tanner correctly, there was a chance the deputy would be left stuck with Annabel and would be delayed in coming after him. In case he left the woman on her own again, however, he was pressing the horses to put as much distance behind him as possible without killing them. He was fortunate in that he had two good horses that seemed up to the task, so he kept them at a good pace, not stopping the first night until he had covered about fifty miles. He had to smile when he thought about having Tanner's packhorse with plenty of supplies to take care of his needs. The old blacksmith said Baxter Springs was eighty-five miles. Larsen planned to make that in two days, and with the ground he had covered on the first day, he was left with a short day to reach the border. Based on the quality of his horses, he saw no problem with that. He knew people in Baxter Springs, men he used to ride with, so he was confident that if he reached there ahead of Tanner, he'd be safe from pursuit. Tanner had no authority out of Oklahoma, at any rate. Just like he and Ben Trout had escaped the Rangers down in Texas, he could leave Will Tanner in Indian Territory. The old hunt for him and Ben by the Kansas authorities should have had time to cool down by now. As far as he knew, none of the gang of cattle rustlers the two of them had ridden with had ever been identified. So there wasn't much risk in going back to Kansas.

With no sign of anyone trailing him, Larsen reached the Spring River early in the afternoon. The busy cattle town sprawled along the other side of the river promised refuge for sure. Once he crossed to the other side, he felt he would have beaten the determined deputy marshal behind him. With no money to his name, he couldn't take the cable ferry across, so he swam the horses to the other side downriver from the ferry. Lack of money was a problem that he had to fix as soon as possible, and he knew where his best bet was to do so.

"Well, I'll be . . ." Ike Bowers started. "Lookee yonder, Earl." He yelled to the bartender, "Hey, Ernie, reckon you oughta close that door? All kinds of trash is blowin' in."

Ernie looked at the man walking into the Trail's End Saloon. "Well, I'll be . . ." he echoed Ike's words. "Brock Larsen, what are you doin' back here? Last time you was in here musta been close to a year. You and Ben Trout was on your way down to Texas."

Ike and the two men seated at the table with him got up and walked to the bar to meet Larsen. "Looks like you've gone Injun since you left here," Ike said, nodding toward Larsen's moccasins.

"It sure as hell wasn't because I had any choice," Larsen replied. "And I aim to buy me a pair of boots just as soon as I can."

He didn't get a chance to explain before Earl Suggins asked, "Where's Ben? Is he with you?"

"Howdy Earl, Ike. How you doin', Jake?" Larsen greeted them all before answering. "Who's gonna buy me a drink? Ben's gone under, shot dead by one of those damn deputy marshals down in Injun Territory. He had me, too, but I got away from him." He grinned. "Stole his packhorse and left him whistlin' in the wind down in Oklahoma." He paused before repeating, "Who's gonna buy me a drink?" No one had volunteered to so far.

"Hell, I'll let you have the first one on the house," Ernie finally spoke up, and set a glass on the bar. "You boys bring your glasses over here and we'll all drink one to ol' Ben Trout, whose string finally run out."

"I know ol' Ben would appreciate that," Larsen said. "And, hell, I'd spring for the next round, but I ain't got a dime to my name. That deputy cleaned me outta all the money me and Ben took in a train holdup down at Muskogee."

"I swear, was that you and Ben?" Jake Roper asked. "We heard about the robbery, but we thought you boys were down in Texas." Everyone wanted to know all about the train robbery and especially the circumstances that led to Ben Trout's death, so Larsen told them about their ill-fated encounter with Deputy Marshal Will Tanner.

"Ben shouldn'ta tried that move," Larsen concluded. "Tanner was holdin' a cocked Winchester on us when Ben decided to draw on him. He didn't even come close to gettin' a shot off."

"Damn fool," Earl said. "He always was a little tetched in the head." It was no secret that Earl Suggins had very little use for Ben Trout. There was no debating the fact that Earl was the leader of the small gang of outlaws rustling cattle in Kansas. The trouble between him and Ben started when Ben decided Earl wasn't running things as well as he could. Ben wanted to start hitting the banks and trains instead of stealing cattle. Larsen had been the only one siding with Ben, and when Trout decided to split from the gang, Brock decided to go with him. "So things didn't turn out so good ridin' with Ben?" Earl asked, his tone thick with sarcasm.

"Well, we had a little bad luck," Larsen said. "We was gettin' along pretty good till that marshal got onto our trail. He even knew about Sartain's, and don't nobody know about that place but outlaws. We was on our way back here, anyway, figured it was better to ride with you boys." That was a lie, but Larsen needed a place to light where he might have a chance to make some money, and at the moment, to rejoin the Suggins gang was his only prospect.

"That so?" Earl replied. "On your way back to the

old gang, huh?" He doubted that, but he needed another man for a little job he was planning. Two more would be better, so he might even have welcomed Trout, too, if the fool hadn't gotten himself shot. "Well, you came back at the right time. I could use another man, and there ain't no hard feelin's, 'cause you sided with Trout."

"I 'preciate it," Larsen said. "I didn't have no hard feelin's when I left here, so I was hopin' I could ride with you fellers again—like old times."

"What about this deputy that was on your trail?" Earl asked. "You think you lost him?" The thought of a U.S. Deputy Marshal so close was cause for concern. He and his men had operated out of Baxter Springs for a couple of reasons. It was a wide-open cattle town, with more than a few who made a living on the wrong side of the law. But also, if things got hot for them in Kansas, they could slip over the river into Oklahoma Indian Territory. This Tanner fellow sounded like he was not one to notice boundary lines.

"I think so," Larsen said with a confident look. That was a lie also, because he had taken no pains to cover his trail. His one thought had been to run for his life. "I had too big a start on him, left him with a woman and child to take care of. Besides, I'm in Kansas now. He ain't got no jurisdiction here. He'll just have to turn hisself around and go back to Fort Smith." He looked from one smiling face to another, satisfied that he was welcome to return. "What's this little job you've been thinkin' about?" he asked.

Earl grunted a chuckle. "This'll tickle you. It's what Ben was always talkin' about doin', only the time weren't right when he was always jawin' about it. But now the time's right. There's a little bank opened up in Independence that's just settin' fat and sassy, waitin' for us to walk in and make a withdrawal. They oughta have enough cash on hand, 'cause the town's been growin' fast since they made it the county seat."

"What about the law?" Larsen asked, already feeling eager over the prospect.

"They got a sheriff and no deputies that we know of," Ike answered. "The sheriff looks like he might run the first time he hears a gun go off."

"Even if he don't," Jake offered, "he won't stand much chance in a shoot-out against the three of us. The four of us now," he corrected. "And the U.S. Marshal's deputies are a hundred and fifty miles away at Fort Riley."

"Sounds good to me," Larsen said. "When you figurin' on hittin' it? 'Cause I need money now."

"We've got time," Earl said. "I figure the best day to hit it is on a Friday, before all the farmers and cowhands come into town on Saturday, lookin' to get money outta the bank. Independence is about forty-five miles from here, so we've got time before then to take two easy days' ride up there. And our horses won't be tired out when we get there."

"Looks like I got back at the right time, all right," Larsen said. "I need to take care of my horses, then I'm hopin' you'll let me owe you for a room till we get back," he said to Ernie.

"I reckon," Ernie replied.

"'Preciate it," Larsen said. "I'll take my horses down to Saul's place."

"Saul ain't there no more," Earl said. "He got took with consumption or somethin' and died last winter. His widow sold the stables to a feller from Kansas City named Holden. We still keep our horses there when we're in town, 'cause it's so close to Ernie's here. But Holden ain't the same as ol' Saul was. You didn't have to be careful what you said around Saul. He was as big a crook as we are. And I suppose I'll have to loan you a little money, so you can pay to board your horses. I doubt Holden will give you any credit, specially since he ain't ever seen you before. It will just be for one night, we're leaving for Independence in the mornin'."

"Much obliged," Larsen said.

"Might be you could loan him enough to pay for his room while you're at it," Ernie was quick to suggest.

"You can just wait till we come back, you greedy ol' bastard," Earl said.

"How do I know you'll come back here?" Ernie asked.

"Hell, we always wind up back in this dump you call a saloon," Earl said. "Don't worry, you'll get your money."

With a few dollars in his pocket, thanks to Earl, Larsen took his horses to the stable. Robert Holden was working on a bridle in the tack room when

Larsen dismounted and led them inside. When Holden heard him, he walked out to greet him. "Howdy, friend, you lookin' to board your horses?"

"I am," Larsen replied. "Just need to leave 'em one night." He sized Holden up while he was quoting his rates, and decided the man might be interested in a bargain. When Holden had finished, Larsen said, "I can pay you for the night, but I'm runnin' short of cash. I'm thinkin' about sellin' a fine .44 Colt handgun that belonged to a friend of mine, includin' the holster. He passed away a short time ago, and I've got no use for another gun. If you think you might have a use for one, this would be a chance to get one cheap." Larsen had judged Holden correctly, and after a minimum of bargaining, he walked out of the stable with thirty dollars in his pocket. "Give my horses a ration of oats each," he said as he left. "They've got a forty-five-mile ride ahead of 'em."

Will arrived at the Spring River ferry after two days of steady riding. When he left Zach Goodson's place on Plum Creek, he had tried to follow the fresh trail he found leading away from Zach's forge. However, he lost the trail after following it across a wide prairie of switchgrass when it led onto a rocky plateau. He lost a good bit of time trying to pick up the trail again until saying, "To hell with it," and striking out straight north to Baxter Springs. It was a gamble, but it was the best chance left to him. Zach told him that Larsen was headed for Kansas, and Baxter Springs was a likely town to head for. The town was a gathering spot for all manner of saddle tramps, but most of them were just wild hell-raising cowhands. Hardened criminals like Brock Larsen and Ben Trout would not normally operate out of Baxter Springs. They might be too well known, so Will figured Larsen was not likely to spend much time in the town. This would be Will's first time in Baxter Springs, so he was surprised to find just how big the town was. Ed Pine had once told him that the popular watering hole for drifters on the run was a shabby two-story building with a saloon on the first floor called Trail's End. That was his only clue, so he asked the ferry operator for directions to that saloon.

The operator looked him over pretty thoroughly before telling him how to find it. "If you don't mind me sayin' so, there's a helluva lot better places in town to buy a drink, or rent a room, or whatever else you want."

"I 'preciate the advice," Will said, "but I've gotta meet somebody there."

"Well, here's some more advice then," the operator said. "Keep your back to the wall and be particular about what Ernie pours in your glass."

"Much obliged," Will said. "I'll do that."

Trail's End was not very far from the ferry, but not too close to what appeared to be the main street through town. Since it was already getting along toward evening, he knew he should take care of his horses, but he decided to check on the saloon first, in case he got lucky. He reached inside his coat, took his badge off his vest, and put it in his saddle-bags. He couldn't help recalling the last time he had done that. It was in Texas, another time when he had found it difficult to respect territorial boundaries. It would be nothing more than wasted time to notify the U.S. Marshal for the Kansas Territory, time that would give Brock Larsen ample time to disappear. Larsen's arrest had become a personal case for Will, anyway. And if the murdering outlaw was to be tried, Will intended it to be done in Judge Isaac C. Parker's court, with Ed Pine there to witness the hanging.

The ferry operator had not exaggerated when he described the run-down condition of the Trail's End Saloon. The only evidence of any attempt at upkeep was a fairly new hitching rail out front—the old one must have rotted away, Will presumed. He dismounted and tied his horses, pulled his rifle from the saddle sling, and walked in the door. Inside, he found a large room with a dozen tables and a set of stairs on one side. There was no one in the place but two men seated at a table close to the bar, and four card players at a back table. He looked quickly from one face to the other in case he had gotten lucky, but none of the customers was Brock Larsen. He shifted his gaze over to the man behind the bar, who was studying him intently as well. A scrawny little man with a drooping gray mustache and bald head down to his sideburns was no doubt Ernie, Will decided, so he walked over to the bar.

Still studying the tall stranger as he approached his bar, Ernie affected a welcoming grin and sang out, "Howdy, partner, what'll it be?"

Thinking the bartender might be more cooperative if he bought a drink, Will said, "Whiskey." He laid his rifle on the bar between them and watched while Ernie blew the dust from a glass before pouring a shot from a half-full bottle.

"Ain't never seen you in here before," Ernie said as he slid the glass closer to Will. "This time of year, we don't see many cowhands come into Baxter Springs. You just passin' through town, or you gonna light for a while?"

"I don't know for sure," Will answered, and tossed his whiskey down. He had to pause while he endured the burn in his throat. It was pretty rough whiskey, rougher that the drink he had taken with Zach Goodson, and it burned all the way down. "I'm lookin' for a friend of mine who was supposed to meet me here. He said he'd most likely be at the Trail's End, and if he wasn't here yet, to ask for Ernie."

"Well, you found Ernie," he said. "I'm Ernie and this here is my place. What's your friend's name?"

"Brock," Will answered, "Brock Larsen. Have you seen him?" He watched Ernie's reaction closely, and it told him what he wanted to know. If he had guessed correctly, that Larsen had been here, he would hardly expect Ernie to tell him. But the look in the bartender's eyes and the suddenly frozen smile on his face could not disguise his sudden caution. If he was reading the man accurately, he was halfway certain his gamble to ride directly to Baxter Springs had paid off. Now it was a question of whether or not Larsen was still in town. He glanced toward the stairs at the side of the room and wondered if there was a chance he was renting one of the bedrooms up above.

Ernie paused a long moment before answering. "Mister, I wouldn't hardly know your friend if he hadda been in here. I don't ask nobody their name. In this town, it ain't healthy to ask questions."

"Well, now, if that don't beat all," Will said, still playing it straight. "Brock said you knew him real well. That's why he told me to ask you."

"Well, I don't," Ernie said, "and that's that." He had no doubt now that he was talking to an Oklahoma deputy marshal, the man that Larsen had assumed would not cross the Kansas border to come after him. So much for what Larsen said, Ernie thought, because the crazy son of a bitch came right on into Kansas.

"I bet you just don't remember," Will said. "Maybe he took one of the rooms upstairs for the night. I'll go see if he's up there." He turned abruptly and walked briskly toward the steps.

Momentarily struck dumb by the stranger's brash move, Ernie yelled, "Hey, you can't go up there!"

With his foot already on the first step, Will ignored his warning and replied, "Why? It's a public roomin' house, ain't it? I'll just go up and see if ol' Brock is up there." By this time the few customers in the saloon were aware of the conversation between Ernie and the persistent stranger. One of the two men seated at the table close to the bar pushed his chair back and started to get to his feet, looking as if he was thinking about supporting Ernie. Halfway up the stairs by now, Will paused, cocked his Winchester, fixed the man with a warning gaze, and shook his head slowly. It was enough to change the man's mind, so he sat back down.

Up on the second floor, Will found himself in a hallway fronting a single row of rooms, four in all. He didn't hold out much hope of finding Larsen in one of them, but he wanted to know for sure. Trying the first door, he turned the knob and found it unlocked. The room was empty. He found the second room unoccupied as well. The third door was locked, so he gave it a firm kick with his boot, sending the door banging open against the wall, startling a prostitute in the process of servicing a client. Before the man could reach for a pistol in a holster on a chair in the corner, Will grabbed him by his hair and yanked his head back to get a look at him. It was not Larsen. "My mistake, mister. Sorry, ma'am," he said, and left them in the state of shock he had created.

The final door was also locked. It received the same opening procedure as the one next door. There was no one inside, but a quick look around told him that this was Ernie's room. There were extra furnishings and clothes, too many for an overnight renter. Returning to the head of the stairs, he prepared himself for the reception that might be waiting for him. With his rifle ready before him, he stopped at the top. As he halfway expected, Ernie was standing in front of the bar, holding a shotgun in his hands. Anticipating a shoot-out, the card players had departed for reasons of health. The other two men were still seated at the table, with no indication they were going to be involved. Will thought it best to keep an eye on the one who had stood up before, anyway, lest he might decide to join in. Looking back at the angry little man holding the shotgun, Will said, "That would be a mistake."

"Who the hell you think you are?" Ernie demanded. "Come in here and raise hell on my property."

"I think you know who I am," Will said calmly. "And what you need to know is that if you even think about raising that shotgun, I'll cut you down right where you're standin'." He paused to let that warning sink in. "Now, I owe you for a drink, and for a couple of doors I damaged. I'll pay you for that, then I'll be on my way. So I'll ask you to put that shotgun on the bar and we'll settle up." He started down the steps, slowly, the Winchester raised and ready to fire.

Unnerved by the deadly calm of the lawman's words, Ernie lost what nerve he had summoned. He laid the shotgun on the bar and backed away from it. Concerned that the two men at the table might think him spineless for having given in, he blustered, "All right. As long as you're fixin' to pay for everythin', I reckon we'll forget about the ruckus."

Will continued down the steps, still watching the two men, who were still silently witnessing the altercation. Walking over to the bar, he reached in his pocket and peeled off a few dollars, laid them on the bar, and said, "That oughta take care of the damage." Before moving toward the door he asked, "How long has Larsen been gone?"

"What?" Ernie started. "I told you, I don't know no Brock Larsen." Will shrugged. It was worth a shot.

Outside, Will wasted no time climbing aboard Buster and leaving the saloon, in case Ernie changed his mind about using his shotgun. At least he had satisfied himself that he was on Brock Larsen's trail. The question facing him now remained, is Larsen still in Baxter Springs or has he moved on? If he is still here, it might take a lot of time searching a sizable town like this one. And if he's already moved on, that search of Baxter Springs would result in giving Larsen more and more distance from here. The situation was not that promising. He shrugged. *At any rate*, he thought, *I'm gonna need a place to take care of my horses and bed down for the night.*

He had not gone a hundred yards from the Trail's End when he came upon a livery stable. It occurred to him that it was handy to the saloon, and very likely Larsen might have stabled his horses there. It would make sense, so he pulled Buster up before the corral and stepped down.

"Evenin'," Robert Holden said as he walked out to greet him. "Lookin' to board your horses?"

"Yes, sir," Will said. "I am, if the rate's fair. I'm

new in town, so I ain't had a chance to compare prices."

"It's the cheapest in town," Holden said with a laugh. "It's the only way I could make it. I'm new in town, myself, been here since last May when I bought this place from the widow of the fellow who used to own it."

"Is that a fact?" Will replied. "Looks like you oughta get a little business from folks on this end of town, like that place just down the road, the Trail's End."

"I get some from that place," Holden allowed. "There seems to be a lot of people coming and going from there. Most of 'em I don't ask many questions."

They talked on for a bit. Will asked about the town and how Holden liked it. Holden was frank in his willingness to talk about the town's strengths and weaknesses. He concluded with a statement that if the cattle business slacked off, the town might dry up. Will came to the opinion that Holden was an honest businessman and had no real connections to the shady crowd that hung around the Trail's End. Because of that, he decided to take a chance and level with him as to why he was in Baxter Springs. "Mr. Holden, you look like an honest man, so I'm gonna be square with you." Holden paused, thinking maybe he had misjudged the stranger, expecting now that Will was going to explain that he didn't have any money to pay him. He was astounded when Will continued. "To tell you the truth, I'm a U.S.

Deputy Marshal out of Fort Smith, Arkansas," he said, and reached in his saddlebag for his badge. "And I'm tryin' to track down a murderer and train robber that skipped over the line here in Kansas. I'm wondering if you've happened to have seen him, since I know he spent some time at Trail's End." Holden, properly surprised, was at first short of words. "It would have been within the last day or so," Will prompted. "His name's Brock Larsen. He's ridin' a red sorrel and leadin' a bay packhorse. You see anybody like that?"

"Yes, sir, I have," Holden said. "Two or three days ago a fellow brought in two horses like that. He just left 'em one night. I don't know what his name was, whether it was the fellow you're after or not. Like I told you, I don't ask a lot of people what their names are." He hesitated for a moment, wondering whether or not he should say more. "He sold me a Colt .44—said he needed the money. I gave him thirty dollars for it."

Will felt certain it had been Larsen—it had to be. He would have been out of money, so he sold Ben Trout's handgun. "I don't suppose he said anything about where he was headin'," Will said.

"No, I'm sorry, he didn't," Holden said. He remembered then. "He did say to give his horses a ration of oats because they were gonna have to make a forty-five-mile trip the next day."

That wasn't much to go on—Larsen could have gone in any direction from there. "Can you think of any town that's forty-five miles from Baxter Springs?" Will asked.

"No, not right off. There aren't many towns that

close that I can think of," Holden said while searching his memory. "Coffeeville, maybe, but Coffeeville's a little farther than that, more like fifty miles. Independence," he suddenly remembered. "Independence is closer to sixty miles from here." He shook his head. "I can't think of anyplace else."

That'll have to do, Will thought. He had been gambling against long odds on every decision he had made since leaving the campsite where Larsen made his escape. So far, his luck was holding out. *Might as well gamble on Coffeeville*, he thought. "You're pretty sure he left town?" he asked.

"I'm sure," Holden said. "When he came to get his horses, there were three other men with him. They rode out west on the road to Coffeeville."

Three men, Will thought. That put a different light on the situation. Now he had four to deal with. It didn't change his objective, however, so he made arrangements with Holden to stable his horses overnight. At least he was familiar with Coffeeville, a little town on the west bank of the Verdigris River. And he knew Jim Davis, the owner of the Border House, a Kansas saloon just across the Oklahoma boundary. If the four men he now chased were in Coffeeville, Jim would surely know it. He planned to get an early start in the morning, so he paid Holden a little extra to sleep in the stable with his horses that night. Before turning in, he rode up to town and ate supper at a hotel Holden recommended.

* * *

Well before noon the next day, he crossed the Neosho River and continued on, not stopping to rest the horses until reaching a creek several miles farther distant. After some coffee and a breakfast of beef jerky, he got under way again and struck the Verdigris early that evening. Crossing over, he rode a short distance north to the Border House. He tied his horses at the rail beside a couple of others and stepped up on the narrow stoop. Opening the door about halfway, he paused to look the room over before entering. When he didn't see Brock Larsen, he pushed the door open and walked in.

Jim Davis, the owner, was tending bar, and when he recognized the tall lawman, he called out a welcome. "Well, if it ain't Will Tanner!" He grinned broadly. "How the hell are you, Will? What are you doin' up this way?"

"Jim," Will returned. "I just thought I'd get up here to see if you were still in business."

"Why, hell yes," Jim said, "and doin' better all the time. This little town is doin' all right. New folks movin' in every month through the summer— slowed down now that we're lookin' winter in the face." He lowered his voice as if to keep anyone from overhearing. "You still ridin' for the Marshals Service?"

"That's right," Will said. "And I'm tryin' to get on the trail of four men that mighta come this way. I thought maybe you mighta seen some strangers in town in the last couple of days."

Davis's face immediately went blank and he shook his head. "Can't say as I have. There ain't been anybody new around here. You say there was four of 'em?" Will nodded. Davis continued. "I don't know how four strangers coulda come into this little town without everybody knowin' it. You sure they were headin' here?"

Will shook his head, disappointed. "I ain't now." He went on to tell Jim about the circumstances that led him to believe Larsen and his new friends were headed to Coffeeville.

"I swear, that ain't much to go on, is it?" Jim speculated. "Maybe it was Independence they were headin' for. But you say your man told the feller at the stable he was gonna take a forty-five-mile ride. That would be more like sixty miles. Maybe he just didn't know how far it was." Then another possibility struck him. "Of course, you rode over from Baxter Springs on the wagon road, straight west. To go on to Independence from here, you have to head straight north for about fifteen miles. That puts it at about sixty miles, but if you knew the country and cut straight across, instead of followin' the road, I expect it wouldn't be but about forty-five as the crow flies."

"You might be right," Will allowed, wondering why he hadn't considered that possibility. Even if he had, however, he didn't know the territory well enough to have known what direction would take him straight to the town. He knew Independence was northwest of Baxter Springs, but how far west and how far north would have been a guess. He was beginning to get the feeling that he was just wasting his time, but he decided to go on to Independence at least. If Larsen and his companions were not there, then he wouldn't have any idea where to look for them next. And he didn't like the bitter taste of the defeat he would have to admit. He offered a silent curse to Annabel Downing and her broken-down old horse, Caesar.

Jim Davis watched the young deputy as he was obviously laboring with his possibilities. "Are you goin' to Independence?" he finally asked.

Will exhaled loudly and answered, "Yep, I reckon so."

"Tonight?"

"Nope," Will replied. "My horses are tired. I'll go in the mornin'."

"If you wanna take 'em to the stable, there's one not too far from here," Jim suggested. "There's a hotel in the middle of town."

"I'll just ride on up the river a piece and make camp," Will said. "This trip is costin' me plenty already."

"Well, you can have your supper right here. Eat with me. I'll have Annie cook us some stew."

"Who's Annie?" Will asked. "Have you gone and got married since I was here last?"

"Nah," Jim said. "Annie's an Osage woman that's doin' the cookin' for me." He chuckled at the thought. "I won't even charge you nothin'."

"That sounds to my likin'," Will said.

CHAPTER 13

Will rode a light snow shower into the thriving settlement of Independence. The town lay along the banks of the Verdigris River, just south of its confluence with the Elk River. He pulled Buster up to take a look at the cluster of businesses lining the main street, before proceeding on. The first place he was naturally inclined to look for Larsen and his companions was in a saloon, and he could see three from where he sat. The biggest one, and the only one with a formal name, proclaimed itself to be the River House. The other two were smaller, rougher establishments with signs that simply read SALOON. The men he searched for would more likely frequent the smaller saloons, but he couldn't know that for sure. He could only guess about the three men Larsen hooked up with, but it was a good bet they were of the same caliber as Larsen. To be sure, however, he guided Buster toward the River House, since it was the first in line.

As was his custom, he drew his rifle from the

saddle sling and walked to the entrance, guarded only by two swinging doors, in spite of the cold weather. He paused for a few moments, peering over the doors to get a look at the room inside. It was a large barroom, with a long bar running half the length down one side of it. The rest of the spacious room was occupied with tables, half of them filled with patrons. Will scanned the room, his gaze quickly skipping from table to table, then back to the half a dozen men at the bar. Brock Larsen was not there, and after looking the saloon over, Will was not surprised. The River House did not look to be the kind of establishment to attract Larsen's kind. It appeared to be a meeting place for the more respectable citizens of the town, judging by the number of business suits he saw at the tables. *Might as well see if I can get any help,* he thought, and pushed on through the doors.

He immediately caught the attention of a good many of the patrons when he walked across the room and took a position at the end of the bar. He was confronted immediately by the bartender, a pleasant-looking man of middle age and the look of a lawyer or maybe a schoolteacher. "Good day, sir," he said. "I guess you're new to the River House."

"That's a fact," Will replied.

"I suspect you didn't notice the sign that said 'No Firearms' posted by the front door," the bartender said.

"For a fact, I didn't," Will said, genuinely surprised, for he had not seen it, having been concentrating on who was in the room. He looked around him then and realized that no one was wearing a weapon. "Sorry, I reckon it's just a habit. I'll leave, so I don't upset your customers."

"It's not your fault," the bartender said. "Tell you what, why don't you let me put your weapons behind the counter till you're ready to leave?"

"To tell you the truth," Will confessed, "I was just lookin' for a cup of coffee and a little information. It's a little too early in the day for me to want a drink."

"I've got coffee. It'll cost you a nickel, and the information is free."

"Fair enough," Will said. "I appreciate it." He handed his Winchester and Colt to the bartender, who put them behind the end of the bar. Then he went to a small potbelly stove near the middle of the bar and poured a cup of coffee from a metal pot resting on the corner of the stove.

"I don't sell much of this, except for first thing in the morning," the bartender said as he set the cup before Will. "The rest of the day, I drink most of it. Now what kind of information are you looking for?"

Will took a sip of the coffee, then looked around the room again, noticing that the hum of conversation had resumed after his weapons were safely out of sight. "I don't see any sense in beatin' around the bush, Mr. . . ." He paused. "What was your name?"

"Harry," he said, "just plain Harry."

"All right, Harry, my name's Will Tanner, and like I said, there ain't no sense in beatin' around the bush. I'm a U.S. Deputy Marshal and I'm lookin' for an outlaw that I think is in this town. And I wanted to ask you if you've seen any strangers in town that don't look like the upstandin'-lookin' citizens I see in your saloon. He's travelin' with three other men, and I'd bet they don't look much like your customers, either."

Surprised, Harry paused to think. "Well, not in here, I haven't," he said. "I can't say about anywhere else in town. Independence has had its share of drunken, unruly cowboys, but more good families have settled on the farm and cattle land around the town. We've built churches and schools in the last few years. The two saloons down the street are about the only places that are left for the riffraff that still wander through town, and they don't stay long after they find out the town doesn't want their kind."

Will considered what Harry had just told him, and it caused him to wonder even more what business the four outlaws had in Independence. "Well," he finally said, "I thank you for the information. It sure sounds like you've got a right ambitious town here."

"Yes, sir," Harry said with a great big smile. "We're growing all the time. As a matter of fact, we've got a new bank just opened up a couple of weeks ago. It's a branch of the Bank of Kansas, from over in Kansas City. They're claiming to have money to lend to settlers who move here and want to improve on their property."

"I reckon that's a good thing, all right," Will allowed. A stray thought crossed his mind as he said it, and he wondered if the new bank had anything to do with Larsen and his friends coming to town.

He thought about the possibility of that while Harry moved down the bar to pour another drink for one of his patrons. The bartender lingered to talk to that customer, until Will signaled that he was ready to leave. "Owe you a nickel for the coffee," he said when Harry came back. But the bartender waved him off when he reached in his pocket.

"I won't charge you anything for the coffee," he said, and pulled Will's weapons out from behind the counter. "I hope you catch up with the men you're chasing, but I hope you don't find them here."

"Much obliged," Will said. He holstered his Colt, took his Winchester, and walked out the door. Outside, he took another long look down the street. About forty or fifty yards north of the River House, there was a crossing street, and there were two banks on the corners, directly across from each other. From where he stood, it was difficult to tell which one was the new one. The thought he had had earlier caused him to decide to have a closer look, especially the new one, but he figured he might as well take a look in the two small saloons on the way. *Just in case ol' Brock Larsen is sitting on a barstool waiting for me,* he thought, so he took Buster's reins and led his two horses up the street.

The first saloon he came to was a single-story building with a rough facade that held a hand painted sign that said SALOON. Unlike the River House, this saloon had a single door and it was closed. He opened it far enough to see one end of the room. Even though the room was dimly lit, he could see well enough to recognize Brock Larsen had he been seated at one of the tables. He was not there, so he opened the door farther and scanned the other end of the room with the same results, so he pushed the door wide and walked in. He was greeted by the bartender. "Hey, close the damn door. I ain't tryin' to heat the whole town." This came in spite of the fact that the air was almost stifling, courtesy of a large iron stove in the middle of the room. It wasn't helped by the low-hanging cloud of tobacco smoke.

"Sorry," Will replied, and pushed the door shut. He took a minute to survey the dozen or so patrons, sitting at the tables and standing at the bar. There were two card games in progress. It struck him that this looked more like the typical saloon in a frontier town, causing him to change the impression of the town he had first formed after visiting the River House. He strode over to the bar.

"You drinkin', or just lookin'?" the bartender asked.

"Still too early for a drink," Will replied as he had down the street. "I ain't ready for a drink of whiskey. How 'bout some coffee? You got any for sale?"

"Coffee?" the bartender responded. "No, I ain't got no coffee to sell. This ain't no dinin' room." He gave Will a hard looking-over then. "You're new in town, ain't you?" Will answered with a nod. "I didn't think I'd seen you in here before."

"That's right," Will said. "How 'bout anybody else? Have you seen any other new faces, besides mine?"

The bartender's eyes narrowed and a suspicious

frown formed on his face. "I don't take much notice of everybody that walks in that door."

"Just me, huh?" Will said.

A man standing close to Will, who had been listening to the word play between the two, spoke up then. "What about them fellers that walked in here last night, Whitey? They was new in town—said they was cattle buyers."

Will turned his attention to him. "Were there four of 'em?"

He nodded and started to reply, but Whitey cut him off. "Hush up, Lem, you're drunk." He looked back at Will and said, "Lem says all kinda crazy things when he's been drinkin' too much."

"Was one of 'em wearin' Indian moccasins?" Will asked Lem, ignoring Whitey's interruption.

Realizing now that he might be telling too much, Lem was relieved to reply, "Nope, they was all four wearin' boots."

Will nodded to the flustered bystander, then smiled at Whitey. They had pretty much confirmed that there were four new faces in town. *Larsen must have bought himself a new pair of boots*, he thought. "Much obliged for the information." He was about to suggest that when he caught up with the four outlaws, he'd be sure and tell them that Whitey had given him the lead. Before he could speak, however, a disturbance erupted at the back corner table.

"By thunder, that's the last card I'm gonna see come off the bottom of the deck!" The warning was bellowed out by a large brute who stood up, knocking his chair over in the process. The object of the brute's fury was the player seated across from him. By his dress, Will speculated that he was a professional gambler. One of the other men at the table made an effort to calm his angry friend, but Will could not hear what he said. "The hell he didn't!" the enraged brute charged. "And it's the last time he's gonna cheat anybody!" He drew the .44 he was wearing on his hip and leveled it at the gambler. There was an immediate hush over the noisy, smoke-filled barroom, accompanied by the sound of chairs scraping on the wooden floor as cautious patrons pushed back to give them room. The irate card player stood, threatening over the table, his .44 aimed at the gambler's face. "I aim to get my money back, or this'll be the last hand you ever deal."

Terrified moments before, but relieved when the huge man hesitated to pull the trigger, the gambler finally spoke in his defense. "I didn't cheat you, mister. I didn't have to, you're just not any good at playing cards." It was the wrong thing to say. The brute cocked his pistol.

"Take it easy, Pratt," his friend pleaded. "It ain't worth killin' him over it and goin' to jail for it."

"That's what you say," Pratt replied. "He ain't took all your money. I'm gonna shoot the bastard. It'll be self-defense. He drew on me." He glanced quickly around him. "Ever'body in here can see that. We'll put a stop to these fancy gamblers comin' in here and cheatin' honest folks."

Will glanced at Whitey. "You gonna put a stop to that, or are you just gonna let him murder that man?"

"Hell," Whitey said. "I ain't gonna get between 'em. It ain't none of my business. Like he said, Pratt'll put a gun in his hand after he shoots him. And when the sheriff comes in, everybody here will swear he drew on Pratt." Whitey snorted in contempt and added, "That lily-livered sheriff ain't gonna ask no questions, afraid he might have to do somethin' about it." As he said it, a smug grin broke out on Pratt's face and the gambler began to cringe, realizing that the menacing hulk really intended to kill him.

Will found it hard to believe that the whole crowd was willing to stand by and watch a senseless murder take place. Unwilling to participate in the entertainment, he moved away from the bar and walked straight up to Pratt, holding his rifle before him in both hands. Astonished to find the stranger almost nose to nose with him, Pratt jerked his head back and demanded, "What the hell do you want?" Without replying, Will suddenly brought his rifle up and slammed the butt against the side of Pratt's head. Stunned, Pratt staggered backward, pulling the trigger as he did, sending a bullet through the tabletop. Will stepped with him, staying right in his face. Before Pratt could cock his .44 again, Will caught him hard against the other side of his head with the barrel of the rifle. It was enough to put the big man's lights out for a few minutes.

Amid the shocked spectators, Will stepped back and turned to the gambler. "Pick up your money. Have you got a horse out front?" The devastated gambler nodded vigorously in answer. "Well, get on it and get your ass away from here." It was not necessary to repeat the instructions.

There was an eerie silence hanging over the barroom as the gambler ran out of the saloon, followed slowly and cautiously by the mysterious stranger. As soon as he closed the door, Will heard the instant resumption of conversation as the witnesses reacted to the violent handling of the threat. It was an unfortunate happening, as far as Will was concerned. He could not have made his presence in town known more if he had printed it in the newspaper. This could make his job a great deal harder than it would have been, had he slipped in quietly as he had intended. It was bad luck, but he figured he had had no choice. The man was preparing to murder the gambler. The question now was, what to do next? He had planned to stop in the third saloon on the chance Larsen might be there.

He took Buster's reins and started walking toward the two banks and the saloon just short of them. After walking a short distance, he decided that he should go talk to the sheriff. He might hear about the incident in Whitey's saloon and be searching him out for an explanation. Better to go to him first, Will decided, and identify himself as a deputy marshal. He didn't have to tell him he was working out of the Western District of Arkansas; let him think he was a Kansas deputy. Maybe the sheriff could help him—he should be aware of any strangers in town. *Should have done that right off,* he thought. He stopped and looked up and down the street until he spotted what appeared to be the sheriff's office. It was across the street and beyond the next saloon. Will hesitated a moment more, then decided he wanted to at least take a look in the saloon, except this time without making such a dramatic appearance.

The scene was not a great deal different from the one he had discovered at Whitey's. There was only one card game instead of two, and evidently no one was cheating. Also, as before, there was no sign of Brock Larsen. Although it was still early in the day, he decided he was ready for a drink, after his visit to Whitey's and his introduction to Pratt. The bartender moved over to stand directly across from him when he stepped up to the bar. A tall, skinny man who bore a striking resemblance to the late president, Abraham Lincoln, the bartender offered no greeting.

"Whiskey," Will said, and received a brief nod in reply, then the bartender produced a glass and poured Will's whiskey. Will reached in his pocket, pulled out a quarter, and placed it on the bar. The lanky bartender raked it off, put it in his cash drawer, and drew out a dime in change. Will had figured as much, having assumed the place to be a one-bit saloon. The River House was no doubt a two-bit establishment. He put his dime change in his pocket and tossed his drink down. The bartender watched in bored indifference, still without having spoken a word. *Well, silence is better than the rude reception I received at Whitey's,* Will thought. *I'm gonna have to see if he really is a mute, or I'll have to find somebody else to talk.* "I just rode into town," he said. "Supposed to meet some friends of mine." A shift of

"Abe's" eyes was the only indication the man had heard him. "Oughta been four of 'em," he continued. "Hit town a couple of days ago. You ain't by any chance seen 'em, have you?" "Abe" shook his head slowly. Will began to have doubts that the man could speak, so he asked, "You can talk, can't you?" The bartender nodded. It was almost getting to be comical. "Well, say something, then," Will said. "My name's Smith. What's yours?" he felt compelled to ask.

"Abe," the bartender replied.

Will almost laughed. "No foolin'? That's not your real name, is it?"

"Nickname," Abe replied, still stone-faced. Then in a stampede of words, he made a comment. "Just like Smith ain't your real name."

"What makes you say that?" Will asked.

Abe shrugged. "Heard about you at Whitey's. You're a lawman."

Will was astonished. How could he have heard about the altercation at Whitey's? He had just come from there. Evidently someone from the other saloon must have run down the back alley to warn Abe that a lawman was in town looking for some outlaws. It didn't take much speculation to decide which side of the law the one-bit saloons were on. He was wasting his time here. "You wouldn't tell me if you had seen four strangers lately, would you?"

Abe shook his head slowly. "Been nice talkin' to you," Will said as he turned to leave. Out on the street again, he headed for the sheriff's office.

* * *

Sheriff Leland Couch looked up from his desk when he felt a rush of cold air tumble through the open door. He did not recognize the somber, sandy-haired man who stepped inside his office, carrying a Winchester rifle in one hand. "What can I do for you, mister?" Couch asked.

Will took a moment to look the sheriff over before he answered. He was not a big man and he had a boyish face that was sparsely covered by a scraggly attempt to grow a beard. Will could imagine right away that the sheriff hardly struck fear in the men who frequented Whitey's and Abe's saloons. He glanced around the tiny office, noticing that the room was neat and organized, telling him that the sheriff spent a great deal of his time in his office. "Sheriff," Will finally stated. "My name's Will Tanner." He pulled his coat open to expose the badge on his vest. "I'm a U.S. Deputy Marshal." This captured the sheriff's attention right away.

"Yes, sir, Deputy," Couch replied smartly. "I'm Sheriff Leland Couch. What brings you to Independence? Nothing real serious, I hope."

"Well, I'm afraid so," Will said. "I don't rightly know if it's gonna cause any trouble in your town or not. I'm trackin' a man wanted by the Arkansas marshal's office for murder durin' a train robbery down in Oklahoma Territory. His name's Brock Larsen and he came up this way. I picked up his trail in Baxter Springs and it led right here to your town." He let Couch digest that for a moment before continuing. It brought a worrisome frown to Leland's brow. "That's not all the problem. He joined up with three other men. So what I wanna ask you is, have you seen four strangers hangin' around here during the last couple of days?"

"No," Couch replied, openly concerned, "at least I don't think so. Whaddaya suppose they want in Independence?"

"Well, I don't know," Will said. "But they musta come here for some reason. Anything goin' on that would attract a gang of outlaws?" Obviously getting fidgety over the prospect, Couch shook his head. It was easy to see that the news was unsettling to the sheriff. "And you ain't noticed four strange fellows in town? Maybe in one of those one-bit saloons up the street?"

"Well, no," Couch said. "I reckon I wouldn't have noticed that, anyway."

Will was quickly getting the impression that Couch never left the office. "I figured you'da noticed four new men when you were makin' your rounds around town." Couch continued to shake his head. "No, huh? Do you ever check the crowd at Whitey's or Abe's?"

"They sorta keep their business to themselves, and I don't bother them as long as they keep it inside and I don't get complaints from the other businesses. I have a deputy who works part-time, and that's kinda what he does, and he tells me if there's anything to be concerned about going on." As if on cue, the door opened and a young man charged inside, heading straight for the small stove in the center of the room. "This is my deputy now," Couch said. "He's been sorta watching the town. Lon, this is U.S. Deputy Marshal Tanner."

Lon Blake had been so intent upon getting out of the cold air outside, he had taken no time to see who the sheriff was talking to. When he heard the words *Deputy Marshal*, he turned to take a look. "You're the feller that laid Pratt Wilson out on the floor at Whitey's!"

Will remembered having seen the young man then, so he figured that answered the question of how the crowd at Abe's got the news about Pratt so quickly. Lon's blurted announcement caused a look of nervous concern on the sheriff's face, so Will turned to him. "He was gettin' ready to shoot a man," Will explained.

"I was fixin' to jump in and stop him," Lon said, "but this feller beat me to it—kinda took us all by surprise, especially Pratt."

"Why didn't you identify yourself as a deputy sheriff?" Will asked.

"Well," Lon hesitated, "the situation was already handled pretty good. I didn't think there was any use in sayin' somethin'."

Will was getting a pretty good picture of the state of law enforcement in Independence. Leland Couch appeared to be an incompetent sheriff who might be a little reluctant to face down a hardened outlaw. And at this point, Will was a bit skeptical about the young deputy. He might even be in cahoots with the rough crowd in the saloons. It seemed to be

the perfect picture of a town that could eventually
be taken over by the undesirable element that hung
around Whitey's and Abe's. That was something
that Couch and the businessmen of Independence
would have to deal with in the future. But for now,
there was an immediate concern that he was defi-
nitely involved in—Brock Larsen, and whatever he
and his three friends were in town for. After meeting the law in the town, Will could readily see why
a gang of outlaws might pick Independence to pull
a big job, if that was what they had in mind. And off-
hand, the first thing that came to mind was the new
bank just opened. His only concern when he rode
in was to find Larsen, arrest him, and take him back
to Fort Smith for trial. But that was no longer his
only option. The town might be primed for a bank
holdup, and he felt an obligation to try to stop it.
He took another look at the sheriff and his deputy,
and hoped like hell he could depend on them for
help. *Doggone you, Annabel Downing,* he thought.

"Sheriff." Will came right out with it. "I think
your little town here is fixin' to get hit by four outlaws, and my guess would be a bank holdup."

His announcement had the same effect on
sheriff and deputy, judging by the expressions of
surprise on both faces. Couch was the first to speak.
"A bank holdup! Why do you think that? We've
never had anything like that in Independence.
We've always been a peaceful town."

"I suspect that's one of the reasons you're fixin'
to get hit," Will said. "That and the fact that you've
got a new bank. These outlaws might be thinkin' it'll

be easy to scare these new employees and they won't have to worry about anybody tryin' to resist 'em."

"What'll we do?" Couch asked, obviously in a shocked state of confusion. He looked at his deputy then. "Lon, have you seen anybody you didn't know in town?"

Lon guessed right away that he was going to have to decide whose side he was on. He didn't want to admit that he was accepted as a friend by the lawless element in town simply because he could be counted on not to divulge all that went on in the rougher saloons and bawdy houses. "There was one or two fellers that I ain't never seen before come into Whitey's." He shrugged indifferently. "But they wasn't rowdy or nothin', so I didn't say nothin' to 'em."

"One or two," Will asked, "or four?"

"Maybe there was a couple other fellers with 'em," Lon reluctantly confessed. "But like I said, they wasn't up to no mischief, so there wasn't no reason to bother 'em."

"Damn it, man," Will demanded, "are we gonna be able to count on you, or not?"

Lon recoiled slightly, having previously witnessed the marshal in action. "Yes, sir," he decided. "You can count on me."

"Good," Will said. "Now, what we don't know is when they plan to hit the bank, but I expect it's gonna be pretty soon. It would most likely be in the mornin' when they're openin' up the safe and gettin' the money out for the tellers. Wouldn't you say, Sheriff?"

"What? Ah, yeah," Couch stammered, still in a state of shock.

"Course they might hit it at closin' time when they open the safe again to put the money away," Will said, halfway talking to himself. "I expect we'd better watch 'em all the time. I figure the best we can do is to sit in the bank and wait for 'em to walk in. And we'll have to watch both banks. I'll take the new bank and you and Lon can take the other one. That all right with you, Sheriff?"

Couch glanced quickly at Lon before answering. "I guess so," he said, thinking that he would have preferred to be with the deputy marshal.

"All right, then," Will concluded, "I've got things to do right now. I wanna take a look at each bank, and I've got to take care of my horses." He looked behind Couch at the clock on the wall. "What time do the banks close?"

"Four o'clock," Lon answered him.

"That gives us plenty of time to let the banks know what we're goin' to do, for me to take care of my horses, and for us to be inside the bank at closin' time," Will said. "Lon, you and the sheriff keep a sharp eye out for any strangers hangin' out around the banks. I'll keep an eye out for Brock Larsen if he's with 'em. I'm 'bout to starve to death. Is there anyplace to get a meal close to the bank?"

"Right across from the old bank at Sadie's Diner," Couch said. "I'll go with you after we tell the banks." They left then to inform the bank managers what they planned to do.

* * *

As Will expected, the managers in both banks were visibly alarmed when they learned of the real possibility of a robbery about to strike them. Will was most concerned about the potential for nervous employees to broadcast their fear and in so doing, tip off the robbers before they could be apprehended. So in talking to the managers, he stressed the importance of remaining calm and letting the lawmen handle the situation. "We're gonna be sittin' right here outta sight, ready to stop the robbery before it gets started good," he told them. Then reminded them that there was a good chance that he and the sheriff had guessed wrong and there was no holdup planned. "Won't hurt a thing to be ready, though." He advised Hugh Franklin, the manager of the new bank, that he would knock on the back door at around three-thirty. "In case somebody's watchin' to see who goes in and out, it might be best to use the back door." Franklin seemed to have calmed down about the possible crisis at his new bank. Will appreciated it, and wished he could say the same about the sheriff. He was inclined to think the newly opened bank would likely be the target, so maybe Couch wouldn't have the occasion to soil his trousers.

While that thought was fresh in his mind, Will heard the back door open. A few seconds later, a rather roly-poly man came through the back room, having just come from the outhouse behind the bank. "Here's our guard now," Franklin said. "Jug Watson, this is Deputy Marshal Tanner."

"How do?" Jug asked with one firm nod in an attempt to convey his readiness to handle any trouble that might befall the bank.

Will was not impressed. Jug appeared to be sloppy in his appearance, in the way he carried himself, not to mention his red, bloodshot eyes. He thought about Couch and Lon then and shook his head in frustration. Deciding to do the best he could with what he had to work with, he instructed Jug on where he wanted him positioned and what his responsibilities would be. When their business was done at both banks, Will took his horses to the stable at the end of the street. He made arrangements with the owner to leave his packs in one of the stalls, but he left his saddle on Buster. He might need the buckskin in a hurry, so he would unsaddle him after the bank had closed. With that taken care of, he walked back up the short street to Sadie's Diner, where Sheriff Couch and his deputy were waiting.

Sadie's Diner was actually a part of the hotel, and was where most of the hotel's guests ate. There was one long table in the center of the room that seated fourteen diners, if the two chairs at the ends of the table were counted. Around the sides and one end of the room, smaller tables were arranged with four chairs each. It was at one of these side tables that Couch and Lon sat, but Lon was the only one eating. The sheriff waved Will over when he stepped inside the door. Will pulled out a chair and sat down at the table. He rested his rifle against the wall and waited for the rather heavyset waitress to look his way. When she did, she didn't bother to come to the table, asking loudly instead, "You gettin' the special?"

"What is it?" Will called back.

"Stew," she replied.

Lon momentarily interrupted his violent attack on the food on his plate to interject. "It's what I'm eatin'," he managed to say before resuming his assault. "It ain't bad."

"Yes, ma'am," Will said. "I'll have that." The food on Lon's plate looked a lot like Mammy's cowboy stew back at the Morning Glory Saloon in Fort Smith. He figured the risk wasn't any greater at Sadie's. "And a cup of coffee," he yelled after her as she went through the kitchen door. He turned his attention to the sheriff then. "You ain't eatin'?"

"Nah," Couch replied. "I've got a little unsettling in my stomach. This cup of coffee will do me."

Will suspected he knew what caused Couch's loss of appetite. He just hoped he would hold himself together until this business was finished. He couldn't help wondering why he wanted the job as sheriff in the first place. Further thought on the subject was interrupted by the arrival of Sadie carrying a plate heaped with stew and two large biscuits riding on top. "I'll bring you some coffee," she said as she placed the plate before him. "How 'bout you, Sheriff, you want a warm-up on that coffee?" Will recoiled slightly when she reached across to pick up Lon's empty plate, exposing a large wet stain down her side from under her arm, this in spite of the chilly air in the room. She was a big woman, and the thin cotton dress she wore was hard put to contain all of her. With Lon's plate in one hand, she pulled a hand towel from around her neck and mopped a bead of sweat from her forehead. "Who's your friend, Sheriff?" she asked. "You ain't never been in before," she said to Will.

"He's not a friend," Couch replied. "He's a U.S. Deputy Marshal." When he realized how that sounded, he hastened to say, "I don't mean he's not a friend, I mean he just rode into town."

Will smiled at her. "I hope you and I are friends after I test your stew."

"Shoot!" she exclaimed. "My stew'll stand up to anybody's. Ain't that right, Lon?"

"That sure is a fact," Lon said.

"You let me know how you like it," she said to Will, and left to fetch the coffeepot. She returned in a few minutes with the pot. "Well?" she aimed at Will.

He took a moment to swallow, then said, "It'll stand up to anybody's."

"You doggone right," she said with a chuckle. She turned to Couch and said, "You're lookin' kinda puny today, Sheriff, you'd best let me fix you a plate of stew." He graciously declined. "You'll wish you had before suppertime," she predicted, and left to attend to her other customers.

Will finished his stew and another cup of coffee before announcing it was time to take a position in the bank, in case today was the day. "I'm wondering if we should alert the mayor and the other citizens of the town," Couch said.

Will paused as he was reaching for his rifle. "I don't think that's such a good idea," he said. "If these outlaws ride into a town where everybody's sittin' at a window with a shotgun, they might get spooked and decide not to try the holdup. Then you ain't got any reason to arrest 'em, except for Larsen, if he's with 'em. And I don't want some excited store owner to start shootin' while I'm tryin' to arrest him. If you and Lon are sittin' back there in that bank where they can't see you when they walk in, you oughta get the jump on 'em. And you won't have to shoot anybody. If we're lucky, we might be able to catch these robbers before the town even knows what happened."

Couch nodded slowly while he considered that. "I guess you know best," he said. Will picked up his Winchester and went to the small counter near the door to pay for his meal. He hoped like hell that his hunch was right, and the outlaws intended to rob the new bank and not the one where Couch and Lon would be waiting.

CHAPTER 14

"I'm gettin' damn tired of settin' around this riverbank, freezin' my ass off," Ike Bowers complained. "When we get that money, I'm thinkin' 'bout layin' up somewhere in a nice warm hotel till spring gets here."

"Hell," Jake Roper scoffed, "winter ain't even hit yet. You just got too soft layin' around the Trail's End, back in Baxter Springs."

"I don't see why we had to get here a day early, anyway," Ike carped. "We coulda rode right into town yesterday and hit them banks and be on our way to Wichita now, instead of settin' here lookin' at this river."

Tired of Ike's complaining, Earl Suggins interrupted to remind him that he was the boss of this gang. "I told you why we got here a day early, damn it. We got a chance to walk in both banks to see what the setup was before we go bustin' in there. That's gonna make it a lot easier to get in and get out faster, especially the new bank. They ain't got nobody workin' in there but one feller who looks like a manager or somethin' and that stumblebum that might be a guard."

"And one woman teller," Ike reminded him.

"And she wasn't bad-lookin'," Brock Larsen commented. "I might wanna tote her off with the money."

"I swear, you ain't changed a lick, have you?" Earl retorted. "Always thinkin' about the women."

"You got somethin' better to think about while we're settin' here drinkin' up all our whiskey?" Larsen said.

"Yeah," Earl replied. "How 'bout the business we came here to do?" Like his partners, Earl would rather be waiting the time out in a room in the hotel, instead of this camp on the bank of the Elk River. But he felt it important that any of the town's citizens who might have been suspicious would've been relieved to see the four of them leave town yesterday. His plan was to strike in the morning when the banks opened up and got the money out of the safes. With what he had seen when he walked in before, it should be fast and easy to knock off both banks at the same time. "I expect it would be a good idea to go easy on that whiskey, too. I'm gonna roust you out early in the mornin'. I wanna get to town right after them banks open."

"What are you worried about?" Larsen answered him. "That loudmouthed deputy in Whitey's said the sheriff ain't likely to be no problem. He don't even like to stick his nose in that saloon."

"Yeah," Ike chimed in, "and the deputy'll turn tail and run the first time he sees a six-gun in the hand of somebody who knows how to use one. He ain't much more'n a boy."

"We've got more to worry about from some hero takin' a shot at us from one of those stores on the street," Earl said. "That's why we've gotta get outta those banks in a hurry before anybody knows what's goin' on."

"You ain't got to keep harpin' on it," Larsen said. "We know what to do. You just take care of the new bank. Me and Ike know what to do in the other one." He grinned at Ike. "Don't we, partner?"

"I reckon," Ike replied.

"Remember what I told you," Earl said. "Don't shoot nobody unless you have to. We don't want no posse comin' after us for killin' somebody. Most town folk don't get as stirred up over a bank robbery as they do a killin'. Besides, the first time a gun goes off, everybody in town will know somethin's goin' on. If we're lucky, we could be ridin' outta town before most of the town knows what happened." His precautions were aimed mainly at Brock Larsen, who had a fondness for putting a bullet hole in someone. Suspecting as much, Larsen shrugged his indifference.

"I'm gonna find some more wood for that fire," Ike muttered.

* * *

Knowing already that the deputy marshal planned to come to the back door of the bank at three-thirty, Marcy Taylor hurried to the door when she heard him knock. As the deputy had instructed her to do, she asked, "Who is it?"

"It's Will Tanner," the answer came back, so she unlocked the door and let him in. Will looked around, but didn't see Hugh Franklin, the manager. When he asked where he was, Marcy said he was out in front of the bank, directing the efforts of two men who were setting up a sign that would proclaim the bank as FIRST BANK OF KANSAS.

"He should be back inside pretty quick," she said. "It's getting close to closing time."

"It doesn't look like you have many customers," Will said, since she was alone in the building.

"We've had a few today," she said with a smile. "Mr. Franklin said he expected it to take a little time for people to get used to us. I suppose he's right."

He suddenly caught himself comparing her smile to that of Sophie Bennett. They were not a great deal different. Both gave a man the impression that they knew a secret that he didn't. Promptly bringing his attention back to the business at hand, he asked, "Those two men puttin' up the sign—you know 'em?"

Guessing why he asked, she quickly assured him. "Oh yes, that's Mr. Peterson and his son. They did most of the work on the building." Her smile faded to a frown then and she asked, "Do you think we're really going to get robbed?"

"I don't know for sure," he said, "but I think there's

a chance you might. I'm hopin' I'll be able to keep it from happenin'."

"I guess I should be frightened," she said, "but you seem to know just what to do."

"You just remember what I told you," he said. "The minute anything starts to happen, you duck down and curl up under that counter and don't come out till I tell you to." He walked to the front window to take a look at the men nailing up the new sign. Turning back to her again, he asked, "Where's that fellow you hired to be a bank guard? What was his name?"

"Jug," she replied, "Jug Watson. He left a few minutes before you came in. Since there were no customers, and we were this close to closing time, he decided he'd leave early for supper." When she saw the expression of exasperation on Will's face, she said, "I know, he should have stayed."

Will started to comment, but shook his head instead. He thought maybe he could hazard a guess that Jug's name was short for Jughead. Just as well, he thought, the clumsy bank guard might get in the way in the event the holdup took place. Seeing that she was awaiting an answer, he muttered, "Don't make much difference, I reckon."

She nodded and a frown of concern returned to her face. "What must your wife think of you out trying to catch robbers and murderers? I should think she would be worried sick."

"I don't have a wife," Will said.

"Oh," she said, and the frown disappeared, replaced by that mischievous smile. At that moment, Hugh Franklin came in the door.

"Well, at least we've got a sign up now," he announced, "so folks coming through town will know who we are." He walked behind the teller's cage to his desk to write a check to cover the cost of the sign and handed the check to Marcy. "Mr. Peterson will be in for his money. Have him endorse it and cash it for him." Turning his attention to Will then, he said, "I guess we're pretty close to closing time." He pulled his watch from his vest pocket, looked at it, then looked at the large clock on the wall to compare them. "Might as well turn the 'Open' sign around, Marcy, and we'll start closing. I told Peterson to come on inside when he puts his tools away." If there was any anxiety about the sudden arrival of four dangerous outlaws, he didn't show it. Will suspected the man had never come into contact with the caliber of killer he might be facing in a matter of moments.

Peering out the window at the empty street between the two banks, Will watched for the first sign of four riders approaching that end of town. After Peterson came in for his money and left, Marcy removed her cash drawer and handed it to Franklin, who put it in the safe. "They'll have a devil of a time breaking into that safe," he said to Will.

"Glad to hear it," Will said, and glanced up at the clock. It was a quarter after four. "Well, looks like they ain't gonna show up tonight." He went to the back door and looked up and down the alley behind the building to make sure no one was waiting there.

"I didn't think they would," Franklin said. "Independence has grown into a respectable town. I would imagine a band of outlaws would think twice before attempting to rob a bank here. They should know we have law enforcement in Independence."

Will suddenly realized that Franklin was so non-chalant about the precautions being taken because he truly didn't believe it could happen. As far as Will was concerned, there couldn't be a better setup for an easy bank holdup than the First Bank of Kansas, Independence branch. Were it not for the fact that he was hoping to catch Brock Larsen, he might have been tempted to withdraw and let Franklin find out how close he was to the untamed frontier. "Well, sir," he said, "I surely hope you're right. But I'll be waitin' at the back door in the mornin' and we'll play it like we did this evenin'." He glanced out the front window just before Marcy closed the heavy shutters to see Sheriff Couch and Lon standing out in front of the bank across the street. *If anybody is watching from anywhere up the street, they sure as hell know we're expecting company*, he thought. When the bank was locked up, he followed Franklin and Marcy out the back door.

"We'll see you in the morning, then," Franklin said. "Are you staying in the hotel tonight?"

"No, sir," Will replied. "I reckon I'll sleep in the stable with my horses."

"The stables?" Marcy exclaimed. "That doesn't sound very comfortable."

Will smiled. "It's not that bad. A pile of fresh hay makes a pretty good bed, almost like sleepin' in a hotel."

"What about supper?" she asked. "Are you going to eat with your horses, too?"

By her tone, he realized that she was teasing him.
"Maybe," he replied. "Just probably not the same thing. On the other hand, I might take another chance with Sadie. I ate dinner there and I'm still standin'."

"I've heard most people say the food at Sadie's Diner isn't bad," Franklin offered. "I've never tried it myself."

"I've had a lot worse," Will said.

"How would you like to have a nice home-cooked supper tonight?" Marcy asked. "If you would, I'll tell my mother we're having a guest come to supper."

"Her mother's a splendid cook," Franklin said. "My wife and I can vouch for that. You'd be wise to take Marcy up on the invitation."

Will was not sure what to say. He certainly hadn't entertained the possibility of getting an invitation to supper. "That's mighty nice of you, ma'am, but I wouldn't wanna show up for supper without your mama even knowin' I was comin'. Besides, I've got to meet with the sheriff now, and I'll have to go take care of my horse. He's still saddled. But I thank you just the same."

"You'll have time before supper to do all that," she insisted. "You can even walk to our house. You passed it on your way in from Coffeeville. There are two little houses on the left, just before you get to town. The one with the picket fence and the barn behind it is our house. Don't worry, Mama will be pleased to have you. We eat about five, but don't worry if you're a little late. We'll still feed you." He started to decline again, but before he could speak, she interrupted. "I'll expect you at five or thereabouts." Giving him no time for argument, she spun on her heel and said, "Good night, Mr. Franklin," then started for home.

"Are you going to the stable?" Franklin asked Will. "I'll walk with you. I have to get my horse."

"I've gotta go meet with the sheriff and his deputy first," Will said. "I'll see you in the mornin'."

Franklin nodded and headed toward the stable. Will stood watching him walk away for a few moments, wondering what it was going to take to convince him of the seriousness of the threat to his bank. "Brock Larsen with a Colt .44 in his hand, I reckon," he muttered, before starting around the corner of the building to meet Couch.

"Well, no sign of 'em today," Couch said when Will walked around to the front of the bank. "Maybe they've thought better of the idea."

"We was ready for 'em," Lon boasted. "We was hidin' in that room behind the place where the tellers stand. They'da sure got a nice surprise when they came in to get in the safe. Anybody tryin' to rob that bank was gonna be dead meat."

"Maybe they ain't plannin' on hittin' one of these banks," Will said in response to Couch's hopeful optimism. "But we need to be here before they open in the mornin' in case they do. And we need to be inside the banks, not out front where anybody can see us." He looked at Lon then. "And nobody else needs to know about this, no talkin' about it in Whitey's or the other saloon."

"You don't have to worry about that," Lon said. "I know how to keep my mouth shut."

"Maybe they're not thinking about robbing the bank when it's open," Couch said. "Maybe they're thinking about breaking in at night."

"Well, there's that possibility," Will allowed. "But if they did, they might have a helluva time tryin' to open those big safes. Even if they tried to dynamite 'em, that might not work, and they'd wake up the whole town doin' it. I think they'll figure it's a whole lot easier to walk in when the money's out and stick a gun in a teller's face."

"Maybe it would be best to shoot them on sight," Couch suggested, "as soon as they show up. That way, none of us would risk getting shot."

Will found himself thinking he might be just as well off without their help. It might be better if Couch and Lon failed to show up in the morning. That would be especially true as long as he was accurate in his belief that the new bank would be the target. But since he couldn't be certain, he didn't want to take the chance of leaving the other one unguarded. "There's a couple of things wrong with that," he said "We won't know for sure they're bank robbers unless they walk in the bank and draw their guns. And number two, I'm plannin' on arrestin' 'em if I can, instead of shootin' 'em. So I'll meet you back here in the morning', eight-thirty." He left them then and went to unsaddle Buster.

Marcy's invitation was worrying his mind as he took care to see that his horses had been watered and fed. It would most likely be an awkward situation if he accepted and showed up on her father's doorstep. It would be quite a surprise for the girl's parents. She had not seemed to be an irresponsible young lady. He wondered if she often surprised them on other occasions. He had to admit, however, the prospect of a good home-cooked meal was tempting. "Hell," he decided, "all they can do is tell me to keep walkin'."

A little less than a hundred yards past the River House, Will came to the two houses Marcy had referred to. He had noticed them when he first rode into town, but had not paid them much attention. Now he discovered the sign next to the gate of the picket fence identifying the residence as that of Dr. Edward Taylor. Marcy had not mentioned that her father was the town doctor. He lifted the latch on the gate and stepped on a walkway of flat stones. *Pretty fancy*, he thought, then saw that the walk split before reaching the front porch, with a smaller branch leading to a side room on the house and another door. Beside that door was a small shingle that read DOCTOR'S OFFICE. A thought occurred to him that Marcy probably worked in the bank just to give herself something to do. *I reckon she didn't want to be a nurse for her father,* he speculated to himself, thinking that would have been the natural thing for her to do.

He continued on the main walk where two steps led up to the porch, which appeared to be as wide as the front porch at Ruth Bennett's boardinghouse back in Fort Smith. There was a large scrub brush on the bottom step, so he reached down to pick it up, only to find that it appeared to have been nailed to the step. *Peculiar,* he thought, and stepped on up to the porch. He stood for a few moments with his fist raised, prepared to rap on the door, but hesitating, not sure he wanted to impose upon the doctor and his family. It occurred to him that he would rather face down a threatening gunman than to have this social confrontation. Suddenly awash in the discomfort of the situation, he decided to retreat. It was too late, for the door opened at that moment to find him facing a smiling Marcy, his fist still raised to knock. "I saw you come in the gate," she said cheerfully. "You looked as if you were still deciding to come in or not. You weren't going to run, were you?"

"Why, no, ma'am," he sputtered, "not a-tall. I was just fixin' to knock."

"I can see that," she said, glancing at his fist raised menacingly above her head. He seemed to have forgotten it until she mentioned it. "I certainly hoped you'd show up after we went to the trouble to cook an extra chicken." She stepped back to let him enter.

"Come on in and I'll let you see my parents aren't nearly as scary as you may have thought."

Totally embarrassed now, and genuinely sorry he had shown up, he nevertheless dropped his saddlebags and rifle on a rocking chair on the porch and followed the slender young lady into the parlor. Before the front door closed behind him, he suddenly remembered the .44 on his hip and stepped back on the porch to remove his gun belt. Back inside, he thought to take off his hat, all the while aware of the amusement he was providing for the girl. He glanced down at his boots and the few traces of his walk along the muddy street still on them, realizing only then why the scrub brush was nailed to the front step. Suddenly feeling unfit to be among civilized people, he considered withdrawing and letting Marcy and her parents think what they wished. Marcy's father came in from the hallway at that moment, trapping him in the parlor.

"Marshal Tanner, welcome to our home. I'm Edward Taylor." He extended his hand. "We were delighted to have you come to supper with us. Marcy has told us why you're in our town. I'm distressed to know the reason for your visit, but I feel we are fortunate that you seem to have arrived on the scene at a most critical time."

"Yes, sir, thank you, sir," Will responded, at once a bit concerned. "I hope your daughter ain't told nobody else why I'm here."

Marcy quickly responded. "No, no one else, but I think it appropriate that Dad knows, since he's the mayor."

It was on the tip of his tongue, and he almost

blurted it out, but Will swallowed the profanity before it passed his lips. This was not good news. He had counted on the sheriff and the bank people to keep this thing under their hats, firmly believing that the fewer people who knew about it, the better the chances he could pull it off without innocent folks getting hurt. He already had the concern of Marcy's and Franklin's safety on his conscience as well as the employees of the other bank. Then there was also the concern of bank customers who might come in at the wrong time. It was a lot to worry about, but the alternative was to let them rob the bank and hope to catch up to them afterward. Even that would not guarantee the safety of anyone, employees or customers. In addition to these problems, he was operating in a territory where he had no legal authority, so he was counting on making an arrest with no one but himself and Brock Larsen knowing his jurisdiction was limited to western Arkansas and Oklahoma.

"I suspect that goes without saying," the doctor said after Marcy's disclosure. "I understand your reasons for wanting to keep this quiet, and I assure you I'll certainly honor your request. I think you're right, the more people involved, the bigger chance someone will get hurt. My one concern is the danger to my daughter, and if you can insure her safety."

"As a matter of fact," Will said, after thinking on it a moment. "I think it would be best if Marcy doesn't come to work first thing in the mornin'. There's no good reason why she should be there.

Larsen and his friends ain't gonna know until they walk in."

"That sounds like a good idea to me," her father said.

"Wait a minute," Marcy protested. "I plan to go to work as usual. I'm not afraid with Will there. Besides, he's already told me what to do if they walk in, and Mr. Franklin has to have a teller."

"Your father's right to worry about you," Will said. "I shoulda told you right off to stay home."

"Good," Dr. Taylor said with authority. "That's settled then, so let's eat supper before my wife throws it out to the hogs."

Avoiding Marcy's eyes, Will followed her father into the dining room. He knew she was not at all afraid to confront the bank robbers and expected she might even think it would be exciting. He was afraid the issue wasn't finished. In the dining room, Will was introduced to Marjorie Taylor, a pleasant woman, slender with streaks of gray in her dark black hair. Will could imagine that he was looking at Marcy when she reached her mother's age.

"This is Deputy Marshal Tanner," the doctor said to her. "He's passing through Independence, sent down here from . . ." He paused then. "Where are you working out of, Mr. Tanner?"

"Topeka," Will answered, having to think quickly. He wasn't certain, but he thought he remembered Dan Stone saying there was a marshal headquartered there.

"Well, you're certainly a long way from home," Marjorie said. "Welcome to our home."

Marcy's mother was a good cook and Will complimented her. "This surely is a treat for me, ma'am. I can't remember when I last ate fried chicken." Marcy was quick to inform him that she had helped cook the meal. "Yes, ma'am, I figured you musta." While he was truthful in his praise, the meal was actually a bit of an ordeal for him. He felt that all eyes were on every forkful he put in his mouth, as if he were a donkey sitting at the supper table. By the time they got to the apple pie, however, he was approaching the point where he didn't care, and he attacked it with a vengeance.

After supper, he was uncomfortable once again, however, when the doctor wanted to learn more about the outlaws. While the two men drank coffee, and the women cleared the table, Will answered Dr. Taylor's questions in as vague a manner as he could. He was reluctant to tell him the potential bank robbery was strictly a hunch on his part, and if it didn't happen, he was going to be searching for one man's trail. And to hell with the other three.

When he decided he could take his leave politely, Will thanked the women again for the fine supper and said that he had things to attend to before calling it a night. "I might wanna keep an eye on the banks tonight, just in case," he said as he went out the door. The doctor and his wife both thanked him again for coming to the aid of their town.

Marcy followed him out on the porch. "I'm so

glad you came to supper," she said to him. "It wasn't so bad, was it—I mean, nobody bit you, did they?"

He laughed, relieved to be going. "I reckon not, and it was mighty good eatin'." He stepped off the porch and started toward the gate.

"Will," she called after him, "you be careful in the morning."

"I will," he answered. "I always am." He said it without thinking, but it brought to mind that it was his usual parting words to Sophie Bennett when he left the boardinghouse in Fort Smith. *I expect she's sitting in the porch swing with Garth Pearson about this time of night*, he thought, *if it ain't too cold.*

Inside the house, her ear pressed against the front door, Marjorie Taylor strained to hear the parting words between the two young people. She turned to shake her head at her husband, who was standing in the middle of the room waiting for Marcy to return. When she heard her at the door again, her mother stepped back a couple of steps.

Finding both parents still in the parlor waiting for her, Marcy protested, "Mother! Were you listening at the door?"

"Don't you go getting any ideas about that young man," Marjorie said, ignoring her protest. "He's just drifting through town and will be gone like a leaf off a tree in a windstorm."

"Your mother's right," her father said. "A man like that lives in the saddle, and most of them don't live very long. He seems like a nice young man, but his type are natural-born killers and don't make decent family men at all. Did he say anything to make you think he was interested in you?"

"Of course not!" Marcy answered at once. "He's a decent man, and I just thought it would be a nice thing to have him come to supper with us. We should be thankful he showed up here in Independence. I hate to think we would have had to depend on Leland Couch and Lon Blake to stop a gang of outlaws from robbing the bank."

"I'm sure Sheriff Couch and his deputy are capable of doing the job they were hired to do," her father said.

"They wouldn't have even known about it if Will Tanner hadn't come here and told them," Marcy said.

"Next time you have a notion to entertain somebody, I'd appreciate a little more notice," her mother said. "Especially if it's a man. Now you can get the broom and sweep up the dirt he tracked across the parlor floor."

Walking under a cloudy nighttime sky, Will passed the three saloons between the doctor's house and the corner where the banks stood. All three were busy, with only Whitey's and Abe's spilling out into the street. Will ignored the few shuffling drunks who wandered out in the dark, to stumble back to their homes or camps. His mind was on the house he had just left, and he thought about how nice they were to invite him to supper. He didn't know why he had felt so uncomfortable.

They seemed genuinely gracious. The sheriff's office was closed when he walked by, so he went on down to make sure there was no one around the banks. Everything was quiet on that end of the street, and he still felt that, if there was a holdup attempt, it would come in the morning. So he proceeded to the stable for the night.

CHAPTER 15

They rode into town on the north road a little before nine o'clock. Most of the stores were open, but there were only a couple of people on the street. When they reached the cross street that formed the corner where the banks stood, they split up—Larsen and Ike pulling up to the First Bank of Independence, Earl and Jake to the new bank. When they had dismounted, Earl looked across and nodded to Larsen. It was the signal to get ready. Larsen nodded back, but at that moment, a woman came from around the corner and walked up to stand before the door, waiting for the CLOSED sign to be turned around and the door to be unlocked. Startled, Ike was about to grab the woman, but Larsen remained calm and shook his head, stopping him before he could act. "Good mornin', ma'am," Larsen said. "The bank's gonna be closed this mornin' for a few hours till we get through with a bank examination. If you come back later, we'll be open for business."

The woman hesitated, confused, for the two of them didn't look like what she imagined bank examiners would. But Larsen's reassuring smile seemed pleasant enough. "Well, I never . . ." she started. "They never said anything about being closed this mornin' when I was here yesterday."

"Well, that ain't so surprisin'," Larsen said. "See, if they was always told we was comin', it wouldn't be a very good examination, would it? If you come back in a couple of hours, they'll most likely tell you all about it. You can ask 'em how they did."

"If you say so, I reckon," the woman said, and walked away toward the sheriff's office. A moment later, one of the tellers unlocked the door.

"Hurry up!" Larsen urged then. "They're already in across the street. We need to get movin' before that woman decides we ain't no bank examiners."

Too late to pull their bandannas up to hide their faces, they pushed the door open, forcing the teller to back up to keep from getting run over. A bald middle-aged man, he wore an expression of fright as if he had seen a ghost, and he continued backing away from the door. The thought went through Larsen's mind that the teller looked like he was expecting them. He reacted at once, pulling his pistol and leveling it at the teller. Ike followed his lead and drew his .44. The bank manager and another teller were caught standing near the cage, having just come from the safe in the other room. "That's right, folks," Larsen announced, "this is a holdup, and as long as you do what you're told, won't nobody get shot."

They did as he instructed, freezing where they stood, all three obviously terrified. The older, gray-haired manager could not help glancing nervously toward the door to the back room. Already suspicious about their unusual reactions, Larsen followed the manager's eyes toward the back room. "Who's back there?" he demanded, threatening with his pistol. "You'd best come on outta there!" he yelled. "If you don't, I'm fixin' to shoot these bastards down!"

"Don't shoot," a timid voice came from the safe room. "We're comin' out." In a few moments, Leland Couch moved cautiously through the doorway, his pistol in his hand. Seeing the weapon, Larsen and Jake both aimed their pistols at Couch. For a moment, there was a standoff. Lon Blake moved slowly out behind the sheriff, but no shots were fired. "I'm Sheriff Couch," he said in as authoritative tone as he could manage. "You two men are under arrest, so drop your weapons."

"What?" Ike blurted in disbelief.

The arrest attempt was so pathetic that Larsen could not help laughing. "Under arrest?" he responded. "You dumb turd, if you raise that pistol, I'll blow you to hell. So if you don't feel like dyin' this mornin', you'd best drop it on the floor. And I mean right now." Couch dropped his gun as if it had suddenly become red-hot. "You, too, sonny," Larsen said to Lon. Lon reached down and slowly pulled his pistol out of his holster, his eyes open wide in the tense moment, as if making a decision. Larsen didn't wait for the weapon to clear the holster, and suddenly the heavy air in the bank was split by the bark of his .44 as he discharged a round into Lon's stomach. The deputy bent double and dropped to the floor, grasping his stomach. Larsen quickly shifted his aim to cover the bank employees. He reached inside his coat, pulled out a folded cotton sack, and pitched it to the bank manager. "Now, empty them cash drawers into that sack, and make it snappy. My finger gets itchy if I have to wait too long."

No one was startled by the shot any more than Ike. "Damn, Brock, what the hell did you do that for? We was supposed to keep it quiet."

"He had the look in his eyes," Larsen said, impatient with the question. "He was fixin' to try to take a shot. Now, take that feller with you and tell him to clean that safe out and put it in your sack." He motioned toward the teller standing closest to Ike. "Get to it. They've heard that shot across the street so they know they'd best get the job done over there." He smiled, feeling very much in control of the situation. "I'll keep my eye on the sheriff, here, in case he decides to be a hero."

Couch was numb with fear. As Will had suspected, the sheriff had never before found himself facing sudden death in the form of a conscienceless killer like Brock Larsen. He stood petrified, with Lon Blake lying at his feet, writhing in pain, wondering if this was going to be the day of his death. While Couch stood helplessly watching the robbery of the bank, Larsen walked over and kicked the two pistols across the floor, in case the sheriff suddenly found the courage to make a try for one of them.

Not altogether confident in Earl's and Jake's ability to control the situation across the street, Larsen glanced impatiently out the window. It stood to reason that if the sheriff and a deputy were waiting for them in this bank, then there were likely a couple of men waiting in the other bank, too. "Hurry up, Ike," he bellowed. "We're runnin' outta time. Take whatcha got and come on."

"I'm comin'," Ike called back while prodding the frightened teller with the muzzle of his six-gun to hurry him along. In a few seconds, Ike appeared in the doorway, pushing the teller before him, a heavily stuffed sack of cash in his other hand.

"Leave him in that room," Larsen said, then motioned toward the back room door with his pistol. "The rest of you get in there." They hurried to do his bidding, relieved that it appeared they were not to be shot. When they were all inside, Larsen grabbed Lon's foot and dragged him in as well. Then he closed the door and turned the key in the lock. Looking at Ike, he said, "Let's get the hell outta this town." He moved at once toward the door.

"What about the other boys?" Ike asked when Larsen wasted no time heading for his horse. The words had no sooner escaped his lips when they heard the report of gunfire from the new bank.

It only quickened Larsen's sprint for his horse. "They gotta take care of it," he exclaimed. "We took care of ours. We need to get the hell outta here. We'll meet up with them later." He jumped in the saddle and kicked his horse into a gallop back out the north road, tying the drawstring of his sack of money around his saddle horn as he rode. Ike followed, likewise abandoning any sense of caring about the fate of his partners.

Things had gone slightly differently in the town's newest bank. Will was waiting at the back door when Hugh Franklin arrived at a quarter to nine. He was relieved to see that Marcy had taken his advice and not reported for work that morning. Franklin and Will were already inside when Jug Watson showed up right at opening time. *At least he remembered to come to the back door,* Will thought as he let him in the door and cautioned him to be quiet because he could already hear Franklin unlocking the front door. "Get over in the corner behind that desk," Will told Jug. Then he positioned himself on the opposite side of the safe room door where he could hear what was going on. He heard Franklin's sputtering reaction when the men with bandannas covering their faces pushed inside. Will suddenly realized that there were only two robbers. *They're hitting both banks! I hope Couch can handle it.*

"I ain't aimin' to kill you if I don't have to," Earl Suggins told the bank manager as he leveled his .44 in Franklin's face and pulled his cotton sack from inside his coat. He looked quickly around the empty bank. "Where's the woman who works here? Is she in the back room? If she is, you better damn sure get her out here where I can see her. Lock that door,

Jake. We don't want nobody disturbin' us before we're done."

Finally finding his voice, Franklin stammered, "Miss Taylor isn't here this morning. There's no one in the other room."

"Mister, you'd better be tellin' me the truth, 'cause I'll shoot you down if you're lyin'," Earl warned him. He wasn't sure he believed him, judging by the anxious look on the banker's face. It was at that unfortunate moment that Jug decided the desk he was hiding behind might not provide him with the protection he might need. So he eased backward with reaching a row of file cabinets in mind. Will motioned for him to remain where he was, but they were both suddenly surprised by the sound of a gunshot in the bank across the street. It startled Jug to the point where he stumbled over the desk chair and went crashing to the floor, firing a wild shot through the ceiling in the process.

"It's a trap!" Jake Roper shouted in a panic, and fired three shots blindly through the open back room door.

Damn! Will thought, knowing the situation was out of hand and Franklin was now in mortal danger if he could not act quickly enough. There was no time to think what to do—his reaction was automatic. He dived through the open door, rolling as he hit the floor and holding his rifle outstretched before him. Afterward, he remembered seeing one of the masked men bringing his weapon up to aim directly at Hugh Franklin, who was cringing with his hands up before his face. Oblivious to the two shots from the other robber's gun that ripped into the floor on either side of him as he rolled, he squeezed off the shot that staggered Earl. Without a pause, he rolled up to a sitting position to level his rifle at Roper, who was frantically trying to reload his pistol. "Drop it, or you're dead," Will warned as he cranked another cartridge in the chamber. With little choice, Jake dropped the pistol. Will knew, without pulling their bandannas down, that neither man was Brock Larsen. He also knew that he had been extremely lucky that the bandit had left one chamber of his six-shooter empty as a safety precaution. Had he not, he might have taken more time to aim that sixth round.

Will scrambled to his feet as Jug came stumbling out of the back room, his pistol in hand. "Watch him," Will ordered, pointing to Roper, at the same time looking back toward the one he had shot to make sure he was no longer a threat. He wasn't. His shot had caught him in the center of his chest and he had dropped immediately. Wasting no time, he rushed to the window, but there was no sign of anyone out in the street, and no horses except the two tied at the rail. Across the street, at the other bank, where two should have been tied, there were none. "Dammit, dammit, dammit," he muttered to himself, knowing that Couch and Lon had bungled it, and Larsen had escaped once again.

He looked to Hugh Franklin, who was white as a sheet and trembling uncontrollably. "You're all right now," he said to him. "Maybe you'd best sit down in that chair, till you get your feet steady again." Back to Jug then. "Keep your gun on that one. Shoot him if you have to, but only if you have to," he stressed, only then having the time to be disgusted with Jug's bumbling.

"I didn't believe it would happen," Franklin mumbled, still trembling from having faced death. "If you hadn't dived out that door when you did . . ." His voice trailed off as he finished the thought in his mind.

"Just sit down and you'll be all right," Will said. "I've got to check on the sheriff." He looked at Jug again, not sure he could rely on him. "Can you take care of that one?"

"Yessir, I sure can," Jug assured him. "He ain't goin' nowhere."

"Good," Will said, and went out the front door. He stepped off the board walkway and started across the street in time to encounter Leland Couch coming from behind the bank. "What the hell happened?" Will demanded, already short of patience.

"They shot Lon and got away with some money," Couch answered. "I guess they got the jump on us and locked us in the back room."

"How the hell did they do that?" Will responded. "Did you set up in that back room like we planned?"

"Well, yeah, we did," Couch answered. "But they knew we were in there waitin' for 'em. There wasn't anything we could do."

"How bad is Lon?" Will asked, not wanting to hear any more reasons for the botched ambush.

"Shot in the stomach—it's bad, but he ain't dead," Couch said.

"Anybody else get hurt?" Will asked. When Couch said no, Will told him what had happened in the new bank. "You've got one dead outlaw in there, and Jug is guardin' the other one. You need to lock him up, and get the doctor to take care of Lon." He glanced at a small number of curious souls who were courageous enough to come out in the street, now that the shooting was apparently over. "Send one of them to fetch Dr. Taylor. I'm goin' after the two that got away." He started to run toward the stable where Buster was saddled and waiting, but paused long enough to ask one final question. "You *have* got a jail back of your office, ain't you?" When he had been in Couch's office, he had assumed the back door led to the jail, but after this operation with the incompetent sheriff, he thought he'd better ask.

"Oh yes, sir," Couch replied. "We've got a dandy cell room." Will nodded, then started toward the stable again. "You're comin' back, ain'tcha?" Couch called after him.

"I don't know," Will answered, even though he knew he would have to, because he'd have to come back for his packhorse.

Bill White was standing at the door of his livery stable when Will came running inside. "What was all the shootin'?" he asked. "Was the bank robbed?"

Will didn't stop, but went straight to the stall and led Buster out. "One of 'em," he answered White as he stepped up into the saddle.

"I swear," White said. "I had a feelin' somethin' like that was goin' on. I saw two fellers ridin' hell-for-leather out the north road."

"I'll be back for my packhorse," Will said as he rode out the stable door.

"I'll take care of him and your possibles," White called after him, then thinking to ask, he shouted, "Was anybody hurt?" But Will was already out of earshot, leaning forward over Buster's withers as the big buckskin horse galloped away.

He caught himself biting his lower lip in anxiety as the thunder of Buster's hooves pounded out a steady rhythm on the hard-packed road. He was not surprised that the bumbling sheriff had not handled the situation in the bank, but it did nothing to ease the frustration he felt for Larsen's escape. *Damn the luck*, he thought, for it was just plain bad luck that Larsen hit the bank where Couch and Lon waited. And now it boiled down to a chase and whether or not Buster could close the distance in the time they had. With that in mind, he reined the big gelding back after about half a mile at full gallop, knowing he wasn't going to catch Larsen if he tired the horse out.

Holding Buster to an easy lope now, he thought about following a trail, since the two outlaws had too much of a head start on him to make it simply a race between the horses. His task was made easier for him, because of the frequent light patches of snow that were still in evidence from the last snow shower. Based on the length of the strides, he concluded that the outlaws had held their horses to a gallop for about half a mile farther than he had. When they did slow them down, it appeared they backed them off to a fast trot. He hoped he would gain on them at a lope, before slowing to a fast trot himself. Buster could maintain that pace indefinitely, as long as he reined him back to a walk once in a while. He continued on for another mile, following an easy trail, before the outlaws left the road and cut back toward the west. It was not going to be so easy from this point on, for they were no doubt thinking about hiding their trail, now that they had been successful in gaining a good jump on any pursuit. Will hoped they would be counting on extra time, thinking the sheriff would have to organize a posse to come after them.

Having always been a skilled tracker, Will was able to follow the trail left by the two horses, but his pursuit was slowed considerably. The trail led him to a shallow crossing of the Verdigris River, but there were no tracks leaving the water on the other side. It was not unexpected. He anticipated an effort by the outlaws to lose their pursuers at the river. With patience that was hard to force, considering the bonehead circumstances that permitted them to escape, he rode north along the river, searching for exit tracks. Knowing he was losing valuable time, but with no alternative but to keep looking, he scouted the west bank of the river for almost a mile before coming to a place where the river spread wide over a shallow bottom. The result was a flattening of the banks for a short distance, creating a wide area of small, shallow pools. The outlaws would have had to leave the river at that point, because they would leave tracks in the sandy expanses between the pools. And there were no tracks indicating that that had happened. He could find no tracks leaving the river before reaching that area, either. He had guessed wrong—more time lost. Also causing him some concern now were the heavy clouds that had begun forming soon after he had started his search. It was still early in the day, and he hoped they would hold off for a good while. If they didn't, he hoped they would drop snow and not rain. Rain might wash away tracks, but a light snow shouldn't cover all of them.

There was nothing to do but turn back and scout the bank south of the place where they had crossed. He nudged Buster into a lope back to the crossing and began his search again. This time he followed the river for no more than a quarter of a mile before coming to a wide stream that emptied into the river from the west. It seemed like a good place to exit the river without leaving tracks, so he dismounted and took a close look to see if he could spot some evidence that he was right. If they had ridden up the stream, they were careful about it, because he could find no tracks to confirm it. *It's still a damn good place to leave the river*, he thought. *It's where I would leave it, if it were me.* So he walked Buster slowly up the stream, his eyes tracing the sides of it. After a short distance, his careful gaze paid off, for there on one side of the stream, one of the horses had stepped too close to the bank. He saw a clear imprint of half a horseshoe. Now it was a matter of

continuing along the stream to find where they left
it, and that was no more than a hundred yards
where a heavy grassy area came down between a
thick stand of cottonwoods, right to the edge of the
stream. The overhanging trees had sheltered the
grass, so there was no snow on it. They must have
thought the grass would conceal their tracks, but
the evidence was still there in the form of bent-
down blades that had not yet recovered.

He found tracks leaving the trees that lined the
stream, and he was mildly surprised that they led
back to the south. He paused to take a look over-
head. The clouds were getting darker and darker.
Hold off awhile longer, he begged silently. Asking
Buster for a faster pace wherever possible, he followed the trail over a rolling prairie between the
Verdigris and its confluence with the Elk River.
Upon reaching the Elk, the tracks led west along
that river, but there was a rumble of thunder over-
head as he turned Buster to follow them. In minutes, a patter of raindrops began a tattoo on the
water and the bank ahead of him. He pressed
steadily on, pleading with the rain to hold off, but it
continued to increase, in spite of his cursing. In a
short time, he was following the bank of the river
blindly, because the downpour of rain quickly oblit-
erated all traces of tracks. Finally, he realized that he
might be riding miles off course if he continued,
so he decided to seek shelter until the storm passed,
and then search again. Spotting a thick stand of
trees on the opposite bank, he crossed over and

rode in the midst of them, surprised when he found the ashes of a campfire.

After leading Buster up under the heaviest of the trees, he unrolled his rain slicker and put it on. Not willing to wait for the rain to slacken, he started looking around what appeared to have been a campsite. By the size of the spot that had been scorched by the campfire, he could guess that it had not been the fire of a lone hunter. So he was quick to decide that he had stumbled upon the camp of the four men who had robbed the bank. To further indicate this to be a fact, he discovered a great many hoofprints that had been partially protected from the rain by the limbs of the trees. Soon he had a picture of the camp in his mind, even to the place where it appeared they had left a couple of packhorses while they rode into town. *So they came back to this camp, picked up their packhorses, and rode off to God knows where,* he thought.

Further scouting turned up a few tracks of horses coming and going from the camp, which would most likely indicate those left on their rides back and forth from town. What he needed to find were tracks of all the horses leaving the camp in a different direction. Those would be the tracks he wanted to follow. With still no letup in the rain, he scouted the perimeter of the camp until finally coming upon a series of tracks leading out of the camp to the west, away from the river. Unfortunately, once he left the trees, the rain effectively worked in Larsen's favor and washed away all traces of the horses' prints. He stood there at the edge of the trees for a long time, staring at the endless stretch of rolling prairie beyond, knowing that they could have gone in any direction. And the odds that he could guess that direction were too slim to bet on. It appeared that he was beaten at the game, but he was not content to call it a whim of fate and figure he had given it his best shot. Now, more than ever, he was determined to settle with Brock Larsen, even though it was going to take a little longer.

When the rain let up a little, he climbed back in the saddle and turned Buster back toward Independence, prepared to undertake another long chase. He figured the outlaws probably planned to go to some town, or hideout, somewhere west of there where they could disappear. And the only possible lead he might have would most likely come from the one outlaw that hopefully Sheriff Couch had jailed. The problem was whether or not that outlaw was willing to sing. It wasn't much of a chance, but it was a chance.

In spite of the rain, there were still a lot of folks milling around the First Bank of Independence when Will guided Buster down the muddy street. He gave it only a glance as he rode on past on his way to the sheriff's office. He could well imagine the concern of the people who might have had their money in the bank. He looped Buster's reins over the hitching rail in front of the sheriff's office and went inside to find Sheriff Couch talking to Dr. Taylor. He figured the doctor's visit was in his capacity as mayor. They both seemed excited to see him.

"Did you catch up with 'em?" Couch asked.

"Nope," Will answered.

His single-word reply was not enough for Dr. Taylor. "You mean they got away with the bank's money, free and clear?"

"Yep," Will said.

"So you've given up the chase?" Couch asked.

"Nope," Will said.

His passive response was too much for Taylor to accept. "Damn it, man, they rode away from here with a substantial portion of the bank's money. I'd like to know there's something else that can be done to catch those outlaws."

It was apparent that he was going to have to give them details of the chase so far, although he didn't see that it was going to help the situation any. "I tracked 'em to a camp they had on the Elk River, but they had too much head start on me. They were gone when I got there, and I couldn't pick up their trail from there because this rain washed their tracks clean. So it's gonna be a longer chase than I figured."

"But now you don't have any idea where they are heading," Taylor said, obviously skeptical.

"I'm hopin' to get a better idea after I talk to the one you're holdin' in jail," Will said. "You do have him in jail, right?" He couldn't help asking.

"Sure do," Couch replied. "But I don't know how much he'll tell you. All he'll tell me so far is his name, Jake Roper. As far as the rest of the gang, or what they were plannin' to do, he won't say anything."

"Jake Roper, huh?" Will asked. "Have you got any paper on him?"

"No. I checked, but I don't have any posters on Jake Roper," Couch replied.

"I'll see what I can get out of him," Will said. "How 'bout your boy, Lon? Is he gonna make it?" He glanced at the doctor. "I reckon I oughta ask you that."

"It's a serious wound," Taylor said. "But I think he'll recover, although it'll take some time. By the way, I think we should thank you for preventing the new bank from losing any money. More important, according to Hugh Franklin, had it not been for your quick action and accurate shooting, he would certainly be dead."

"I was lucky, I reckon," Will replied. "I'm gonna go talk to your prisoner now, Sheriff."

Couch walked over and opened the door for him. Will stepped inside and pulled the door closed behind him. Inside, the room was divided into two small cells with a cot in each one. Jake Roper was stretched out on one of them. "Who the hell are you?" Roper asked.

"I'm a U.S. Deputy Marshal," Will answered.

"You're a lucky son of a bitch," Jake shot back. "If my gun hadn'ta been empty, you'd be dead right now. And it looks to me like them other two fellers musta give you the slip, 'cause they'd be in here with me if you'd caught 'em." He favored Will with a cocky smile. "If you're wantin' to know who them other fellers are, I'll tell you the same as I told that chicken-foot sheriff: I don't rightly recall."

"I know who they are," Will said. "You and your two friends partnered up with the wrong man when you hooked up with Brock Larsen. It's kinda funny hearin' you takin' up for Larsen, like he was gonna treat you fair and square. I can't believe you and your friends believin' Larsen was gonna split that money with you. Did he tell you about shootin' his partner, Ben Trout, down in the Nations? By that look on your face, I reckon not." Will could already see that the story he was concocting was raising a little doubt in Jake's simple mind.

"Shit," Jake responded when he couldn't think of anything else to say.

"I found your other friend," Will went on with the lie. "He didn't get very far. It wasn't more'n a mile outta town. I found him beside the road, shot in the back—turned his back on Brock Larsen one too many times." He was satisfied to see a flick of surprise in Jake's eyes, so he continued. "I brought his body back with me just now. Sheriff Couch'll more'n likely prop it up in front of the jail so other bank robbers can see it—soon as the undertaker fixes him up." He paused to shake his head as if astonished. "It's hard to believe he talked you fellers into robbin' that bank for him."

"How do I know you ain't lyin'?" Jake finally managed.

"Maybe I am," Will said. "Tell you what, why don't you ask your friend when you see him propped up in his pine box tomorrow?" Will shrugged indifferently. "I reckon I can see how you got gulled. Ol' Brock's a smooth talker, all right. But I'll tell you this, I found that little camp you boys had on the Elk River, and it was plain to see that Larsen didn't lose a second waitin' around for you boys to show up. He was already cleared out—took everything, horses, the money—took it all, and laughin' about you and your partner in the new bank. He wasn't plannin' to wait to see if you two got out all right or not."

By the time he had finished the story he created, he could tell that the simpleminded outlaw was struggling to mask his dismay. So he figured the time was ripe to go for the one question he needed an answer for. "Maybe ol' Brock will have a drink to thank you and the other two for makin' him a rich man when he gets to, what's the name of that town?"

"Wichita," Jake murmured low, the picture of Larsen celebrating in his mind.

"Right. Wichita," Will said, turned promptly around, and left the cell room.

Sitting on the side of his cot now, Jake was still in a state of shock, having been convinced that he had been double-crossed. He realized that he had spit out the name of the town they had planned to go to after the bank holdup, but now he didn't care. "That back-shootin', double-dealin' son of a bitch," he muttered. "I hope they catch him."

Will found the sheriff and the mayor still waiting in the office when he came out. "You gonna take Roper back with you?" Couch asked him.

"Nope," Will said. "I'm headin' for Wichita first thing in the mornin'. I've gotta take my horse to the

stable now and let him get a good rest. I rode him
pretty hard today."

"You're leavin' Roper here with me?" Couch asked
to be sure.

"Yep," Will replied, then paused. "Here's what
you do. Wire the marshal in Topeka, tell him you
want him to send a deputy with a jail wagon to transport a bank robber back."

"I figured you'd do that," Couch said.

"I would, but I've gotta go to Wichita to arrest
those other two. Maybe we can get some of the
bank's money back to them." He didn't want to con-
fuse him and the mayor by telling them that, if he
did recover the money, it might come back to them
from Judge Parker in Fort Smith.

"Well, good luck to you, then," Dr. Taylor said to
him as he went out the door. "The town of Independence is certainly in your debt, and the U.S.
Marshals Service as well."

Will looked up to see Marcy Taylor walk in the
door and wondered the occasion for the young
woman's visit to Sadie's Diner. Her purpose was
soon evident when she paused for a moment to
survey the room, and upon spotting him seated at
one of the smaller tables, made straight for him.
"Evenin'," he said when she stopped before him.
"Were you lookin' for me?"

"Yes, I should have guessed you'd be here," she
replied. "Papa said you were leaving in the morning." When he appeared puzzled by her remark, she

explained. "I expected you to have supper with us again. We surely owe you something for what you did. I got to the bank this morning shortly after you went after the two men who got away. Mr. Franklin told me you saved his life."

Not quite sure how to respond, Will merely shrugged and said, "I reckon we were all just lucky— except Lon and the feller I shot. Maybe my luck will hold out a little longer, and we'll recover some of the bank's money." She continued to stand there for a long moment until he thought to ask, "Would you like to have some supper—maybe some coffee or something?"

"I've already had supper," she said, "but I'll take you up on that cup of coffee." She pulled a chair back and sat down. He suddenly found himself in an extremely uncomfortable situation and was glad when Sadie came to the table.

"Well, hello there, Miss Taylor," Sadie greeted her. "We don't see you here very often. What brings you in—gettin' tired of your own cookin'?"

Marcy laughed. "No, ma'am," she replied. "I just came in to have a cup of your coffee with Mr. Tanner—that is, if it's fit to drink," she teased.

"Well, I would say it's strong enough to put hair on your chest," Sadie responded. "But I reckon that ain't real important to a lady." She chortled at Marcy's pretend display of shock. "I'll be right back with a cup."

Marcy was pleased to see the little flush of embarrassment on Will's face. It confirmed to some degree the opinion she had already formed of the sandy-haired young lawman. "I guess you have no idea when you might be back this way," she said.

"Reckon not," Will replied.

"Do you ever think about doing something other than being a deputy?" she asked.

Surprised by the question, he shrugged. "I don't know anything else, except workin' with cattle."

"There are a lot of cattle ranches close around Independence," she said. "A man like you could probably build a ranch of his own after a while."

"As a matter of fact, I already own a ranch down near Sulphur Springs, Texas. It's not an awful big spread, but it's a workin' ranch. I might figure on goin' back there one day."

"Texas," she said. "That's a long way from here."

"Yessum, I reckon. But it ain't far below the Red River." In truth, he had not thought about the J-Bar-J in quite some time. It prompted him to wonder how Shorty Watts and the boys were doing. Then bringing his mind back to the table, he wondered how in hell he had gotten into this conversation. It was interrupted then when Sadie brought Marcy's coffee.

They talked for a while, mostly about the town of Independence and the potential it was showing. Most of the conversation was carried on by Marcy with one-word responses from him. At the conclusion, Marcy thanked him for the coffee and made him promise to call on her when he came back this way.

"I surely will," he promised, but he had no plans to ever visit Independence again. Not until she stood up to leave did he think to offer to escort her home, since it was now dark outside, and she would have to pass two rowdy saloons on her way.

"That would be awfully nice of you," she said. "Are you sure you don't mind?"

"Not at all," he replied. "It would be my pleasure," he said in his best attempt to be gallant.

He escorted her past Abe's and Whitey's saloons, glad that he had thought to offer, for there were a few drunks loitering in front of both places. He walked her as far as the gate to her father's house and bade her a good evening. "Thank you," she said. "And don't forget, you promised to come to see me when you come back." Then, on a sudden impulse, she stepped up to him and kissed him on the cheek. Stepping back as quickly, she opened the gate and went inside. "You be careful, Will Tanner."

"I will," he said, still confused by the kiss. She turned away and hurried to the house, leaving him wondering what had happened on this night, if in fact something had happened. He had never been wise in figuring women out, except the kind he found in saloons, but now he was more confounded than before.

Chapter 16

At first light, Will was in the saddle, his horses well rested and fed. He had a journey ahead of him that he could only estimate how long it would take—four days of hard riding, if he was lucky. It might take him longer, because he was not that familiar with the country between Independence and Wichita. Consequently, he was bound to follow the Elk River to its head, which was actually many different streams flowing together to form the river. From that point, he planned to head due west until reaching the Arkansas River, thinking to follow the Arkansas until reaching Wichita.

As he left the buildings of Independence behind him, he gave some thought to the journey he was starting on. There was little doubt that his boss, Dan Stone, would be fit to be tied if he knew Will was pushing deeper into Kansas Territory. Dan would be inclined to turn the problem of catching Brock Larsen over to Kansas authorities. At the same time, there would be little chance Dan would be surprised that Will had taken a personal interest in the capture of Larsen. Will was driven by the responsibility he felt for Larsen running free, even considering the fact that the murderer's escape was made possible by the intervention of one Annabel Downing. These thoughts weighed on Will's mind, but not heavily. All he knew was it was his job to recapture Larsen, and he was prepared to follow him anywhere the chase led, knowing there was the possibility he would be out of a job by the time he returned to Fort Smith. *To hell with it,* he thought. *If Dan fires me, I'll go back to Texas and working cattle.* Behind him in Independence, Mayor Taylor was staring in utter astonishment at the telegram he had received from Topeka.

"This doesn't make much sense," Taylor said to the telegraph operator. He had wired the U.S. Marshal in Topeka requesting a deputy to pick up the prisoner. In the wire, he had expressed the town's appreciation for the heroic actions of Deputy Will Tanner. The wire he had received back said that a deputy marshal would be sent as requested. But then it informed him that there was no deputy marshal on any Kansas rolls by the name of Will Tanner. "Maybe I'll go see if Leland knows anything about this," he mumbled to himself as he walked out the door.

Leland Couch was just as puzzled by the news as

the doctor. "Well, forever more . . ." he started. "If that don't beat all—he was wearin' a marshal's badge. What would make him wanta help us prevent a bank holdup, if he wasn't really a deputy?"

"He said he followed one of them from Baxter Springs," Taylor said. He paused to think about all that had happened since Will arrived in town. "The only facts we are left with tell us that two of the men got away with over twelve thousand dollars of the bank's money. And the man who has supposedly gone after them is not a real deputy marshal."

"Are you thinkin' he was just after the money all along?" Couch asked. "That don't make any sense to me at all. Hell, he shot one of his own friends, if that was true—and put another one in jail."

"Less ways to split the money," Taylor replied. "Doesn't surprise me." He shrugged. "Well, I don't know that there's anything we can do about it now. Maybe when the real deputy gets here, he'll know more about Will Tanner." The doctor was looking forward to one thing, however, he couldn't wait to inform his daughter what he had found out about the man she had scandalously flirted with. "I doubt we'll ever see Mr. Will Tanner again," he said, thinking that news would be comforting to Marcy's mother.

Brock Larsen and Ike Bowers rode into the cow town of Wichita on a blustery afternoon with light snowflakes swirling about their horses as they crossed the Atchison, Topeka and Santa Fe railroad tracks. Commonly known as Cowtown by the cattle drovers, the town started as a trading post on the Chisholm Trail. It was now a bustling cattle town that was host to all manner of drovers, outlaws, prostitutes, and gambling houses. Although Larsen and Bowers appreciated all that Wichita had to offer two men on the run, they had no plans to light there. Their destination was across the Arkansas in the little town of Delano, where there was no law to challenge outlaws and murderers and men of their kind.

"I'm thinkin' I'd like to have a little drink before we cross the river," Ike said as they turned their horses down the main street.

"Reckon you can afford it?" Larsen joked.

"I reckon I can," Ike replied with a chuckle. "Why don't we go in the Parker House and get some supper after we get a drink—have us some fancy fixin's? We'll be eatin' that slop at Roy's soon enough."

"That sounds fine to me," Larsen said. "We'll rub elbows with the swells at the hotel bar, then go on in the dinin' room to eat."

The two outlaws already felt reasonably safe in the crowded town of Wichita, but they would cease to worry altogether once they had crossed over to Delano and took a room over Roy Bates's saloon. Too old to rustle cattle anymore, Roy was spending his later years as the owner of the Rattlesnake Saloon. It was known among outlaws as the "Ask No Questions Saloon." When asked why he named it the

Rattlesnake Saloon, Roy would always respond with, "'Cause the whiskey I sell has got a bite like a rattlesnake."

"Reckon how Earl and Jake made out?" Ike wondered as they tied the horses up in front of the hotel.

"Don't know," Larsen replied. "Maybe they'll be along pretty soon. I ain't worried about it."

"You reckon we shoulda left one of the pack-horses by the river for 'em? Wonder what they'll think if they get to that camp and find out we took the horses."

"They won't think nothin' but maybe they'd best get theirselves over to Roy's," Larsen said. "Hell, we couldn'ta left a horse tied up there by the river without knowin' if they even made it outta that bank. There was some shootin' goin' on, and the last shot I heard came from a rifle. And neither one of 'em took their rifle when they went in the bank."

"I reckon you're right," Ike said. "I woulda liked to see how much they mighta got away with, although I ain't complainin' 'bout what we got away with." They had counted the money when they had camped the first night, and it came to a total of $12,427. That was more money than Ike had ever seen before. That was $6,213 all his own. They matched for the extra dollar, but Larsen won. The only worry he had was, if Earl and Jake showed up at Roy's and they hadn't gotten away with as much. That would call for another split, but he was think-ing the same as Larsen, that their partners hadn't made it out of the other bank. If they had, they should have been right behind them, riding hell-for-leather. He had to admit, he hoped that they hadn't made it. He didn't wish them any bad luck, but he'd never really been rich before and he wanted to stay that way. That thought caused him to trouble his mind with another. "You reckon we ought not be stoppin' here in Wichita? I mean, settin' around in the hotel bar and dinin' room, somebody might remember us if a deputy marshal comes lookin' for us."

"I don't know," Larsen said. "You might be right. It wouldn't do for anybody rememberin' seein' us." He had been unconsciously counting his share of the money, just as Ike had, and it occurred to him that he might have a chance to double it. "Hell, we don't need to waste none of our money on this fancy hotel. Let's mount up, and we'll just camp on the riverbank tonight—get over the river to the Rattlesnake Saloon in the mornin'. I'll just go in the bar here and buy us a bottle to take with us. Shoot, I'll even spring for it. Whaddaya say?"

"Hell, fine by me," Ike said.

"We've got a lot to celebrate tonight," Larsen said as he filled both of their cups again. "Maybe I shoulda bought two bottles, instead of one." While Ike took another big gulp of the fiery liquid, Larsen threw a few more limbs on the campfire. "It's kinda peaceful here by the river, ain't it?"

"I reckon," Ike said. "But I feel like I'm gettin'

drunk. We'd better fix somethin' to eat pretty soon to soak up some of this whiskey."

"Hell, go ahead and get drunk," Larsen blurted, his speech slurred as well. "Payoffs like we hit don't happen very often."

Getting to his feet, Ike staggered unsteadily as he announced, "I gotta take a leak." He paused for a moment. "Damn, I'm drunker than I thought," he said, and walked only a few yards away from the fire to relieve himself. When he came back, he sat down heavily on his bedroll and picked up his cup again, but he didn't drink from it. He didn't say anything else for a long time, until Larsen realized he had fallen asleep sitting up.

"Ike," Larsen called his name. There was no reaction in the glazed eyes staring blindly from under half-closed eyelids. Larsen got to his feet, no longer showing signs of drunkenness, and walked over to stand by Ike. After still no reaction from the sleeping man, he lifted his foot, placed it against Ike's shoulder, and pushed him over to crumple on his side. "If you ain't somethin'," he said softly. "You're makin' it pretty damn easy." There was still no response from the sleeping man, so Larsen drew the long skinning knife he wore on his belt. One quick slice across Ike's throat caused his eyes to flash wide open as he suddenly realized his final moment. Then he was still. "No hard feelin's," Larsen said.

"Well, ain't it surprisin' what the bad weather will blow into town?" Roy Bates drawled. "I swear, Brock

Larsen, I didn't expect to see you around these parts again."

"Howdy, Roy," Larsen replied. "I just stopped by to see if you were still alive. I thought you'd be dead or in prison by now." It had been a while since he had been back to Delano, but he knew he could hole up here for a while with no worry about the law. Roy was an honest man, at least honest in the sense that he was admittedly dishonest.

Roy chuckled. "They'll play hell tryin' to put me in prison. They don't want folks as old as I am takin' up space in prison, anyway." Without asking, he set a glass on the bar and reached for a bottle to fill it. "What brings you back this way? Musta been a year or more since you've been here. You still ridin' with Earl Suggins and them boys?"

"I was," Larsen answered after he tossed his drink down. "But we come up on some hard times of late. Me and Ben Trout went down to Texas for a spell, but Ben got shot by a deputy marshal in Muskogee, Indian Territory. I came back to Kansas and joined up with Earl and the boys. They had a little bank job lined up in Independence, but that went sour. The law got wind of it somehow and they was waitin' for us. I reckon I can thank my lucky stars for that one, 'cause there was four of us and I'm the only one that got away. You remember Ike Bowers? He got shot for sure. Earl and Jake Roper either got shot, or arrested, I ain't sure which, but I just got out by the skin of my teeth."

"Damn . . ." Roy drew out and shook his head. "That's hard news."

"Yeah," Larsen lamented, nodding solemnly. "They was all good boys."

"So I reckon you didn't get away with any money," Roy said, accustomed to drifters showing up at his saloon dead broke and down on their luck.

"Not much," Larsen said. "A little bit that was in one of the cash drawers. I didn't have time for any more before the shootin' started. But I got enough to pay for my drinks and maybe a little tobacco." *And more than twelve thousand besides*, he thought to himself. It wouldn't be smart to brag about how much money he got away with.

"Well, that's good," Roy said. "In that case, that first drink is on the house." He poured another shot in Larsen's glass, set another glass on the bar, and poured one for himself. "I'll have a drink with you to remember them boys that didn't make it outta there."

"Amen to that," Larsen said. "Sometimes I wonder why I was the lucky one that got away." He held his glass up in salute, then tossed it down. Smacking his lips in appreciation of the cheap whiskey, he said, "I've got enough to rent one of your rooms upstairs for a few days until I decide what I'm gonna do."

"Fine," Roy said. "Always glad to get the business. Ain't nobody in that last room at the end of the hall. There's a feller stayin' in one of the other two rooms up there. Maybe you know him—Johnny Moody?"

Larsen shook his head. "I don't, for a fact, but I mighta heard of Johnny Moody—think I heard he was wanted by the law in Missouri."

"That he is," Roy said, "and Colorado Territory as well. He was workin' with some other fellers over that way before the law got too hot on their tails."

"What about the law around here now?"

"Still the same," Roy assured him. "There ain't much across the river in Wichita, and there still ain't none over here. And what law there is over there ain't interested in comin' over here to get shot."

Larsen nodded, thinking that he might be interested in hooking up with Johnny Moody. "Is he upstairs now?"

"No," Roy said. "He's been gone for a couple of days, but he'll most likely show up before long."

Larsen nodded again. "Who's runnin' the stable next door?"

"Seth Thacker, same as when you was last here. Go on over and take care of your horses," Roy said. "Then, why don't you come on back and you can move your possibles into your room and take supper here. I'll tell Flo you're gonna eat here. She's halfway expectin' Johnny back here by suppertime, anyway."

"Thanks just the same," Larsen said. "But I've got to go back into Wichita tonight. A feller over there is fixin' the firin' pin on a spare pistol of mine, and I'll just catch some supper over there while I'm waitin'." It was an outright lie, but Roy's wife was not a great cook by any stretch of the imagination, not much better than Larsen could do for himself. He felt like havin' a good supper tonight, and he could certainly afford one. He slapped a quarter on the bar to pay for his second drink, glad that Roy didn't ask why he had left the gun in Wichita.

Seth Thacker walked out to the open stable door to meet Larsen. "Wanna stable 'em?" he asked, eyeing Larsen up and down, trying to recall having seen him before.

"Yep," Larsen replied. "I expect so. I need an extra stall, too, 'cause I've got a lot of supplies in these packs I wanna leave here while I'm stayin' at Roy's place next door."

"If you've got the money, you can rent 'em all, and my shack out back, too," Seth cracked.

Larsen ignored Seth's attempt at humor. "I've got food and stuff in these packs that I wanna keep dry." He had a problem that was of most concern to him, and that was two large cotton sacks holding the stolen money from the bank. After leaving Ike's body in a gully cut into a bank of the Arkansas River, he had repacked the money, hiding it in half a dozen different packs, underneath flour sacks, coffee sacks, rain slickers, clothes, and anything else he could find. He figured it would be less likely to be found in the stable and better than leaving it in the room at Roy's. He felt pretty sure that either Roy or his wife would most likely take a look in his room as soon as he was not around. So after he had stacked his packs in a corner of the stall he stepped up into the saddle and headed for Wichita.

* * *

U.S. Deputy Marshal Will Tanner rode into the wide-open cow town of Wichita late in the afternoon. As he reined Buster to a stop and sat there at the head of the street looking at the busy town, it occurred to him that it wasn't going to be an easy task to find Larsen and his friend. There was nothing to do but start a search of every saloon in town, in hopes of sighting Brock Larsen. Thinking the two outlaws might stop at the first saloon they saw as soon as they hit town, Will decided that he would start there. And that would be the Chisholm Saloon, an establishment no doubt named in honor of the man the Chisholm Trail was named for.

Accustomed to seeing new faces in town, bartender Barney Smith favored Will with a bored glance, and asked, "What'll it be?"

Will didn't particularly want anything to drink, but he figured one wouldn't hurt. "Whiskey," he said. "Maybe that'll take a little of the chill outta my bones." He took the drink Barney poured and turned around with his back to the bar to survey the room again, in case he had overlooked something the first time. He didn't see Larsen in the saloon, nor did he expect to, and he wouldn't know the other bank robber if he was standing at the bar next to him. The room was not especially crowded, considering it was getting along toward suppertime. Most of the customers looked to be typical cowhands, probably riding the grub line after delivering a herd up from Texas. The one exception he saw was one table closest to the bar, occupied by a thick-shouldered brute of a man who seemed to know

Barney pretty well, for he walked over to the end of the bar several times to exchange a few words with him. After one of these trips, Barney stopped to ask Will if he was ready for another shot.

"I reckon I could use one more," Will answered. He watched while Barney filled the glass, then reached in his pocket to pay. "I reckon I'd best cut it off at two drinks if I'm gonna find a couple fellows I'm lookin' for tonight." Barney didn't seem interested, but Will went on. "I'm new in town and I'm supposed to meet a friend of mine. He's ridin' with another fellow, that I don't know." Barney waited him out, although not at all interested. "My friend's name is Brock Larsen. I don't reckon he's showed up in here, has he?"

Barney raked the coins off the bar. "Brock Larsen, huh? I couldn't say if he has or not. A lot of strangers come in here every day. I don't ask 'em their names. Sorry."

"Thanks just the same," Will said. "I reckon I'll just keep on lookin'." He started to leave, then paused. "Where's a good place to find supper?"

"The Parker House," Barney said, "right down the street on your left."

"Much obliged," Will said, and started toward the door.

"What was he jawin' about?" Johnny Moody asked when Barney came down to the end of the bar to talk again.

"Nothin' much. He said he's lookin' for some feller and asked if he'd been in here. You know a feller named Brock Larsen?"

"Brock Larsen?" Moody repeated. "Nah, I don't know nobody by that name."

Will continued his rounds of the saloons, with the same results he had gotten at the Chisholm Saloon. After the third inquiry, he decided to play it straight and told the bartender in the fourth saloon that he was a deputy marshal, and he was after a murderer and bank robber. The bartender told him that he was probably wasting his time in Wichita. "You'd most likely have better luck in Delano," he said.

"Where's Delano?" Will asked.

"Right across the river," the bartender said. "It's a little ol' town where all the hell-raisers congregate, 'cause there ain't no law to bother 'em. And I expect you'll find all the outlaws you can handle over there, but I'd think twice about tellin' anybody you're a lawman."

"Any particular place in Delano?" Will asked.

"Any of 'em," the bartender said. "Maybe the Rattlesnake Saloon, that's about as rough as they come."

"Much obliged," Will said, and took his leave.

Outside, he stood by his horses for a few moments while he thought about what the bartender had told him. He was probably right about wasting his time in Wichita, but Jake Roper said Larsen was headed to Wichita. Maybe he meant Delano, but he said Wichita. For that reason, Will was reluctant to leave the town without taking a closer look around, even though Delano sounded a lot more likely the place that Larsen would be drawn to. According to what he had just learned, Delano was not that big, so it shouldn't take long to find out if Larsen was there. *If it's as bad as the bartender said,* he thought, *maybe I'd best get myself a good supper. Might be my last one.* He stepped up into the saddle and turned Buster toward the Parker House.

CHAPTER 17

"I'll have to ask you to leave that gun belt here at the desk," the manager of the hotel dining room informed the rugged-looking customer who stood in the doorway.

"I'll just hang on to it, I reckon," Brock Larsen replied. "Kinda feel nekkid without it."

"I'm afraid that's the rule here in the dining room," the manager said. "Weapons in the room tend to unsettle the hotel guests. So we don't serve anybody wearing a sidearm."

"Is that a fact?" Larsen huffed, prepared to challenge that rule. Roy Bates had told him that the Parker House was a fancy hotel, but he felt like he was in possession of enough money to buy the place. He was about to tell the manager that when a man wearing a badge and armed with a double-barrel shotgun stepped out of the door behind the counter. He was enough to cause Larsen to hesitate. "How come he's totin' a shotgun if nobody else can?"

"He's a deputy sheriff. He works here part-time to make sure everybody follows the rule and doesn't disturb the other customers," the manager said politely.

Larsen was tempted to test the deputy. He didn't like the idea of backing down, even if the man was a deputy sheriff. He continued to stand motionless for a long moment, making up his mind. When the deputy stepped closer to the desk, Larsen decided it wouldn't be good for him to stir up trouble the first week in town. He planned to hang around Wichita for the winter, and shooting a deputy down in a public place wasn't a smart idea. *What the hell*, he thought, and started to unbuckle his gun belt when he was suddenly stopped cold by someone he caught out of the corner of his eye. He turned to stare at a man seated at a table in the far corner of the dining room. Not trusting his eyes at first, he blinked several times, certain that it was an illusion, but the image remained. *Will Tanner!* Sitting at the table, eating supper right there in front of him. *The relentless hunter had followed him!* Larsen's brain was too stunned to think. Then it registered that Tanner had not seen him, and the next thought was to pull his .44 and kill him before he did. His hand dropped to the handle of his pistol, but the move caused the deputy to take a step forward, raising his shotgun, alert to Larsen's strange hesitation. It was enough to jolt Larsen's common sense. "I don't reckon I'll eat here," he mumbled, realizing that his best option was to leave before Tanner spotted him.

He turned and hurried out the door, still in a serious state of shock.

Outside, he hastened to step up into the saddle. He started to gallop away, but held up when he recognized the buckskin horse that Tanner rode. Again, he considered waiting for Will and shooting him down as soon as he came out the door. He looked around him at the busy street, crowded with witnesses, and decided it too risky. His instinct was to run, anyway, so he decided that was best. Then, thinking to prevent the lawman from coming after him, he reached down and quickly pulled Buster's reins from the rail. Then, reluctant to waste any more time, he kicked his horse hard, headed for the sanctuary of Delano across the river.

Unaware of the closeness of a confrontation with the outlaw he hunted, and the possibility of a bullet in the chest when he came out of the dining room, Will finished his supper. He picked up his gun belt and rifle and walked outside. He had enough money to put Buster in the stable and rent a room in the hotel, so he decided to spend one more day checking out all the likely spots in Wichita before going across the river. He was mildly surprised to find Buster's reins untied from the hitching rail, thinking he had been careless. It didn't really matter, however, for the buckskin would not wander away from the spot where Will had left him. The bay pack-horse was another story. He would have probably wandered down the street. He stepped up in the saddle then and took his horses to the stable.

"You sure it was him?" Roy Bates asked Larsen.

"Damn right, I'm sure! The son of a bitch hauled me halfway to Fort Smith in chains before I got away. I ain't likely to forget him."

"You said he was a marshal outta Oklahoma," Roy said. "What's he doin' here in Kansas? Hell, he ain't got no authority to arrest anybody in Kansas."

"That's just how crazy he is," Larsen replied. "He don't know when to stop. He probably ain't interested in arrestin' me no longer—more likely lookin' to shoot me."

"Like I said," Roy repeated, "he ain't no lawman here. He's just another gunhand fixin' to draw down on you. You shoot him down, and it's just self-defense. The way I see it, you've got what you oughta been hopin' for."

Larsen nodded as he thought about that, then had second thoughts about his decision not to ambush Tanner when he walked out into the street in Wichita. He was interrupted when he started to say as much by the arrival of a horse out front. He immediately drew his gun and stepped behind the bar for cover. "Hold your horses," Roy said, "That ain't nobody but Johnny Moody." He walked to the door to be sure. "Don't want you shootin' my customers," he added, half joking.

"Whoa!" Johnny Moody sang out when he walked in to find a stranger with a drawn pistol behind the bar with Roy. He took a couple of quick steps backward as he started to reach for his .44.

"Hold it, Johnny!" Roy exclaimed. "Ain't no trouble here." He turned to Larsen and told him to holster his weapon. He waited until Larsen did so, then explained to Moody, "This here's Brock Larsen. He just thought you mighta been a lawman that's tailin' him."

"Is that so?" Moody replied. "For a minute there, I thought I'd walked in on a holdup or somethin'." It occurred to him then. "Brock Larsen did you say? Damned if I don't believe that's the name a feller in the Chisholm Saloon was askin' Barney about. Said he was lookin' for a friend of his, name of Brock Larsen. That's what he said."

"I ain't got no friends," Larsen said. "Was he a big feller with kinda sandy-colored hair?" He didn't wait for Moody's answer. "That was Deputy Marshal Will Tanner."

"Deputy marshal," Moody replied, "and you led him to Wichita?"

"I didn't lead him anywhere," Larsen retorted. "He just happened to come to Wichita. Maybe one of the fellers I was ridin' with on a bank holdup told him I was headin' here."

"Bank holdup?" Moody asked. "Where? Was it that bank job in Independence?"

"What if it was?" Larsen responded, not sure he liked Moody's tone.

"I heard about that holdup, heard a couple of fellers got away with over twelve thousand dollars," Moody said. His remark caused Roy's eyebrows to raise in surprise as he recalled the modest amount Larsen had claimed. He also remembered Larsen saying that he was the only one to escape.

"Twelve thousand, is that what they said?" Larsen responded, forcing a chuckle. "I wish there hadda been that much. I reckon the bank would say they lost a lot more than was actually took. You know, for insurance or somethin'. They're just a bunch of crooks, too, not much better'n the rest of us."

A long moment of silence fell over the room as Roy's and Moody's eyes were focused on Larsen. He realized that he was going to have to come up with something quickly. "There was a pretty good little haul from that job, all right, but there wasn't near that much—closer to four thousand."

"Well, that ain't a bad little payday," Moody said, "is it, Roy?"

"It was too much to tote around," Larsen lied. "So I buried it where won't nobody find it."

"Four thousand dollars," Moody drawled. "And you've got a deputy marshal comin' after you." It was obvious that he was already thinking about how he could get a piece of Larsen's haul.

"Yeah, but there's a little more to it," Roy said. "That deputy's ridin' outta Injun Territory. He ain't got no authority in Kansas. He's climbed his butt out on a mighty skinny limb, comin' up here on his lonesome."

"Whaddaya figurin' on doin'?" Moody asked. "You fixin' to start runnin' again? If you asked me, I'd say it's a pretty good chance to teach that Oklahoma lawman a little lesson about comin' into Kansas territory to arrest somebody." He studied Larsen's face for his reaction to his suggestion and after a moment he continued. "Maybe this lawman is a lot for one man to handle, and you could use a little help. Well, I'm for hire. It wouldn't hurt to have a little insurance, would it? We could let that son of a bitch walk between the two of us, and he wouldn't know what hit him till his hide was cooked." He let that sink in for a moment, seeing that Larsen was thinking it over. "And I work cheap, too. You say you got away with four thousand? Hell, I'll help you put that deputy in the ground for a thousand. Whaddaya say?"

He *was* thinking it over. He wanted more than anything else to finally put a stop to Will Tanner's relentless search. And what better way to do it than to gun him down in a blaze of gunfire? "That's a high price," Larsen said, "since I'm the one that robbed the bank and damn near got shot gettin' away." He was well aware that he could normally hire a two-bit outlaw like Johnny Moody to kill someone for a lot less than a thousand—more like a couple hundred. "But, what the hell," he said. "Fine by me. Course, all this depends on him findin' me. After all, he might not."

"Oh, he'll find you, all right," Moody said. "I'll make sure of that."

That sounded an awful lot like a threat to Larsen, but he figured the money was worth it to better his odds against Tanner. And then there was always the possibility after the job was done that the same thing that happened to Ike could happen to Moody. "I reckon we've got a deal then," he declared.

"Good," Moody said. "I say, let's have us a drink on it. Then we can decide how we're gonna set a trap for this jasper."

The planning went on for some time that evening, and when it was done, Larsen was satisfied that he could once and for all be rid of the menace of Will Tanner. He found that Johnny Moody was an enthusiastic conspirator, and he was satisfied that he could count on him to do his part. Moody seemed especially eager to get a chance to shoot a deputy marshal in the back, which would be his role while Larsen had the pleasure of facing Tanner. He was counting on Tanner to attempt to arrest him first. He would enjoy the confrontation. Before the planning was over, Roy managed to talk Larsen into a couple of hundred for using his saloon to stage Tanner's assassination. Larsen agreed to it, because he intended to eliminate Moody when the job was done—and the same treatment was planned for Roy. When it was all taken care of, he would take his fortune and head for California.

After a hearty breakfast at the Parker House dining room, Will strapped on his pistol, picked up his rifle and saddlebag, and walked out on the street. He started to head down to the stable to get his horses when a heavyset man got up from a chair in front of the hotel and walked to intercept him. Will recognized him as the man the bartender in the Chisholm Saloon had been talking to the night before.

"Mornin'," Moody said as he approached. "You probably don't remember me, but I was in the Chisholm Saloon last night when you came in."

"I remember," Will said.

"I know it ain't none of my business, but I couldn't help hearing you ask Barney about a feller named Brock Larsen. In spite of what Barney told you, he knows Brock Larsen. He was just scared to tell you, in case you was really a lawman lookin' for Brock."

"Is that right?" Will responded, more than a little leery of anyone stepping forward to volunteer information about an outlaw, especially one who looked the part of an outlaw himself. "And you know Brock Larsen, too?" Will asked.

"Well, I reckon so," Moody replied, "and a meaner son of a bitch ain't ever been born. I know him and I know where he is."

"Is that a fact?" Will asked, more suspicious than ever. "And I suppose you want some money to tell me."

"Not a red cent," Moody replied at once. "I got a feelin' you ain't no friend of Larsen's, and neither am I. If you've got a score to settle with that bastard, then I say, go to it and good luck. Me, I'm headin' outta town right now, so I don't care what happens to Mr. Larsen. Name's Johnny Moody."

"Well, that's mighty considerate of you to help a stranger like me, Mr. Moody," Will said. "Where is Larsen?" He was playing along, but he figured he knew a scoundrel and a liar when he saw one. One thing he was now certain of was that Larsen knew he was in Wichita and he had evidently decided to face him, but on his terms. And the part of this jackass confronting him now was to set up the ambush.

"He's holed up at a saloon in that little town across the river, a place called the Rattlesnake Saloon," Moody said.

"How do you know he's there?"

"What?" Moody stammered, having to think quickly. "'Cause I just came from there, and he's the reason I'm leavin'." He could tell that Will was not prone to trust him. "Listen, you can do what you wanna. I don't care. I just thought I'd tell you where Larsen is." He turned abruptly and walked briskly toward one of the horses tied to the rail.

Will watched him ride away, thinking, *Well, I know for sure that I'm being set up for Larsen to take a shot at me.* Still, there was no thought of not going to the Rattlesnake Saloon to seek him out. The fellow whipping his horse into a fast lope up the street was no doubt to be a part of the bushwhacking. How many more would he be facing? It was such a pathetically obvious ambush that he felt he would be playing the fool to walk into it. But he wanted to settle with Brock Larsen too much to play it safe. He was going to Delano, but he would go with his eyes open and his rifle cocked. It was time to bring this thing to a close, capture or kill, he no longer cared. It had become a personal matter between them.

* * *

He stood in the trees that lined the bank of the river above the old two-story building with a weathered sign that read RATTLESNAKE SALOON. He had been watching the saloon for a good while since having circled around the little settlement to approach it from the north. In the corral behind the saloon, next to a small barn, he recognized the sorrel Larsen had ridden, as well as his packhorse, so he knew Larsen was there. The question to be answered was if Larsen was waiting inside to face him, or was he hiding somewhere to bushwhack him? The next question was to determine the whereabouts of the man who had come to him at the Parker House, because Will was convinced he was still a part of it. In the approximately thirty minutes he had watched the saloon, there had been no sign of anyone entering or leaving, and there were no horses tied at the rail in front. He looked again at the corral. In addition to the two horses he recognized, there were two others, but neither was the ragged paint that Johnny Moody had ridden from the hotel that morning. Could he have been wrong—and Moody had not been lying? The only way to know for sure was to go in the saloon and find out.

Before riding down to the saloon, he scanned the riverbank in front of it to spot any likely spots for a sniper, and decided there was no place where a gunman could hide. So he nudged Buster to a fast walk, coming out of the trees directly in front of the saloon, his rifle held ready before him, prepared to shoot. Still there was no sign of anyone. He dismounted at the rail and stepped quickly to the door. Before entering, he pushed the door open with the barrel of his rifle and scanned the room. An old man stood behind the bar, and at a table at the far end of the room, his back to the wall, sat Brock Larsen, his hands in his lap.

Thinking the top of the stairs at the side of the room to be the logical place for the back-shooter, Will checked to make sure there was no one there before going in. That left the old man at the bar as the potential bushwhacker. So Will stepped just inside the door and motioned for Roy to walk out from behind the bar, while covering Larsen with his rifle and keeping an eye on the top of the stairs. "Go on over against the wall and sit down," he told Roy, who obediently did as he was told. To this point, those were the first words spoken in the tension-filled room. Addressing Larsen then, he said, "I can't see for sure, so I'm thinkin' you've got a weapon in your lap. If I see you so much as blink an eye, I'm gonna cut you in two." Larsen's only response was a wry smile. "I'm willin' to give you a chance to surrender peacefully, and I'll take you back for trial. But if I don't see both your hands on top of that table right now, I'm gonna open fire. And I mean do it slow."

Larsen brought his hands up and placed them on the table, smiling cynically as he did. "So you finally caught up with me," he said. "You know, you ain't got no authority to arrest me here in Kansas. Up here, you ain't nothin' but a pain in the ass. Not only that, you're a damn fool to walk in here to face me all by yourself—especially with that Spencer carbine aimed right between your shoulder blades."

Will felt the blood in his veins freeze, stunned to think someone had managed to get behind him. He realized at that moment, too late, that he had failed to make sure there was no one hiding behind the counter. "You walked right into it, didn't you, lawman?" Johnny Moody scoffed.

"I expect you'd best drop that Winchester on the floor," Larsen said, "while I decide what to do with you. You've caused me a helluva lot of trouble." It was obvious he intended to amuse himself since he had the advantage. "Maybe we'll give you a trial, then hang you. Whadda you think, Johnny?"

"I say we just go ahead and shoot him down, if he don't drop that rifle like you said," Moody replied.

So this is the mistake that cost me my life, Will thought. *It was bound to be some dumb-ass thing I should have been looking for.* "Well," he said, "I reckon I'd just as soon die from a bullet, so I'm gonna make sure I put one in you while you're tryin' to get that gun outta your lap."

Larsen suddenly realized he had overplayed his hand. "Shoot him, Moody!" he yelled.

"You do and you're dead, Moody," a voice came from the door.

Moody reacted without thinking. He whirled around and fired, his shot thudding into the doorjamb. At almost the same time, he staggered backward, knocked off balance by the .44 slug that cracked his chest. In a panic, Larsen reached for the pistol in his lap, only to fire a shot into the floor a second behind the slug from Will's rifle that tore into his gut, followed by the lethal shot in his chest. In the span of a few seconds, the ambush was finished. As a precaution, Will looked at Roy to make sure he wasn't armed, still not sure what had just happened. He turned then to confront a scowling Oscar Moon. For a long moment neither man spoke, until Will nodded and said, "Moon."

"Will," Moon returned.

"Glad you happened by," Will said.

"Me, too," Moon allowed.

"How in the hell did you happen to be here?" Will asked, still not believing the miracle that sent the gruff old trapper to watch his back.

"I was just as surprised to see you as you was to see me," Moon admitted. "I brought a side of meat for Flo. It resembles beef, but if you was to look real close, you could see that it's really a fat deer. I bring her game from time to time and she gives me a little money for it, or trades some supplies."

Will couldn't help laughing, even though his nerves hadn't fully settled down from the close call he had just had. "Well, you picked a helluva good time to bring it." He could readily guess that the venison Moon brought most likely had a strong beef flavor. He looked toward Roy, sitting with the passive expression of a man having just watched a cockfight. "Reckon we just cost you a couple of customers."

Roy shrugged. "Don't matter to me. They wasn't

much more than trash. I never cared much for Moody in the first place." He didn't show it, but he truly mourned the loss of the two hundred dollars he had been promised. "What do you aim to do now? Ain't none of this my doin'."

"Not even the part where that jasper was hidin' up under your bar?" Will couldn't resist asking. When Roy was at a loss for an answer, Will set him at ease. "Like Larsen said, I don't have any authority in Kansas, so I don't give a damn what goes on here after I'm gone. So I'm fixin' to relieve Mr. Larsen of his weapons, pack up all his belongings on the horse he stole from me, and leave you to dig a grave for these two. You can keep whatever horse that one was ridin' for pay." He paused and winked at Moon. "But I expect you owe Mr. Moon, here, for that fine side of venison he brought for your wife to cook up." Roy shrugged. At least he had gained a horse from the unsuccessful ambush.

Will was pleased to find the missing bank money when he went through Larsen's packs, while Moon remained in the saloon to make sure Roy had no ideas about causing more mischief. When he was packed up, he led the packhorse to the hitching rail along with the extra horses the outlaw had and waited for Moon to mount up. Larsen's horses would compensate him a little for his trouble, since he would collect no mileage expense for transporting a prisoner back. When Moon was in the saddle, Will said, "I'm thinkin' we need to ride into Wichita and get us a good supper at the Parker House."

"If you're payin', that surely goes to my likin'," Moon replied.

"Oscar," Will said as he turned Buster away from the rail, "I think you and I are gonna be friends for a long time."

CHAPTER 18

On the afternoon of the third day after bidding Oscar Moon so long, Will slow-walked Buster down the main street of Independence. His mind was on the thin, little man with his gray-streaked hair in braids, Indian style, and the bushy mustache to match. He owed a lot to Oscar Moon, not only the location of the hideout called Sartain's, but his life as well. Thinking back, he realized that his chances of coming out of the Rattlesnake Saloon alive had not been worth a handful of the snow now accumulating on the muddy street he rode. He couldn't help smiling when he thought Moon hardly looked like the angel he turned out to be on that day. Will made sure Moon was generously outfitted with supplies and ammunition when they parted, courtesy of the First Bank of Independence. He considered the money spent as simply the cost of doing the business of returning the rest of the bank's money. Pulling Buster to a stop in front of that institution, he dismounted and untied the saddle packs that contained the stolen money.

When he walked in the bank, the first person he saw was John Seeger, the manager, who was stopped cold upon seeing the rangy deputy. Seeger had no doubt found out by now that Will was not a legal lawman in Kansas and probably never expected to see him or the bank's money again. "I recovered most of it," Will said. "What hadn't been spent, anyway." He dropped the packs on a table near the cages.

Seeger was speechless for a few moments longer before he found his voice. "Well, I'll be doggoned. I never expected to see you again." As soon as he said it, he realized what it implied. "I didn't mean to say I thought you were dishonest," he quickly apologized.

"Don't matter," Will said. "Hell, I did give it some thought. It's a lot of money. Now, I'll ask you to write me some kinda receipt, sayin' that I gave it to you."

"Of course," Seeger said, "but we'll have to count it first, so it'll say how much we received."

"Fair enough," Will said. He took a seat by the window and waited while Seeger and one of his tellers counted the money."

Across the street, Marcy Taylor walked to the window to get a better look at the horses tied up at their competitor's. The big buckskin looked like a horse she recognized. She stood there for a few moments until she saw Will come out of the bank, folding a piece of paper. "I'll be right back," she said to Hugh Franklin, and hurried out the door before her boss could ask where she was off to. "Will Tanner," she called out just as he was stepping up into the saddle.

"Marcy," he acknowledged, and stepped back down.

"I knew you'd come back," she said. "Everyone said if you caught up with those bank robbers, you'd probably keep right on going. They said you had no obligations concerning Kansas, and the temptation to keep the money would be too much to resist. I told them they had not taken a true measure of you as a man true to his word. And I knew you'd be back."

Her statement of praise left Will not sure what to say in response. "I told Mr. Seeger what I was aimin' to do," he finally responded.

She smiled at his modest response. "That you did," she said. "Now, are you going to be in town for a while?"

"Ah no, ma'am," he said. "I expect my boss is about ready to mark me off as dead, so I'm leavin' right away."

"Not even long enough to eat supper before you go?" she asked, obviously disappointed.

"Reckon not," Will said, suddenly aware of a desire to stay. "I expect I'd best get back to Fort Smith."

"Then I guess we won't see you up this way again," Marcy said.

He found that he didn't want to say that was true. "I don't know. I might get up here again one day."

She nodded, her eyes locked on his. "Don't wait too long. Things change." She stood back then, turned around, and marched back to the bank. "You be careful, Will Tanner," she called back without turning her head.

He stepped up onto Buster, feeling at home as he settled down in the saddle, and yet part of him wanted to extend his stay here awhile longer. *Maybe her smile isn't that much like Sophie's after all*, he thought. It struck him then that Independence could sure use a more capable sheriff than Leland Couch. It gave him a lot to think about on the long ride ahead of him, and where his road might eventually lead.

AUTHOR'S NOTE

In this book, the name of the town of Okmulgee is spelled *Okmulkee,* since this is the way it was spelled until November 15, 1883, when it was changed to the present-day spelling.

Smoke Jensen Returns!

Keep reading for a very special preview of
Brutal Night of the Mountain Man
coming this December.

Big Rock, Colorado

Smoke, Pearlie, and Cal had left Smoke's ranch, Sugarloaf, earlier that morning, pushing a herd of one hundred cows to the railhead in town. Shortly after they left, Sally had gone into town as well, but she had gone in a buckboard so that she could make some purchases. Her shopping complete, she was now on Red Cliff Road, halfway back home. The road made a curve about fifty yards ahead, and for just an instant, she thought she saw the shadow of a man cast upon the ground. She had not seen anyone ahead of her, and the fact that no man materialized after the shadow put her on the alert. The average person would have paid no attention to the shadow, but one thing she had learned in all the years she had been married to Smoke was to always be vigilant.

"I've made a lot of enemies in my life," Smoke told her. "And some of them would do anything they could to get at me. And anyone who knows me also knows that the thing I fear most is the idea that you might be hurt because of me."

Smoke had also taught Sally how to use a gun, and she was an excellent student. She once demonstrated her skill with a pistol by entering a shooting contest with a young woman by the name of Phoebe Ann Mosey. The two women matched each other shot for shot, thrilling the audience with their skill until, at the very last shot, Miss Mosey put a bullet half an inch closer to the center bull's-eye than did Sally. It wasn't until then that Sally learned the professional name of her opponent. It was Annie Oakley.

Sally pulled her pistol from the holster and held it beside her.

As the buckboard rounded the curve, a man jumped out into to road in front of her. His action startled the team of horses, and they reared up, causing Sally to have to pull back on the reins to get them back under control.

Sally had not been surprised by the man's sudden appearance, nor was the fact that he was holding a pistol in his hand unexpected.

"Is this a holdup attempt?" Sally asked. "If so, I have very little money. As you can see by the bundles in the back, I have been shopping, and I took only enough money for the purchases."

"Nah, this ain't no holdup," the man said. "You're Smoke Jensen's wife, ain't ya?"

"I'm proud to say that I am."

The man smiled, showing crooked, and tobacco-stained teeth. "Then it don't matter none whether you've got 'ny money or not, 'cause that ain't what I'm after."

"What are you after?" Sally asked.

"I'm after some payback," the man said.

"Payback?"

"The name is Templeton. Adam Templeton. Does that name mean anythin' to you?"

"Would you be related to Deekus Templeton?"

"Yeah. What do you know about 'im?"

"I know that he took as hostage a very sweet young girl named Lucy Woodward and held her for ransom."

"Yeah, he was my brother. I was in prison when your man killed him."

"Actually, it wasn't Smoke who killed him. It was a young man by the name of Malcolm Puddle."

"It don't make no never-mind who it was—Jensen was there, 'n as far as I'm concerned, it's the same thing as him killin' my brother."

"Why did you stop me?"

"Why, I thought you knew, Missy. I plan to kill you. I figure me killin' you will get even with him."

"Will you allow me to step down from the buckboard before you shoot me?" Sally asked.

Templeton was surprised by Sally's strange reaction: not so much the question itself as the tone of her voice. She was showing absolutely no fear or nervousness.

"What do you want to climb down for?"

"I bought some material for a dress I'm going to make," Sally said, "and I wouldn't want to take a chance that I might bleed on it."

Templeton laughed. "You're one strange woman, do you know that? What the hell difference will it make to you whether you bleed on it or not? You ain't goin' to be makin' no damn dress, on account of because you're a-goin' to be dead."

"May I climb down?"

"Yeah, sure, go ahead."

Holding her pistol in the folds of her dress, Sally climbed down from the buckboard, then turned to face Templeton.

"Mr. Templeton, if you would put your gun away and ride off now, I won't kill you," Sally said. Again the tone of her voice was conversational.

"What? Are you crazy? I'm the one holdin' the gun here. Now say your prayers."

Suddenly, and totally unexpectedly, Sally raised her pistol and fired, the bullet plunging into Templeton's chest. He got a look of total shock on his face, dropped his pistol, then, as his eyes rolled up in his head, collapsed onto the road.

Cautiously, Sally walked over to look down at him.

Templeton was dead.

Connect with Us

Visit us online at
KensingtonBooks.com
to read more from your favorite authors, see books
by series, view reading group guides, and more.

for sneak peeks, chances to win books and prize packs,
and to share your thoughts with other readers.

facebook.com/kensingtonpublishing
twitter.com/kensingtonbooks

Tell us what you think!

To share your thoughts, submit a review,
or sign up for our eNewsletters, please visit:
KensingtonBooks.com/TellUs.